A Condor Brings the Sun

A Condor Brings the Sun

A Novel

by Jerry McGahan

SIERRA CLUB BOOKS ⌒ SAN FRANCISCO

The Sierra Club, founded in 1892 by John Muir, has devoted itself to the study and protection of the earth's scenic and ecological resources — mountains, wetlands, woodlands, wild shores and rivers, deserts and plains. The publishing program of the Sierra Club offers books to the public as a nonprofit educational service in the hope that they may enlarge the public's understanding of the Club's basic concerns. The point of view expressed in each book, however, does not necessarily represent that of the Club. The Sierra Club has some sixty chapters coast to coast, in Canada, Hawaii, and Alaska. For information about how you may participate in its programs to preserve wilderness and the quality of life, please address inquiries to Sierra Club, 85 Second Street, San Francisco, CA 94105.

Copyright © 1996 by Jerry McGahan

Library of Congress Cataloging-in-Publication Data
McGahan, Jerry, 1943–
    A condor brings the sun : a novel / by Jerry McGahan.
        p.   cm.
    ISBN 0-87156-354-1 (cloth : alk. paper)
    1. Mothers and daughters — Peru — Fiction.   2. Indians of North America — Peru — Fiction.   3. Human-animal relationships — Peru — Fiction.
I. Title.
PS3563.C363575C65   1996
813'.54 — dc20   96–2770
                                                                                      CIP

Production by Janet Vail
Jacket design by Sharon Smith
Book design by David Peattie

Printed in the United States on acid-free paper containing a minimum of 50% recovered waste paper, of which at least 10% of the fiber content is post-consumer waste.

10 9 8 7 6 5 4 3 2 1

For Mom and Jany

Each day it is the condor that brings the sun to the sky,
raising it aloft from its resting place in the sacred lake Waynaqocha.

— Runa legend

Pilar

A Timeline

Pilar's Mothers

1	Warkari	1440–1491	
2	Mita	1462–1483	
3	Soona	1480–1518	
4	Tangara	1496–1550	
5	Phuyu	1514–1573	
6	Rumi Pachak	1532–1586	
7	Karu	1553–1582	
8	Askha	1567–1609	
9	Iphu	1590–1648	
10	Puylla	1607–1637	
11	Layqa (comadre)	1625–1690	
12	Payita	1641–1676	
13	Araullu	1671–1713	
14	Kusi	1694–1758	
15	Isabel	1721–1751	
16	Ninakuru	1739–1804	
17	Titu María	1761–1790	
18	Leonor	1776–1827	
19	Killa	1808–1866	
20	Enriqueta	1835–1918	
21	Genera	1865–1904	great-grandmother
22	Catalina	1890–1941	grandmother
23	Hilario	1922–1963	mother
24	Pilar	1955–	

I

I AM PILAR. One name in front of the sun. I know the names of twenty-three of my mothers, and I know their stories. My first three mothers lived in a place named Pomba along a river called the Juanuru. But I live in Wasi, as my other mothers did, a place far, far away from Pomba. The Inca's soldiers took my people from Pomba and brought them here to Wasi. It was my second mother, Mita, who was in Pomba when the Inca's warriors invaded. Her daughter, my third mother, Soona, was the only one of all the mothers who saw both Pomba and Wasi. She was the one who began the stories and started the line that reaches here now. Soona brought Pomba with her in her accounts of her grandmother and mother. She was the one who made us promise to keep the line.

When the Incas moved my people from Pomba to Wasi, it took more than two months, or moons as Soona called them, even though they walked there on Inca roads. She said we would lose our home but not ourselves. The stories would keep us. All the mothers in Soona's line taught their daughters the stories of the mothers before them. While we were watching the llamas or planting or shucking corn or hilling potatoes, we daughters told these stories to ourselves, all of them. I am twenty-seven years old, and Wasi is almost five hundred, but our story is the same one.

When the white men came and killed the Incas, it was another beginning for us. Soldiers came and told us what to do. The corregidores —the governors then—and their tax collectors came and ruled and took from us. So did the hacendados, the landowners. And the priests came to clean away our sins. They, too, told us what to do and asked for our land, our animals, our money.

Now comes Sendero Luminoso—Shining Path—and behind them, the soldiers once again. Just as my people could not keep the Inca's warriors out of Pomba or Wasi, nor the soldiers and priests who came later, we cannot keep Sendero from walking in and out of our midst or keep them from hurting or killing us. But we can keep them out of our families, out of our village, out of that part that is inside us like a song.

We let the invaders have the plaza. That's our place for them. The Runa—we are about three hundred families—live in the space between the plaza of foreigners and the savage place high above. In the plaza, the peeled ones (that's what we call the outsiders, because it's as though they have lost their own skin and can wear any skin they want) build their stores, their government places, and churches.

The soldiers killed the Incas on the plaza. In Cuzco, on the Plaza de Armas, they chopped off the head of Tupac Amaru, the last full-blooded Inca, the last male born from the union of an Inca king and his sister. Two centuries later, when my mother seventeen lived, they took another rebel descendant of the Incas, José Gabriel Tupac Amaru, and killed him there in the same plaza.

In the plaza of our little Wasi, Shining Path took the one I loved and made us watch while the woman from Ayacucho put a knife into him. The Runa told her they would punish him if that was necessary but said no one should kill him. The people of Shining Path said that they had to kill him, and we had to see it. That we watched was the important part. Our punishment mattered more than his.

He was looking at me when she took the knife out, and I saw the spirit leave his eyes. It was in the plaza, and I could do nothing. Slick and silky, the blood came out of his chest in bumps as if pouring from a jug. His heart pumped life out of him and splashed it on his shoes and on the shoes of the peeled ones who held his arms.

I ran away to the savage place. A condor came to me as a sign, and I knew that I had to leave Wasi that night. Shining Path would kill me if I didn't run away. I knew that the Senderistas would have to kill more people in Wasi than they had killed in any of the other villages of the canyon.

The people of my village, especially those of the lower barrio, thought of themselves as the Runa of Wasi, but really, they were the children of Pomba. We spoke the same language as the Runa across the canyon and in other villages; we wore the same clothes, grew the same crops, raised the same animals, but we weren't the same people at all. After twenty-three generations, the river Juanuru and the songs of Pomba still flowed through us.

It wasn't easy to see, that difference. In the other villages the Runa there, like us, lived between the invader and the high savage places. They, also, let the peeled ones come and go in their midst but kept them shut out of their families and out of the songs of their village. They were like us and did what we did. But not as well. We were the most alone. This is what we had learned to do to keep ourselves.

There was a man who lived in the lower barrio, in the house next to ours, who was a sorcerer. His name was Isidro. He spoke in rhyme, and he could see through time, behind and ahead, even when he didn't know what he was seeing or what it meant. I knew that he had this power, because I knew from my stories that some of the things he saw had happened. Once, I was going to tell him what I knew from my stories about his visions, but I stopped.

Isidro smiled his lusty smile. "Pilar ran. She almost fell. Pilar has a secret she won't tell."

"Pilar has plenty of secrets," I teased.

"Yes." The little sorcerer watched me from the corner of his eye. He looked at me as if I were roasted meat he was going to put in his mouth. "Pilar, the loveliest of Wasi when she lies, lets the hand of no man between her thighs."

He had seen the golden pot of the priest in the Wasi plaza, he said. That pot was on the Inca stone where the finger-pointing-at-the-sun had been before the first black-robed priest had broken it off. Isidro said the golden pot was full of blood. I knew that picture was two pictures, one from the stories behind and one yet to come.

That picture was a warning.

~

One more thing. The condor. In some of the stories, a condor comes. In mine, I was in the savage place, high on the open ridge crossing to the magic spring where my mothers' illas—those little stone animals— were hidden. It was the place Soona had found almost five hundred years before, the place where she had hidden the little stone condor and deer from Pomba that had belonged to my first mother. None of the invaders, neither the Incas nor the priests, nor Sendero most likely, wanted us to believe that the illas spoke to the spirits. One of those illas came alive and flew above me.

I was crying and running. Below, in Wasi, Sendero had just done its killing in the plaza. The wind came at my face. I lost my shawl from one shoulder and stopped to sling it back around. As I straightened, I heard something. I stopped, arm out, and didn't move, for I knew what the sound was and what it meant. It was a kind of humming sound, a high single note, that grew louder and louder. I drew in my arm, wiped the water from my eyes, and looked up into the wind at the giant bird that had come to speak to me.

Her wings covered the sky and sun. I knew it was a she-condor, for the bird had no crest on her head and her eyes were red. The collar of feathers on her neck was soft and white. Her black beak curved to a white point. The rest of her was black beneath. Very slowly she came over me. Her wings were still as stretched cloth. At the end of her wings, the feathers made long slender blades that turned upward. It was from them, the wind cutting through there, that the humming sounds came. Above me, she turned her head to the side and gazed at me. It was the gaze of a mother, a look of courage and kindness. When she was straight above, she lowered her legs from beneath her tail and seemed to be standing on an invisible rock. Then she no longer moved forward but slowly dropped toward me. The whining, whistling sounds grew louder and louder. I could see the little feathers on the front edge of the wing peel up. Down, down, she came. When she tipped her head to watch me, I saw the hole that went straight through both nostrils on the soft part of her beak. One wing nearly touched me. That wing, by itself, was as long I am. I could see the white waste caked on her legs, smell the bitter chalkiness. Her body in that wind rose and dropped in little steps, went forward and then fell back, but her head did not move. Her eye was tied to mine, anchored there.

She could see that I knew her. I saw it in her eye when she recognized it in mine. At that moment, she untied herself from me, lifted her hanging-down legs back to their place beneath her tail, and up she rose, straight up, the loud whine fading as she grew smaller and smaller. Then, high above, when she was no wider than my fingernail at arm's length, she swept her wings down once and arrowed across the sky in a straight line away from the sun. I watched her disappear, followed her until she turned into nothing.

The line of her gliding pointed toward Cuzco.

2

*i*N THE SCHOOL, we had three teachers, all peeled ones from Ayacucho. Reynaldo was the dangerous one. Behind those tiny eyes and mouth ran a deep current of rage. Reynaldo's wife lived in Ayacucho, where he kept her safe from the dirty ways in Wasi; she needed electricity and running water. Reynaldo had helped organize the union in Ayacucho, but when it began to stir up interest among the people there, other peeled ones from Lima quickly moved in and quashed it. As an outcast in Wasi, Reynaldo suffered. He hated our dirty ways. He wanted to change things, to have a revolution that overthrew the government and the church and the hacendados. But here he was in Wasi, where the Runa, particularly those in the lower barrio, wanted nothing to change the way we were. We'd let no one rend the web we wove and mended every day. Reynaldo called us brutes. For people like Reynaldo all Runa were Indian brutes—those two words went together. He never heard the song inside us, the one that made us a village.

There will always be peeled ones and among them, the dangerous Reynaldos, their faces shining with the weight of so much that must be done. I know that when people carry these loads, eventually, the storm rises. The storm answers, it always does. Sooner or later. When these people find that what they carry is enough to kill them, when they find it necessary to die in this way, they will kill us, too. They will kill us first.

Knowing that, I knew to never trust a peeled one. I knew not to talk to them. I knew to keep my eyes from them, to keep my watching so far away that no peeled one could ever say I glanced at them. People can occupy the same village but live in different countries. I could step out the door of my home in Wasi and throw a stone that would hit the homes of men whose gaze I had never met. It all depended on the eyes.

Alejandro, one of the other teachers, changed that. I loved him. He was Runa and a peeled one who I thought at first had forgotten the song. In a way he had, but he knew what was happening. He said the peeled ones were coming to kill us if we didn't let them in. But we were ready to let them in all the time—let them live there just as we had allowed all the other peeled ones, let them walk around among us, let them do their buying and selling, their counting and taxing, the washing away of our sins, whatever they did with us that made them feel better. We were ready for that. We had practiced. As always, we thought that they wouldn't hear our songs or know of them, so it would be as it had always been, with their coming and going, and the Runa of Wasi carrying on as they always had, singing to each other.

When my brother, Lazario, went to school, the first of all our line to do so, he brought Alejandro and me together. It began when Lazario told Reynaldo why the fiestas were different in the two barrios. Reynaldo grew angry with his story of our mothers and questioned him about which year, which century, these happenings Lazario described had taken place. Lazario said he didn't know any of the years. Reynaldo said it was all made up and stalked away. But Alejandro had been listening. He tested my brother. Who was the Inca when mother three came to Wasi? Huayna Capac, Lazario told him. And which mother when the last Inca died? Mothers five and six,

Phuyu and Rumi Pachak. And when José Gabriel Tupac Amaru and Micaela Bastidas lived? Seventeen, Titu María, Lazario told him. Titu María thought she was the last one, Lazario said. She thought that the world would end then.

Alejandro sat down with pencil and paper. At length, he returned to Lazario. "You know all these stories?" Lazario said that he didn't, nor his father. His mother was dead. Only his sister knew them.

I was with the llamas high in the savage place when Lazario and Alejandro found me. Nearby was the magic, the illas my mothers had hidden in the hands of the stone man. When there is power in the savage place, it shows in the light. The ichu grass is gold, and there is no orange in it, nothing warm like the light in cooking fires. The spears are cold like starlight that shivers in night's sky. I could feel the power, the changes coming, even though I couldn't see Lazario and the peeled one he was bringing.

I knew who Alejandro was, but as with all the peeled ones whose place was in the plaza, I had never let my eyes meet his. He had a nice face; it was something I had noticed before. He wore shoes and slippery trousers and a sweater. My eyes saw in that face the smooth water of kindness.

Lazario and Alejandro were a long way off, two flecks against the blackness inside the canyon, two dots on the edge of this golden blanket of puna. Even before there was color, I knew there was a strangeness about them, maybe the distance between them or something I knew about the motion of a man without a poncho. It took them another hour to reach me. From the beginning, I knew they were coming to me.

I was scared. We shouldn't have let Lazario go to the school. Here was this man from the plaza. Now he would invade our savage place. The first thing he would do would be to ask me my name. And if I told him, I would be lost. I could hear my mothers calling. But it was too late. This man was here. He knew my face. He wanted to talk to me. He already had my name. It was how everything before had been lost. I could feel everything slipping, the song, the stories, the silence and power of the savage place and the illas. The peeled ones had found me.

"Pilar," Lazario cried, grinning, "this is my teacher, Señor Alejandro Pinta." He spoke in Runasimi.

Exhausted, Alejandro gasped. He tried to say something, gave up, and stood bent over, his hands braced against his knees. Lazario looked at me awkwardly. Alejandro's pain didn't completely hide that quiet-water way of his.

"Your brother," Alejandro said, casting about miserably as if looking for his wind, "has told me something about you that's so amazing . . ." puff, puff, ". . . so amazing that I had to talk to you."

"Yes," I said, "I'm sorry. Lazario shouldn't have told you. They are just the stories of our mothers," I said, pleading a little. "Lazario's and mine."

"They are the stories of our people," Alejandro said.

"Yes," I said, "but telling them to someone else changes what they are."

"I want to ask you to tell me some, just parts of some, whatever you would tell me, but I . . ."

"No," I said. I walked up the slope a little. I liked his face. I wanted to talk to him. He would like my stories. I would love telling them. But they were mine; they were all I had. Maybe, as Alejandro said, they were the stories of our people, but they were the stories of me first. Pilar. And partly, Lazario's. But Lazario would be like Father and find interest only in the wars and the fighting, when the truth was that the story of our people was the story of women. I was afraid to see those stories in the hands of men.

Lazario and Alejandro went back down. Alejandro looked disappointed, and Lazario, regretful. I watched them until they disappeared at the rim of the savage place and went into the darkness of the canyon on down toward Wasi. When I lost sight of Alejandro, something inside my breast kicked and ached.

⌒

A month later, my father Oqoruro, Lazario, and I went to the savage place for our herranza ritual, where we branded three heifers. At the stone-walled corrals, Tio, our compadre, and my father performed the first evening ceremonies. Tio's other compadres came, too, with their children. Alejandro Pinta, who was a baptismal godfather for one of the children, was among them. I could feel Alejandro watching me. While father unwrapped our ceremonial bundle and took out the illas that we kept in our house, Alejandro moved around to stand behind me.

Father set out two llamas, a cow, and a ram. Then, he laid out the magic corn and coca seeds and the small bottles of corn beer and cane liquor. He opened the tied cloth and exposed the sea shell containing the llampu, the sacred red powder. "I don't think there is enough llampu," Father said. Tio agreed. If we ran out during the ceremony, the spirits would be offended.

Tio brought out the grinding stones. Father poured some of the liquor in the sea shell then emptied it on the ground. For Pachamama, Mama Earth. Then, he refilled the shell and we all sipped from it. I handed the shell to Alejandro. He looked at me with a question in his eyes. I couldn't tell what my eyes replied, because I didn't know what I was thinking.

We went into the hut. Father and Tio went through a bag of corn to find the best ears with large white seeds, none missing. They removed every seed and Tio began grinding them.

Alejandro leaned toward me and whispered, "Your face tells me you want to say something."

"Maybe . . . I . . ." I stopped, confused.

Father looked at us, frowned at our talking. Tio was still grinding. If any grains of corn were spilled or lost, the spirits of the high places would see to the death of our herds. Tio was sweating with concentration. He added two vilca seeds and two wayluru seeds to the corn. Father put in the coca seeds, the white carnation flowers, the pinch of gold and silver, and then the red stone that gave it the color. Tio's wife played the sacred drum.

I could feel Alejandro's eyes, but I wouldn't look at him. I was thinking that maybe if I told him only a few of the stories it would do no harm. I watched the sweat on Tio's temple and wondered if the tension I felt was for him or for myself.

When the llampu was smooth and soft and red, Tio poured liquor into the shell again, and Father sprinkled a little llampu in with the seed from the achita plant that grows alongside the corn. We all drank from the shell. As soon as the llampu had been put back into the shell with the old llampu and tied back into the cloth, everybody felt easier.

Alejandro moved to my side. "Tell me what you were going to say."

"Maybe I'll tell you a little of my stories. If you will do something."

"Anything."

"Will you teach me Spanish?" The question popped out of me.

"Of course," Alejandro said. Lazario watched me curiously.

The others were singing. I sang with them. It scared me to see how quickly I had come to this new idea. I will not leave my language, I told myself and my mothers. This will only be a little journey for me in the way that Mother Soona's was a big journey.

Alejandro didn't stay for the branding. Before he left, he told me that he would find me in the savage place. The rest of us drank and sang all night.

∼

The next day I could feel unseen clouds forming in the wind. It was a different kind of wind, rounder, smoother than the wind of the dry season. In another month the rains would come. I could feel them coming, invisible lines of water pulling, spinning, making out of empty blueness something thick, heavy, inescapable. Beneath all this invisible working, I stood in the savage place near enough to feel the hidden illas of my mothers and watched as a condor must watch, from the rocks above, the rising of another bird far beneath.

Alejandro came alone. He didn't call or speak until I could see the tiny pores of his face. "Good day," he said in Spanish. "Good day," I answered him in that tongue. He sat down beside me. The wind was cool, but the air on the ground was warm. I could feel the currents stirring around us.

"First," he said, "I will tell you words of Spanish that you already know but thought were Runasimi, and then I will tell you some new words."

"And then I will tell you a little story," I conceded.

And so with as little introduction as that, my small journey with Alejandro began. I told him the story of Soona. Watching his face as I acted the story—which I did very well, as I have practiced it aloud often—excited me more than if we had touched each other. It was like being drunk. I told it with strength and spirit. I stood. I gestured. I hollered. I whispered. My voice as the invader was deep. My face as Soona's lover was clever, wicked. I made them alive again. I swallowed the blood of her slain lover. Alejandro was in my power, power that I did not know one could wield, power that I did not know could fill one with such certainty and direction. The wind blew. The power of the illas rose up inside me. And I was Soona. I could see her reflection in Alejandro's wide eyes. Soona back from the dust.

*M*Y NAME IS SOONA, mother three. I always got into trouble, and I liked other people who got into trouble. Maybe it was because my mother died before I could remember her. Maybe it was because my grandmother, Warkari, who raised me, was grim as a vulture. She thought it was our burden to nurture and nourish everything right out of nothingness into being, and that if we did not work with earnest and worshipful regard for every stem and straw, the river Juanuru would cease to flow and the clouds would fall out of the sky. I, in contrast, thought life was all delight, and the only mistake was to miss it.

I was a child of change. My mother, Mita, died when I was three, and I do not remember her. Four years later, my father and grandfather were killed, one with stones, the other with a spear, when the Knot Counters came to rule. We suffered only a small war in this valley. We did not fight, except to protect ourselves, whereas the Knot Counters had been fighting for years. I remember the crying and the fear in those days and the talk of being slaves to another nation, but it was different, I think, than anyone thought. They taught us how to build with stone instead of adobe and how to make roads and walls and buildings that did not weather with the seasons. They took two-thirds of everything we grew, but half of that went into the store-houses for the people in places where it hadn't rained or had rained too much. One year it didn't rain at Pomba, and the storehouses opened for us.

For them, everything was a collection of knots on a string. That is how they remembered all their numbers, and they had many to re-member, thousands of knots on thousands of many-colored strings. But when we became so many knots on a mess of strings, we found ourselves cared for too well. Nevertheless, it wasn't always like we were slaves. They left our sacred wall standing, and when we were told we had to go to the south, they let us take the illas with us, our little stone animals. I had a little stone condor and a little deer. We could keep the illas and trust them so long as we admitted that everything sacred was beneath the sun, which always made sense to me. I think the Knot Counters thought that our magic would be magic for them, too, which seemed strange for a people who knew nothing but knots and numbers and rocks. And change. That was the other thing the Knot Counters knew about—change. That's all they did. Everyday and everywhere, they changed everything.

The first change, of course, came with their first army, when they killed the Pomba men who tried to stop them. All of us had more work then, but the Knot Counters watched over us. They knew what we grew, what we ate, even what we hid. Anyone found hiding food got whipped. We never stopped hiding food; we just got better at it. Some of the caves we used were on cliffs that they didn't know how to climb. With boulders and brush, we concealed the openings of other caves and holes where we put caches. Still they knew, because they watched over the planting and harvest, and with all their counting, they knew how much there should be. They killed Talon, our eldest leader, tied him and speared him. As he died, he told our people to never stop resisting, that the other death they wanted from us was worse.

Still, they couldn't find what we hid. When the killing threat failed, they decided to make the biggest change of all—to move us. Whenever a village on the frontier of their empire gave them trouble, they pulled it up like a seedling and moved it across the long back of the earth, up to the center of their empire, where they could watch its people. A village from the center, one that did what the Incas wanted, came to the frontier to take the place of the renegade village. For us, it was the worst threat. Who could leave their home and not be changed forever?

Young and resilient as I was then, I did not know how terrible it would be. Thinking of other things, I saw opportunity in that change. When we left Pomba, I knew I had a chance to subvert what the elders and my grandmother, Warkari, had planned for me. I saw no future as the bride of the one chosen for me, a man named Yataban. When we were on the long road and far from Pomba, the elders lost their charge as overseers. What they had sworn to Warkari on her deathbed meant little in the wake of an exile so huge and irrevocable. I was free. It was Kuyor I wanted. Kuyor the butterfly. I wanted to show him my wild heart, how it beat like his, and what pleasures the universe had not yet beheld, because no one else had the imagination for love that I had. I was fifteen.

We walked in three groups. Half of the Knot Counters, then our people—two hundred scared, soft as the insides of a snail—and then the other half of the Knot Counters. At night they camped together, and we camped alone by ourselves. At first, they tried to mix the camp; they told us we were going to be like Knot Counters and live in their land so we needed to learn to mingle with them. But it didn't work, partly because most of the older people did not speak the language of the Counters.

Early on, before the second full moon of the journey, when we were still pretending to mix, I was at one of the fires with the Counters and with Kuyor. He and I had to translate for the Pomba elders. I was ready to do more than make soft eyes. Kuyor knew what I had in mind; it didn't take much to see it. I looked all over him. Other girls didn't do such things; Warkari always said I was wild as a deer. Kuyor laughed at my ranging eyes and looked all over me. I could feel his eyes, and the spirit of my body went out to meet them. At the fire, the Counters were talking about corn and the rainy season.

"We tried growing seed from your corn at the village where you are going," a Counter said, "and we got as much as you do. But we get more with our own kind there, even though it doesn't grow very well in Pomba."

Kuyor translated for him.

"But you told the women to bring our seed," our elder said. I translated. Kuyor watched me with interest.

"We will pass the people of that village in a few days and you will give them your seed. We didn't want to leave it for the mice. The seed you will use waits there. Another village protects it." As he translated, Kuyor winked at me.

"And the squash, the beans?" our elder asked. I translated, and then on my own account, added, "And that sweet little boy who translates for you?" The Counters were startled. They gawked at me. Kuyor laughed out loud. Our elders, who had no idea what I had said, looked puzzled. "And the squash, the beans?" I repeated hurriedly.

One Counter understood. He smiled. "We haven't tried your squash and your beans in Wasi. We will see how they do with you there to tend them. If they do well, we will send them to Cuzco. They will raise more seed to be sent to the other quarters of the empire. And what does the Pomba girl have in mind for the sweet Pomba boy? In our empire, it's the man who seeks the woman first."

"In our empire," Kuyor said in their language, "we don't do things in any particular way that might mean passing something by. Sometimes it's better to let the water flow toward you." Then he translated for our elders about the beans and squash. Giggling, all of the

Counters at the fire understood by then. Our mystified elders were uncomfortable. It had been a difficult time. They said something inconsequential about squash and I translated, and then I asked, as the Counter had, what the sweet Pomba boy had in mind for this daughter of Pomba.

All of the Counters stared at Kuyor with suppressed glee. Slyly, Kuyor repeated the question our elder had posed, extracted a reply, and translated it. I could see him thinking many things. Then, without looking at me, he said to the Counters in their language, "These are cold, rainy mountains for a naked love, but with a fire there is no secrecy. I saw a place that's hidden and warm enough. From here it's half as far as from the El Cuntur point to the Juanuru, and from here in the same direction one goes from the river to the grave of Warkari. I will be there tonight when the den of the lion is upside down."

This time I laughed. The den of the lion is a picture in the stars. I knew where to go. I knew when to go there. I knew what I would do when I got there. The Counters were laughing, too. Then Kuyor and I pretended nothing had happened, and even though the Counters urged us again and again, we refused to enliven their boring conversation about seasons and beans.

That night, when I found the grassy cleft, Kuyor was already there. There was no moon, and I couldn't see him. He growled, but I knew who it was. I let him find my legs and pull me down. I wanted to make it last, but we couldn't wait. It was like running as fast as we could. We raced for the high place. The feelings were too large to hold back. Straight to the top we went. We laughed and laughed, and then, without hurry, I explored his body, and he, mine.

Days later we crossed a high wet place where the plants looked like weapons, big rocks with blades. The ground and the air were wet, and it was always raining. It was a place for night spirits. I didn't like it there. Mostly, families walked together, but the elders had given up most of their watching, so I had found Kuyor, and we walked together.

In the last valley behind us, the Knot Counters had filled our bags again with potatoes taken from a stone storehouse there. All of us had heavy loads, so no one talked much.

"Soona," Kuyor said from behind me, "I've got an idea for a trick."

I didn't say anything. The load I carried wanted to fill my mind, so that I was slow to answer. Kuyor waited. "Tell me," I said finally.

"A Knot Counter, one of the young ones, told me that tomorrow we will meet the people who go to Pomba to live, the ones who have left their village for ours."

I thought about this. We had been walking many days, more than a moon, our village forever gone. Others had also been walking many days, their village gone from them. Tomorrow we would see them. Once, one time, that would be it, and then they would go to live in our homes and fields, and we would go to theirs.

"So my idea," Kuyor broke in, "is to find someone in their camp who will change clothes with someone in ours. One of theirs can go back to their old home with us. One of ours can go back to Pomba with them."

I smiled. "Will we understand them? Do they speak the language of the Knot Counters?"

"Yes. But who of us would want to go back home without the rest of us?"

That was easy. "Yataban." My planned marriage. Yataban was a worker, that is true—like his father with the biggest and richest fields— but I saw more spirit in a grinding stone.

Kuyor smiled. "Yes, Yataban would agree to it. Is there a Yataban in every village? If there is, they will know him." He wagged his head. "Yataban would go back with them as long as he could believe he would get in no trouble for it."

Maybe I was already rid of Yataban, but there was no harm in making certain of it.

Much happened the next day. We met the other village at noon. The Knot Counters let us stop and make camp early so that we could talk a little with these others. These people spoke the language of the Knot Counters, but they weren't Knot Counters. They were another people like us, a people the Knot Counters had overthrown three generations before. But they seemed beaten. No life in their eyes. There were no warriors among them. They were farmers like us, and among them was their equivalent of Yataban, a man named Maetin who cared more for his fields than he did for his own people.

We made the switch. Yataban and Maetin were happy to do it, especially when the rest of us and those of the other village agreed. It would make it easier for everybody to start out with a guide, someone who knew when to plant, how and where everything went together.

Not until after talking long into the night had we come to see that our two villages, even though they were far, far apart were much alike: both were built inside an open canyon halfway between an open highland and a river below. Both had one rainy season and one dry season every year, although their rainy season was a little longer than ours had been. They told us of a great mountain desert we were yet to cross. It did not seem possible that we would ever see anything like Pomba again.

The next day, we broke camp and left in our opposite directions. Yataban went back to Pomba, and Maetin came with us to return to his Wasi. Maetin seemed more human to me than Yataban. He had lines around his eyes from smiling. But I didn't talk to him. I would never understand anybody like him, it seemed to me. I loved Pomba as he must have loved Wasi, but I could never leave my people.

At the end of that day we had to cross one long pass. From the top we could still see the line of people from the other village with the Knot Counters guiding them. They looked like a string on the far horizon. I have never let myself get very sad, but looking back from the pass that evening, I was as sad as I had ever been. For the first time, I knew I would never see Pomba again and that I was losing something important.

Being sad was a strange feeling for me. Whenever it happened, I looked around for a little trouble, a wasp nest I might poke with a stick. It was the same for Kuyor. He would fight the long face of the exiles around him with a little mischief.

This time, it was a mistake.

The leader of the Knot Counters had big ears. A gold or bronze medallion, one for each side, fit into a hole in each lobe that stretched his ears to more than twice normal size. Big Ears was a serious leader, one of those uneasy with the duty. Either someone told him about the Yataban-Maetin switch, or he suspected it simply because he did not recognize Maetin. At any rate, his perplexed eye seemed always on the man.

Maetin was scared. Like Yataban, he was one who wished the least change, the least attention to his comings and goings, who wished the least trouble with any authority, and having made a choice to further that inclination, now found himself under scrutiny, a mosquito on the nose of Big Ears. Patiently, Big Ears maintained his vigil: one day, three days, ten days. It sucked the life out of Maetin. His eyes sank, his body softened, his features gathered like cloth.

Then Big Ears struck. We were descending into a canyon. On the road there, three could walk abreast. Big Ears moved in to walk beside Maetin. The others around moved away, but Kuyor and I, seeing what was coming, came up behind to listen. Big Ears said nothing until we had crossed the valley and were ascending again.

"What's your name?" he asked Maetin.

Maetin's answer was shaky. He wouldn't look at Big Ears.

"Speak in your own language," Big Ears said. He turned to look at me. "Say something to her."

Maetin looked like the trapped animal he was.

"Maetin," Kuyor broke in in our language, "Babble, babble. Just babble. See, like this." And Kuyor babbled. It must have sounded like babble to Maetin and Big Ears, too. Comprehension showed on Maetin's face when Kuyor went on making empty noise. His voice cracking, Maetin made the same baby noises back at Kuyor. Kuyor smiled. "Maetin sends you his warmest regards." Kuyor beamed at Big Ears.

"Why doesn't he translate for me, then?"

"Maetin speaks two languages, but he's not quick enough to translate. He can never remember what he just said. He's a little simple."

Maetin looked apprehensively at Big Ears, then at the ground.

But Big Ears was losing interest in Maetin. Kuyor represented honest, immediate provocation. "Yes, maybe Maetin's simple enough to understand the trouble he courts. Maybe that's wisdom."

"Yes, that's the kind of wisdom some people appreciate." Kuyor seemed unable to stop himself. I elbowed him hard.

Big Ears looked at me. As Maetin had done, I looked at the ground. "This one has no sense," Big Ears said, turning to Kuyor again. "He likes trouble. And I will give it to him." With the flat of his hand, Big Ears struck Kuyor on the chest. Kuyor staggered. Big Ears was older, bigger. And he had no practice at holding his anger.

When I saw the look of surprise and then temper on Kuyor's face, I stuck my elbow into his ribs again. He drew back as if to slap me. "Hit me," I said in our language. "Do it, but watch out for that snake. He wants to kill you."

Kuyor swung his head. He looked at Big Ears, who was smiling now and spinning his spear in his fingers so that, as it turned, it made little circles in front of Kuyor's chest. Kuyor's eyes smoldered, so I poked him once more in the same place. "Soona!" he shrieked at me. "I'll knock you down if you do that again."

Big Ears laughed. He laughed more than he felt like laughing. He threw his head back and guffawed, and then holding the spear at

Kuyor's neck, he stopped laughing and sneered. We had stopped walking on the stone road, and people piled up behind us. Kuyor glared at
Big Ears, and Big Ears answered with an expression of certain retribu-
tion. Then he turned and walked away.

The next day Big Ears killed Kuyor. It was just after dawn, and our
camps were rising. I saw Big Ears running with his spear, and I
screamed to Kuyor, who was kneeling at the edge of a stream and
washing his face. He stood, turned, his arms out a little, mouth open.
Big Ears's spear went into his chest. Big Ears could not stop and he
toppled onto Kuyor into the stream. When they pulled Kuyor out,
blood was pouring out of his mouth, and he was choking. I ran down,
fell on him, and kissed him. I swallowed the blood that I took out of his
mouth. He could not speak. He was already dead. They pulled me
away. Big Ears's face was jerking. He pulled his spear out of Kuyor and
put it through Kuyor's neck. I ran back to our camp.

I hadn't noticed, but one of Big Ears's medallions was missing from
his ear. Something else I hadn't noticed the day before, but something
Kuyor *had* noticed, was that each medallion in the ears of that Knot
Counter had two little holes in the center. In the half-darkness of that
moonlit night before, Kuyor had sneaked into the Knot Counters'
camp, found the sleeping Big Ears, threaded a sinew through his ear
medallion and tied the other end of the sinew to his spear. Then,
Kuyor, without waking the man, had put a big rock on the spear and
crept off. All of this, the others—several of our people and a Knot
Counter—told me later. Something else I did not see was the medallion still dangling from the spear that went into Kuyor's neck and
chest.

⌒

Kuyor's baby was born in the rainy season in Wasi, our new home. I
named her Tangara, which, in our old language, meant trickster.

 4

*f*OR A TIME, Alejandro came every day to see me in the savage
place. Sometimes it didn't feel right to give away one of my mothers, and I wouldn't do it. I did tell him about Soona and Phuyu and
Payita, because they were the ones most like me. Always though,
when he came, he taught me words and phrases in Spanish and made
me speak with him in silly little conversations. On the days when I
would not give him a story, he would tell me about how we were as
Runa, what we did differently than the peeled ones, and how it kept us
as we were and apart from the others.

"The Runa share and barter their food, themselves. You don't use
money, not to live on," he said. "That's the difference, the one that
matters."

"Yes," I said, "but that's only different because they have so much
of it, and we have none."

"No. There is no wealth in money. That power is false. A person
can go anywhere with it and get anybody else to do just about anything they want done to them or for them. That's true, because all it
takes is the exchange of something that looks the same in anybody's
hand. It always works best between strangers, because it keeps them

strangers. Money never pulls a stranger into your family, and sometimes, it goes backwards and makes your family into strangers."

I had never considered these things. It had always seemed to me
that it was a matter of bones and blood that made the Runa and the
peeled ones different. That it was like the difference between alpacas
and llamas.

"Money," Alejandro held his finger before my eyes. "Money is a
dangerous way to trade because it asks for no honor, no truth, simply
an agreement of price. After money, then all the other dangers come,"
he said. "Suspicion is the first one."

I listened in wonder, my mouth open. He laughed at this expression of mine, and it made me angry. I closed my mouth, and then I said
his words were silly. I was mad because he had laughed at my listening
ways, my mouth full of sky. I thought, I will never open my mouth
again for you Señor Pinta. But he didn't understand.

"Look," he said, casting his hand toward the valley beneath, down
toward Wasi. "Look at what makes a Runa family wealthy. Maybe they
have a field of one-day's plowing down low by the river where they
grow squash and fruits, and another by Wasi for corn, one- or two-
day's plowing, and then one more between Wasi and the savage place
for quinua and potatoes. Yes, they have those fields. They belong to
the family, perhaps inherited father-to-son or mother-to-daughter. But
who plows them? Who plants them? Who harvests them?"

"I plant them. We harvest them. Oqoruro and Lazario. Our
comadres and compadres. You know these things."

"You don't plant your corn."

"Of course not. It wouldn't grow if I did." A comadre, not the
woman of the house, plants the corn. Corn will not grow if it's not put
in the ground by a woman, but the woman must be from another family. My mother had planted many fields of corn but never her own.
When we harvested the corn, dried and shucked it, when we shelled
the beans and threshed the barley, it was always a ceremony of many

families—all the comadres and compadres who sponsored the weddings and the baptisms.

"See," Alejandro explained, "when a man and woman marry, all those who will sponsor come forward." I knew this, as any child knew it. "But look who they are." Alejandro spoke with much spirit, as I had when I'd been Soona for him. "They aren't ayllu," he said. That's our word for family. "They aren't karu ayllu," our word for distant family, second cousins and beyond. "Nor are they even awra," those families joined by marriage. "The ones who come forward to be compadres or comadres for each marriage are people who aren't in any way related. You see," Alejandro waved a hand at me, "these others, maybe six or ten stand up for the bride and another six or ten come forward for the groom. There they are, those who commit themselves for life to help you plow and plant, to help you harvest. And you, when you are married, will step forward to be comadre for the other weddings." Alejandro pointed toward Wasi again. "You see, what it does? It marries the village in a way. It makes everybody married to everybody else."

"What about the 'orphans'?" I argued. I was ready to show him that he was wrong. I didn't like this talk. "They aren't married into the village." The "orphans" were the Runa who had no fields, nor any compadres or comadres. They were Runa who had treated their mothers and fathers badly and so inherited no fields from either. They lived in the savage place where all the land belonged in one piece to the Runa of the village. The savage place was only pasture. It was too high to grow anything.

"That's what I'm saying," Alejandro argued. "It's the worst thing that can happen to you. You are poor, the poorest anyone can be—no land, no friends to help or be helped by."

"Father says that if we had money, it would cost less to pay others to work than it does to pay them food and corn beer and corn liquor and coca when they all come to work in our fields."

"That may be," Alejandro conceded. His face looked pained. "That may be. But that's the price of any marriage. It's more than just a matter of efficiency. A married village keeps out the invaders. It can take any kind of weather. When there is a drought, the Blancos' fields, the Lunas' fields are the driest, but their compadres take care of them, as they take care of their compadres when there is too much rain for those other fields by the springs. The hacendado does fine as long as he has money, but if something happens to the money in Lima, something the government changes, and his money is no good, he still has the land, but he can't do anything with it. Probably he would sell the land. Right now, he is rich and we are poor, but our people will always be here. Nothing is so sure for him. There are different ways of being poor."

I had never heard anyone talk this way before. I hated the hacendado. I hated what he had done to my mother years before. Alejandro was a peeled one, I thought. No Runa would have such crazy ideas. "There is no one in Wasi who wouldn't rather have what the hacendado has, his animals, the land he has taken from us."

"The hacendado doesn't have the perdonakuy."

"The perdonakuy!" I cried. Never had I heard such ideas. "What is that to anything? The perdonakuy?"

"Think about it," Alejandro said. "There it is in the very last part of the wedding. What do the groom and his godfather do when they kneel on the shawl? When they embrace with the crucifix between themselves? They apologize for any wrong that either has committed against the other. That's what they do. Then they kiss each other's hand and then embrace again. But that's only the beginning. That's what makes it Runa. The godfather goes on hugging and apologizing to all the new compadres of the groom and then to all of the groom's family. Then the Runa on the bride's side go through the line. Everybody does it. Every person in each family forgives each other.

"You see, it is that marriage of the village. It's the way that the

Runa of Wasi keep themselves as one family so that outsiders cannot break in and steal what they have."

"Who would want to steal what the Runa have? It would be like stealing the sky or the wind. There is nothing to take."

"Ha!" Alejandro said. "Yes. Stealing the sky from the Runa." Alejandro waved at the sky.

"How can you say these things and be a peeled one?"

That changed Alejandro. A cloud went into his eyes. "I'm not . . ." He stopped to look at me. I still could not meet his gaze. After all, he *was* a peeled one. He watched me a while. "And why do you want to learn Spanish?" he asked.

"I am not the one who says stupid things about the Runa and the hacendado and the perdonakuy."

"You will be the twenty-fourth mother."

"Yes," I said defiantly.

Inside, I felt something shake. There was something wrong with those words about my mothers, about the line of them, those words coming out of the mouth of a peeled one. It was as if I had told him a secret that all my mothers had kept, as if they were all watching me betray them. They were frowning inside me.

"You must go. I want to be alone." I wanted to tell him to never come back, but I couldn't say it.

Alejandro looked at me as if I'd hit him. I kept my eyes hard, so that he wouldn't say anything. He left. He went down the slope like a peeled one, slowly and bent forward a little to keep from falling. Those narrow, shiny shoes are for the plaza, I thought, not for walking on the mountain. Those feet inside shoes must forget what it is to walk on the earth. I wanted to think things about Alejandro that would make it good that he was gone, but by the time he had reached the rim of the canyon, when he was a speck of color on the edge of darkness, I wanted to have him back. The desire went from my heart into my loins, and I felt a terrible hunger.

〜

A month before I had surprised Isidro, the sorcerer. He had said that I let the hand of no man between my thighs. Always he teased me, but that day I'd teased him back.

Isidro was a tiny man with lean arms and legs and wicked eyes. He drank more chicha than anybody in the lower barrio, and he hunted all the girls. The women liked him back, even though they knew he would be nobody's husband and nobody's father. Most of the prettiest women in both barrios had been to the savage place with him.

The things *that* man does, they said to one another and rolled their eyes and giggled. Maybe he was no different than any other man in the ichu grass, but enough had been said so that most women wanted to see what it was like with the little man who talked in rhymes. Their interest in Isidro made me think of mother seventeen, Titu María, the whore of Wasi, who said that what she did to make a man excited came as much from what she said as what she did with her body.

In the week of vida michiy, when the young men and women went to the savage place to sing and dance and lie with one another in the ichu grass, Isidro always came to me first to ask all his little questions. At the same time, the other boys were stealing the shawls and belts and hats of the other girls.

When a girl doesn't try hard to take back what has been stolen, it's her way of telling him that she will go off with him into the grass. This flirt-stealing seals the agreement for what they will do in the dark after all the dancing and singing and drinking. But Isidro, like the rest of the boys, had never snatched away my hat or my shawl. Maybe he feared me, too, as the other boys did.

Some said that I was a sorceress, and although the girls desired after Isidro the sorcerer, the boys and the men did not lust after any sorceress. I knew from the stories that it had been this way in Wasi for most of my mothers in the last few generations. It was known in Wasi that we were different from other people. Women, and even sometimes men who had problems with their wives or husbands or other kin, would often come to my mother, my grandmother, to me and the mothers before, for our advice and wisdom.

But women with wisdom scare men. The boys and men of Wasi seemed afraid of women who might know too much. I wanted to tell them that we knew some stories about our forebears, which was no different from knowing what many of the old people knew.

For whatever reason, the women of my family had to wait longer for a husband, even though most had been regarded for their beauty. As for me, no man other than Isidro had showed an interest. That is, before Alejandro.

Every year I went up to the vida michiy, the sex games, on the savage place without anything in mind, except a kind of ready disappointment when Isidro would not snatch away my hat and my halfway innocence. When I was younger, maybe sixteen or seventeen, I went to the grass with a few of the boys. But now I think it was Isidro I wanted, not just because of what had been said about him—his little body made of vines and roots and magic—but because I knew he would not go further than the games, than what flesh wanted. I was old, twenty-six years, but I wasn't ready yet, not to be a wife or a mother. But I *was* ready to do some things with the body of a man, to put his root inside me, to have his hands on me and mine on him, to have his sweat running with mine, his breath in my ear, to feel two people join like rivers.

So it was at the vida michiy, early in the same year that I met Alejandro, and there I was, talking to Isidro, while the other girls, the young women, were running and chasing after their clothes, after their desires, and I was thinking all these hungry thoughts for Isidro but still only talking to him. There was happy music. Some of the boys played quenas, panpipes, and a drum. One had an old trumpet.

"Pilar isn't here for the long fight," Isidro teased. "She only wants a man once, and that's tonight."

"You watch out, Isidro! You're the one who's had them all," I tipped my head back at the laughing and singing.

Grinning, Isidro drew back. He had black curls in his hair and black curls in his eyes. His teeth were white and sharp as a lion's. "The men of Wasi say she is a sorceress. But how different is she under that dress?"

With that, I squatted to pee. He could hear the sound of my water. "To me, she sounds like any other woman," I said. "And the sorcerer, is he the same? Or do women marry the other men who can stay on longer?"

Isidro pushed me on the shoulder. "Don't pee on your foot. You will—"

I straightened and snatched his hat. ". . . see his root," I finished his rhyme. Pleased with myself, I started off with his hat for the ichu grass. It wasn't even dark yet. I glanced back at Isidro, and his mouth was open. I was being crazy, but with all the chasing and shrieking going on, I thought I could do what I wanted. Isidro followed at a distance.

Out of sight of the others, I stopped to wait. "You didn't run fast enough to get your hat back. So I suppose this woman will take you. And as the man. So I will be on top. I was the one who stole the hat. I will be the one to plow the root."

Isidro grinned, but he said nothing. I took his hand and pulled him into the grass, and then I put his hand between my thighs. We wrestled around, and I waited until I had his animal in my hand. He started to climb onto me, but I stopped him. "I took your hat," I said panting, sliding on top of him. I put him in me, and we didn't last long. At the end he cried, "Together we run, we run, and now . . ." he groaned mightily, "we are one."

"Isidro," I whispered. I still had him wrapped beneath me. We were spent, but I held him hard. And I still had him inside. "Isidro," I hissed, "why do I know that's the same rhyme you say to all of them? Next time . . ." I squeezed him a little with myself down there, "next time, Isidro, if there ever is a next time, I want it to rhyme with Pilar."

5

*M*Y NAME IS PHUYU, mother five. In my lifetime all the world changed.

Our village had always belonged to the empire of the sun. We tried to make ourselves unseen to the Incas, but they knew what they wanted. They wanted all any people could ever give: our work and our food and—the most terrible of all tributes—our children. When the tribes of people are small and they quarrel, a person is slapped or a garden raided. When the tribes of people are enormous empires and the leaders quarrel, whole families and villages disappear; they are the rocks that emperors throw at each other.

Before that quarrel, the Incas met our needs too well. They made sure that we did not starve; they put the stone images of our spirits in their palaces with their own sacred objects; they counted us and watched over us. But we were like well-tended animals raised for the slaughter, although we didn't want to be tended any more than we wanted to be slaughtered.

Then, in the smallest breath of time, there came a new invasion, this time by a kind of men none of us had ever seen before. Hairy-faced men with pink skin killed the Incas and stripped their cities of stone. We had to make ourselves unseen to these new invaders, which we could not always do.

When my father, Kanchay, died, Mother Tangara married his youngest brother, Chipchiy. Chipchiy served as a father for my brother, Huaman, and me for a year, until The Year of the Counting, when the Incas took Huaman away. But Chipchiy was only a father in the sense that he slept with my mother and he dug and harvested our fields. Mother told us what to do. They had no children. But they had no children not because they didn't couple. We listened often to their struggle. At the end, Chipchiy made a rattling sound. Sometimes my mother cried out like the bird in the savage place. It always made me breathe harder.

Every five years, in The Year of the Counting, the tucuyricoc—The One Who Sees All—came to see what we had done and what promise of tributes he could take back to Cuzco. We saw these Knot Counters for the first time when they were across the canyon. Taking water to the squash plants, Chipchiy had been in our fields by the river. He saw a llama train of ten animals and five men appear on the rim of the canyon. As they descended on the far side, he ran up the other side back to Wasi. They watched him running.

After Chipchiy had warned us, the sun crossed half the sky before the llama train reached our village. This gave us time to bury the illas we kept in the house. The One Who Sees All would take our little stone animals if he found them. The Inca would keep them for us in a palace in Cuzco where he kept the sacred carvings taken from other people. The men of the Inca took our sacred objects, just as they took us, the children, as hostages. What can people who plant the land do against such a force?

We hid as much of the quinua and corn as we could, but it was difficult. We had to stow these supplies of food in places where they weren't likely to be found, but if they were, they wouldn't seem to have been hidden. If the Incas thought we had hidden them, they would have killed us. We hid some in pots under piles of alpaca wool and some under a llama hide.

With the illas, it was otherwise. We hid them not to be found. They were smaller, easier to conceal, and of another, ultimate essence —one of holiness—which, by nature of the risk we took, gave them even more magic.

When we had the illas safely hidden, I ran to the homes of three compadre families to warn them. They, too, would spread the word to other compadres. The first home I ran to was Aqola's. His parents were there, but Aqola was not. He was in the savage place with the llamas.

Aqola was the one I wanted to see. I hoped that he and I would be husband and wife someday. Years later, he was the only boy I let inside me. Our parents saw our hearts were strong for each other. I knew that Mother would allow it. My inheritance would be more than Aqola's, so it would be a fine match for him, enough to please his parents. As for Aqola, he didn't care as much about my inheritance as he did about the way I danced. He had an eye for any dancer who could tell stories in the way she moved. And I got better as I got older. I could dance a good story.

As I ran with my warning, I dared not shout for fear those in the upper barrio might hear me and report it later to The One Who Sees All. Some of the people of the upper barrio, many of them in fact, were our people once, that is, descendants of Pomba, our old home. But they were also compadres and kin of the descendants of Maetin, a man of Wasi who had lived here before we came. He had traded places with one of our people from Pomba and, in that disguise, came back to a place where the language and ways were his own. Maetin's dealings with the empire won him favors, and he became, by Wasi standards, a wealthy man. He had many different crops, because he planted large fields in all three levels of the canyon. He had been granted sanctions of power for his allegiance and for his almost mystical transformation from the helpless foreigner to a canny, productive citizen of the empire. My grandmother, my mother, and the other people of Wasi had to take their disputes to him for judgment. Such advantages of power did not go without reward. Maetin had his choice of mates and of compadres. The upper barrio lived in his shadow.

While the upper barrio courted their closeness with Maetin and—in my time—his grandson Paqarin, the rest of us spurned them and their loyalties. They would do anything for advantages. We would not betray the ways of our families and our ancestors for temporary privileges. These collaborators had been entitled not by the eternal vitality of the earth but by the power of outsiders, a dangerously whimsical authority that wanted to rule life rather than nourish it.

A crowd from the upper barrio met these messengers of the empire at the edge of the village. The One Who Sees All, a tall nobleman, stood in front. He asked, "Who was the man running out of the canyon when he saw us?" No one knew. The One Who Sees All looked with the rest of the villagers at Paqarin. "I want everyone from Wasi here."

Paqarin obeyed. He went through the village calling. We all assembled in Paqarin's fallow field. The One Who Sees All asked, "Who ran out of the canyon when we came?"

Chipchiy stepped forward. The outsider looked in Chipchiy's mouth at his teeth, then at his hands and his feet. He felt Chipchiy's calves, then lifting the tunic, he brushed Chipchiy's thighs with the back of his hand. Chipchiy's eyes widened, but he did not move. Then The One Who Sees All examined my brother, Huaman. And then he looked at me. I was eleven then. He touched neither of us with his hands, but his eyes ran about poking everywhere. He wore a gold disc fit to a hole stretched in each earlobe. These pendants dragged on his shoulders when he turned his head. His eyes, black and small, were like those of a meat-eating bird. He had a sore in the corner of his mouth, one that oozed blood and yellow crystals at the split.

The next day, he called us all—every person in both barrios—out in Paqarin's field again. They divided us into groups: men, women, aged, those in the middle life, the young, and babies with their mothers. Two teams went among us. One asked, "How many fields do you have? How much do you grow?" The other recorded with knots on their quipus, colored strands of string. They made a clay model of the canyon around Wasi, etched in the location of everybody's plots, and then fired it. Then The One Who Sees All married five couples from the upper barrio. One couple had waited two years, just for the honor of being married by this outsider in the name of the sun.

On the third day, The One Who Sees All went door to door, inspected our homes, and assessed each family their food tax and assigned them their period of communal labor. A train of llamas from Cuzco would arrive later to pick up the corn and quinua we owed. They would come every year for the same amount. Our labor project for the next five years (when the tucuyricoc would return) was to build and maintain a suspension bridge over the river and to begin work on a road to Huinga, the next village on the canyon face.

On the day of the Knot Counters' departure, Mother Tangara hid Huaman and me out on the savage place. When the tucuyricoc came to our home, he stared at Mother Tangara. "Where are your children?"

"In the savage place."

"Bring them here." He turned to Chipchiy.

Chipchiy obeyed. He found us where we were hidden and told us to come.

"Have they left?" Huaman asked. Chipchiy said nothing.

Coming down the canyon, we could see that the tucuyricoc had finished his work. At the road they were loaded and ready to go. Chipchiy stopped. "Stay down," he said, "we'll go through the canal where they can't see us. I'll take you to our house. That's all he told me to do."

But one of the Knot Counters was waiting at home. He escorted us to the llama train. Mother was there, crying. I had never seen her cry before. It scared me as nothing ever had or did again. She did not make any sounds, nor was her head bowed. She stood erect, her eyes and her nose streaming, her shoulders jerking silently.

"Mother!" I ran and hugged her, pushed my face into her belly. She would not touch me.

"Huaman," she whispered, "you must go with them. They are taking you to Cuzco."

I whirled to look at Huaman. All the people of the lower barrio stood in a half circle around us. Huaman frowned. I could tell he was trying to be brave, trying to think of something that would change what Mother was saying.

"Chipchiy," Mother went on, turning from her son to her husband, "in another year, you will leave for the North Road to Cuzco. You will be a runner for the sun. For two years."

"Mother," Huaman's voice cracked, "how long will I . . ."

"Go now," Mother said firmly.

The One Who Sees All had been listening intently, as had the other counters from Cuzco. "Tell the little girl," he said to my mother. It was as if my mother would be his voice.

She looked at The One Who Sees All like she was looking at a poisonous snake. His face was impassive. Her voice broke with a choking sound. She knelt beside me. "In five years, when The One Who Sees All returns, he will take you to Cuzco where you might be a chosen daughter of the sun." Her breath was wet and hot.

"I don't want to be a chosen daughter," I whispered, pushing myself around her. I clasped her with my thighs. Everything inside me ached.

Chipchiy spoke up. "Why will you take so many from one—"

"Quiet," my mother called out. I could feel her body tense. We all understood the nearness of great danger.

The One Who Sees All smiled. He turned and led the train on the road out of Wasi. One of the counters waited for Huaman to step in front of him. Huaman's face was like a leaf falling over the cliff into the canyon. Mother's hands writhed. She started toward him but pulled back. I could see the condor illa in her hand. She couldn't give it to him. The counter was waiting, watching. Huaman went down the trail. He was still looking back, but the counter stepped in to block him from view.

In the late afternoon we saw them again across the canyon. Mother Tangara cried all night. But the next day her eyes were dry and hard. Chipchiy seemed to wander instead of walk.

The tribute we paid in food went into a stone storehouse on the edge of Wasi. Young Paqarin—he was only sixteen then, but he was the grandson of Maetin—oversaw what went in and what came out. Because Huaman was gone, Paqarin had been instructed to take no tribute from our family. A year later when the runner came to take Chipchiy away to be a runner, a chasqui, then Paqarin issued us an allotment of corn and quinua every moon. "You see," he told Mother, "the sun cares for its children."

We carried our allotment in three large squash shells. On the way home, Mother spoke to me, as if to herself. "We don't want to be anybody's children. The quinua from the storehouse has worms in it. The corn paid in tribute isn't as fresh as ours. We didn't ask anyone to care for us. They will keep us as slaves and call us something else." Her face was pinched. "The sun cares for its children," she mocked under her breath.

⌒

Paqarin, who received all messages from the province ruler, told us that Chipchiy lived in a village six days' journey away. In that village Chipchiy rested one quarter of the moon. Then, for two quarters of the moon, he worked. He ran barefoot whenever there were messages or quipus, the knotted strings, to relay. Every runner on the main road to Cuzco lived in a little basket-shaped hut in the middle of his stretch of road, a stretch he could run in the dark of a moonless night, if need be. Every chasqui had his own horn, a great shell from the big waters where the sun set. He listened for the call of the runner coming and then blew his own call to warn the runner on the other side. Chipchiy memorized whatever message was to be carried and took the quipus, if there were any, and made his delivery to the next runner. Running messengers covered in one day what men walking covered in five.

Chipchiy was gone for two years, as had been promised. Just one moon before he was to return, the civil war began. When the sickness of little scabs killed, first the Inca, Huayna Capac, and then the son he had picked to succeed him, two other sons battled for the empire. Huascar ruled from Cuzco while Atahuallpa reigned over the northern part of the empire. When Huascar conscripted men to fight, Wasi had to send thirty, and Paqarin chose them.

He chose Aqola first, and I knew why. Paqarin had been watching me. Even though he was from the upper barrio, I saw him look at me with hunting eyes. Mother Tangara's fields, my inheritance, were not what narrowed his eyes and moistened his lips when he stared, nor were they a hindrance either. Paqarin knew about Aqola and me. Everybody did. We had no reason to hide anything. So we thought. After Paqarin picked Aqola to fight for the empire, he grinned messages at me. But I knew Mother Tangara hated Paqarin and the soft and fearful ways of the upper barrio. I knew she would agree to no arrangements there. But we both knew that I lived under a curse and that I dared taunt no one.

I was fourteen when Aqola left Wasi. I was there to say goodbye, but I could not watch him go. I remembered the face of my brother, Huaman. I ran to the savage place. In the afternoon I looked for their party to cross the canyon. A tiny flickering square of color, they seemed like men who were going to work on the empire's road or storehouses. They did not look like men and boys who might never come back.

Then, ten days later, a girl from the upper barrio, Mayu, slipped at the river's edge and hit her head on the rocks. She fell in the water and was gone. We never found her body. When we were coming back from the second day's search, I saw Mother Tangara talking to Paqarin, and I was alarmed. Paqarin was smiling. He wasn't looking at my mother as she talked. He was looking at me.

Waiting in the house for Mother Tangara, I tore at my face with my fingernails. I didn't want anyone but Aqola waiting for me. Maybe if I disfigured my face Paqarin and the men from Cuzco would let me be.

When Mother saw me, she went for water. We sat on the llama hides, and she cleaned the blood from my scratches. She made little sounds in her chest, but her face, still and grim, scared me.

"Mother," I sobbed.

"Shh," she said. "You will be brave. You are the granddaughter of Soona, and you are my daughter, and you *will* be brave." She looked at me as if she were angry with me. I quieted. "Mayu drowned yesterday. Now you will be Mayu. When The One Who Sees All returns, Phuyu will be dead, two years drowned."

"Mayu lives . . . lived in the upper barrio. And Paqarin—"

"Yes, Paqarin. Those in the upper barrio must accept you as Mayu. That's the only way."

"But The One Who Sees All? Won't he recognize me?"

"Not with certainty. Not enough to question the word of all the village and of Paqarin, who is spy and envoy for The One Who Sees All."

"Wouldn't they kill Paqarin if they knew?" I pleaded.

"No," Mother Tangara said. I could see she had already made many plans out of my questions. It crossed my mind that she might have even pushed Mayu into the river, except that she had been with me in the corn when Mayu died. "The One Who Sees All wanted you for the empire of the sun. Paqarin is part of that empire. I suggested to Paqarin that it would be wise to have The One Who Sees All join you in marriage when he marries all the other couples who are waiting. There would be nothing secretive about it. I didn't tell Paqarin, but I think even if the tucuyricoc had any suspicions about who you were, he would go through with the marriage as a favor for Paqarin's loyalty. We all know that no one else here would do for the empire what Paqarin does."

Lying there in Mother Tangara's lap, I tried to think of some other way I could avoid Paqarin and The One Who Sees All.

"If you go to Cuzco, you will never come back. Perhaps they would kill you there in their ceremonies. Here, you will be Paqarin's wife. You will be in the upper barrio. Those things you can never change, but you will be near your family, near your people. I know that we will never see Huaman again."

"I'll tear my face up," I hissed and raised my hands toward my face, even though I knew I could do no more that day. My face, my eye, hurt too much.

Gently, Mother put my hands back upon my chest. "Then Paqarin will not marry you. The One Who Sees All will have his vengeance upon you to keep other women from trying what you would do to save yourself. There's no other way, Phuyu . . . Mayu, I call you now. I told Paqarin what it would be like having you live in his house when he held your life in his hands, how you would be caring for him, lying with him, raising his children, all the time owing him your life. Paqarin will not pass up that kind of power."

I shuddered. I could not understand her cruelty. "And if Paqarin changes his mind. After all this?"

"Then I would tell Paqarin that I will tell The One Who Sees All what we had schemed."

"The men from Cuzco would kill us all."

"Paqarin is not so desperate to sacrifice his life for anything. Remember how much he has, how much more he wants."

I couldn't talk around her. Tears welled in my eyes, and everything looked warped.

"Phuyu . . . Mayu . . . we are people, women, who live. Things hurt us, but the pain will not last long enough to kill us. Tomorrow will be better, no matter what happens, it will all be better than it is today. We are made to live and made to smile again, despite ourselves. You will see how strong you are. You will laugh again, though not without knowing the cost of everything. Just remember that angry people always laugh better. I think they live better."

We did not talk about it again. Mother Tangara called me Mayu. Our compadres and comadres looked at her curiously. But my mother would not explain. Eventually, they, too, called me Mayu.

Paqarin looked upon me as if I were his. I could not answer his gazing, even if he would be the one to save me. On the night of the corn-planting fiesta he waited for me outside the light of the fires. I didn't see him, and he caught me. Holding me hard with one hand, he slid the other along my leg and went up to find me. I didn't resist, but I didn't answer by looking for him under his clothes. He probed at me. Panting hard, he said, "Phuyu—"

"Mayu," I said fiercely. He was the only person I wanted to be Mayu for. There would always be a Phuyu, but not for him. Paqarin was the kind of person who could live with someone who did not love him. He was on this earth, walked upon it, but that earth was not in him. With his hand on me, coarse fingers scraped. For what? The feel of flesh, as warm and loving as the meat of a butchered llama?

He could see that I would neither resist nor answer. He knew that it wasn't right to take me there in the darkness of the village. He could have me in the savage place, but it wasn't right for a man to take a woman anywhere in the canyon unless they were married. So I did not resist Paqarin's fingers. That was an answer yes, one I had to give to live with my people in Wasi. But I did not take his shaft in my hand or in any way answer the cravings I could hear in his breathing. That was my answer, no.

Mother Tangara was right. After you see death, see what you can imagine of it, and exile, or what you can imagine of that, nothing is so frightening again. Neither the death, nor the exile. And out of that comes a firmer, less helpless sense of oneself, enough to see that nothing about the forces outside, the ones that would kill your body or put out your soul, matter at all compared to the power inside. It is true, those other people might kill you, but it would be better dying by them than by your own hand, by putting your own mind and will to sleep.

Chipchiy came back, and Mother Tangara was happier. I understood. She was ready to lose everybody, one at a time. She had made herself ready to live with nothing, and then when Chipchiy reappeared, it was like an unexpected gift. He came at night. He had been a chasqui for two years, so he could run day and night. It got to be like breathing or even sleeping, he said about running, a kind of quiet concentration that went on beneath thought, beneath any distress or any wish.

He lifted the cloth at the doorway and stood there in the firelight as if he were in the wrong house. Mother Tangara kicked over a pot of water on her way to him. They hugged. I could see their hands wild to touch each other. I pushed between them and held Chipchiy for a moment, and then I went out under the moon so they could be alone.

Just as Chipchiy had done, Aqola came back after two years. But Aqola could not stay. The Inca brothers were at war, and Aqola, who was a trained warrior by then, had to fight their quarrel. He was in Wasi for only three days. Almost five years had passed since the last Year of the Counting, and soon I was to be married to Paqarin.

When I first saw Aqola in the street, I couldn't run to him, I couldn't kick over a pot of water as Mother had getting to Chipchiy.

"Hello Phu . . . Mayu," he said. He was so pretty. Aqola had always been a pretty man, small bones and smooth skin with tiny pores, but hard as an illa with a sharpness that glinted from his eyes and cheekbones, from the ledges beneath his collarbones.

"Welcome home, Aqola," I returned, trying to be gay, trying to warn him of the danger. There was no one near enough to overhear me. Five houses down, the old woman, Qoto, was scraping hair from a scalded guinea pig. I touched Aqola's hand. Making myself smile, I looked over Aqola's shoulder and said, "I'm sorry. It's the only way. Paqarin . . . I couldn't . . . you are the one I love."

"I know," Aqola choked. "I know."

I looked all around to see who was watching us. It scared me to see Aqola's face tearing apart; he didn't seem to realize the danger. All of Wasi, especially tattlers from the upper barrio, would want to see Phuyu greet Aqola. "In the savage place," I whispered, still working at a smile, "tomorrow night, just after the moon rises." I didn't wait for a reply. His face was dangerous. I hurried down the street. I smiled at Qoto. I smiled at her dead guinea pig. I smiled at the piles of llama shit behind Qoto's house. I smiled my way home, and then I cried all day.

The next night I surprised Aqola with the wetness of my body, with this heart on fire. I took him with a fury that had only one night to spend itself.

"When I come back . . ." he said. In the darkness he did not see me shake my head. Nor the tears. This was it. I looked at it as the measure of my life. It *was* the measure of my life. Everything else I have held up against it. I held his head in both hands and squeezed, and then I ran back to Wasi.

One moon later The One Who Sees All came to Wasi, but he was not the same one as before. He wore brass pendants in his ears and his eyes were as loveless as a spider's, but his lip had no sores, and he did

not know who Phuyu or Mayu were. Apparently, he had been instructed by the other tucuyricoc, for he did ask for Phuyu. When
Paqarin told him Phuyu had drowned two years before, he did not
question it. After the census on the second day, The One Who Sees All
married nine couples, Paqarin and me among them, in the same field
where we had assembled to be counted and interviewed. By the authority of the sun, the empire, and the Inca, the new One Who Sees
All joined us.

～

I went to live with Paqarin. My name was Mayu. I lived at the bottom
of a river. My hair swam like thin snakes in and out of my mouth. But
eight moons later I gave birth to a daughter. I named her Rumi
Pachak. I told Paqarin that Rumi Pachak would be an impatient girl,
for she came a moon early. But, in fact, Rumi Pachak had been in me
for all nine moons, and she would grow to be a woman known for her
serenity.

In my marriage, I submitted to Paqarin's peculiar appetites, those
of his body and of his thinking, and after a time, found myself content
enough with the care of my daughter and the fields. A year later, Rumi
had a brother, and in another year, another brother. At the same time,
Paqarin's peculiar ways of lovemaking, all the different things I could
never imagine possible with the stick and hole of sex, gave way to the
simplest, hastiest, and least frequent of acts. I knew that he made frequent journeys to the savage place where he could continue with his
strange couplings. A perfect solution, I thought, although I was careful
not to imply it. I even went so far as to complain about his lack of interest, just enough to feed his pride, too.

And then Aqola, without one foot, came home for good. He and
one other man were all that remained of the thirty that had been sent
from Wasi. Hungrily, I listened to his stories. But never alone with

him; I was always part of a group of people listening. Four women vied for Aqola and waited for him. And I wanted him to be happy. Moreover, it was inevitable that he would marry and have children with another woman and live in the lower barrio. The sooner, the better, for me.

Aqola told us all of his long journey to the northlands where they went to defeat Atahuallpa's army. At the last battle they were near the land of Pomba, our ancestral village. That's what the commoners told him there. They might have gotten all the way to that lost valley of ours had not Atahuallpa's troops been so many and so experienced.

"They slaughtered us," Aqola said. "When we attacked, they didn't run. They were accurate with their spears and arrows and their slings. When we shot and threw at them, no one fell. When they threw at us, hundreds fell. We ran. They charged after us and killed us like we were insects. After a while we didn't even fight. We just let them kill us. I thought I was dead. I was under other bodies. But when night came and I could feel the cold and the pain of my wounds, I crawled out. I crawled all night, and I crossed the canyon. I couldn't walk. I found a tangle of thorns that I could get into on my belly. No one looked for me there. In the daylight I could see them across the canyon. They piled the bodies of our men into a mountain and left them there. It was a mountain of dead you could see from far away. Thousands. The smell was horrible. When the other army left, I came out. For a quarter of a moon, I had lived on the water in roots and on ants and beetles. The common people of that land helped me when they saw my foot and when I told them I hadn't chosen to fight for the Inca. I didn't find a camp of our fleeing army for another moon."

I wanted to ask Aqola about the land and the people, if they were like us, but I dared not speak. Everyone would watch. They watched us anyway. I went back to my home with Paqarin. But before I left, I nursed my little girl. I sat turned so that Aqola might see her face. I think he saw her face but did not understand who she was. Which was good. I could never tell him. He would show a love for her that would tell others. One moon after he came home, Aqola was married.

⌒·

One day a runner came to Wasi and said that one of the white ones was coming to Wasi. He was atop a giant llama and soon would be on the far side of the canyon. We all ran down to see and then laughed and laughed to see all of the people of both barrios there. If The One Who Sees All had been there, he could have counted us all.

When the pink one and the giant llama appeared on the other side, we couldn't tell much about them except that they were huge, one atop the other. One sound came from all of us, one great low sound that made my head and neck prickle.

We waited there at the edge of town. A few women had brought their grinding stones and sat down to grind corn. Most of the women, as I, spun wool as they waited. It was something to see, thirty or forty drop spindles spinning and whirling nervously. Whenever our eyes met, we giggled. Several men repaired and sharpened their hoes and digging poles. Aqola sat by the sun's stone and stared at the ground. He picked up pebbles and made a design in his hand with them.

Then we heard the rock-banging sounds of the feet of the giant llama cracking on the cobble of our walking road. The women snatched up their spindles. The men, who had been sitting, stood. There we were, all of Wasi, waiting to see this new pair of creatures.

We made no sound. When they came around the corner, there was so much to see. First the hair on his face, the skin that wasn't white like ice but pink and yellow, something like the skin of a scalded guinea pig when the hair is scraped off. The head of the giant llama, all bone and nostrils and eyes and teeth with leather and metal in its mouth, breath like gusts of wind, a slick belly like a bladder skin filled with water, legs like trees and the long-haired tail. The man—it was a man

—with leather leggings and a metal hat and a red tunic with parts that wrapped around his arms.

His eyes! That was the surprise for me. Those eyes were the color of the sky, the eyes of a blind man. But he was looking at all of us. When he saw me, I pushed myself back in among the others. He spoke in another language. No one understood. Paqarin asked him if he understood Runasimi. The man answered with strange words. He shrugged and then spoke to his llama. The giant animal moved toward us, and we moved apart like waves of water. The two of them went up and down the lanes of Wasi. We followed at a distance. Then the man and the giant went back to the road out of Wasi and left.

A year later, three of the pale ones came. One of them spoke Runasimi. He told our people that we wouldn't be the slaves of the Inca anymore. We already knew that. We hadn't paid tributes for three years. One of the men dressed in black went to the Inca stone, to the finger-pointing-at-the-sun, and attacked it with a boulder. Three times he hit it before it broke. The one who spoke our language said that we were not to worship the sun or believe in any magic again. We were to worship the spirits they taught us to worship. He showed our people the black-covered pack of square-cut corn sheaths, each sheath covered with tiny tracks. He showed us a sacred metal object like two sticks crossed and tied together. When the three men left, they said they would come back.

Paqarin had told them he was Wasi's leader, but no one paid him any mind. He couldn't see that, without the empire, the rest of the villagers didn't care what he thought or said. He didn't see them laughing.

But I didn't care what they said about my husband. One-footed Aqola was the one I loved, he and our daughter, Rumi Pachak. Aqola had his own family by then, three sons and a wife who seemed to love him. His sons were beautiful and kind, and I think I may have liked them from afar more than my own sons, the boys I had with Paqarin.

But I had learned many things by then, and one of them was how to live like I was inside somebody else's skin.

By this time, Huascar and Atahuallpa were dead, Huascar captured and killed by Atahuallpa's men, and Atahuallpa by the pink ones after they took all the gold he had delivered. The pink ones chose Manco Inca, another Inca brother, to rule. Thinking to master him, the pink ones demanded more gold, but Manco Inca rebelled, and following a war that lasted ten years, the pink ones killed him, too. After that, the pale ones came regularly to Wasi, the man in black to teach us about a new spirit, and a tribute man to take much of what we grew. It was their land now, and to use it, we had to pay them. The pale ones had divided up our world and divided up our work. Some of our people had to work in deep holes to bring out the metals for the pale ones who owned them, but in Wasi we only had to give them corn, squash, and beans. It was better for us because most of those who had to work inside the ground died there.

I didn't watch much of what the pale ones were doing to my village. I had Rumi. I watched my daughter grow to be a beautiful woman. When Rumi Pachak was eighteen, she married a man from the upper barrio. Mother Tangara and I had tried to find her a husband in the lower barrio, but Paqarin wouldn't consent. It would have been a loss for Rumi Pachak—she would not have inherited the fields I brought to the marriage, not without Paqarin's consent—but she would have been among her own people, the descendants of Pomba, of Warkari, Mita, and Soona. For three years Rumi remained without child. The year after Mother Tangara died, Rumi Pachak carried a child inside her. It was as if the spirit of Mother Tangara was coming back. Rumi named her daughter Karu.

Karu had eyes that crossed.

That was my chance. I made Rumi promise me that Karu would marry in the lower barrio. Karu would inherit Rumi's fields, those inherited from Mother Tangara and me, which alone would have been enough to hold her above any match from the lower barrio. But her crooked eyes, that fault, would make it a fair match. The husband below would get a woman with crossed eyes, but the fields would compensate. By then I would be dead. Paqarin would be dead.

Rumi promised. I thought to tell her my secret then, but I waited.

⁓

In the old empire, the pale ones fought on against two of Manco's children still hiding with a small army in the jungle. One of the Inca sons died there, and then the second and last one took power. The pink ones went down into the dark lands to find this last Inca, the one who was called Tupac Amaru. He fled with his wife. They ran deep into the forest, but the pink ones went after them and found them. The wife of Tupac Amaru was carrying a child about to be born. Tupac Amaru had with him a sacred statue of gold that was filled with dust from the hearts of the Incas before. With this sacred statue of all the Incas, the pale ones believed they had all of the Incas' hidden gold. They took this last Inca into the middle of Cuzco to show all the other invaders and all the native people that the end of the empire stood there before them in the body of that last Inca, Tupac Amaru. There, they cut off his head. But they couldn't chop Tupac Amaru's head from his body until he had quieted the crowd for them.

Everyone knew that the time of the pink ones had come.

I was an old woman then. That year, when I could no longer weed the corn, I stopped eating so I would die. I told Rumi Pachak my secret. I made her promise that she would try to arrange a marriage between Karu and a grandson of Aqola. I told Rumi that we were not like the Incas or the Knot Counters, as Soona called them, but that we could do something like they did with royal blood, that is, in part. By marrying sister and brother, the children of the sun kept pure their blood of the sun's spirit. They were not people like the rest of us. If Karu married a grandson of Aqola, I told Rumi, it would be something like the Incas, a return to her own blood, a mixing back to their ancestral mothers whose stories I had made her memorize.

"My father . . ." she said. "Aqola?" Her face was full of wonder. Such things change the house inside our heads so much that when we look out the door all has become different.

 6

*t*HE SEASON OF RAINS was coming. For days, I—Pilar—and all the other women of Wasi had been braiding the coyo grass that the men had cut and gathered. We had pounded the grass with rocks to flatten it and make it bend easier, and then we braided it into long thin ropes. We braided the ropes together again, then those in turn once more. In the canyon at the place of the bridge, the men twisted four of these heavy ones into a giant rope thicker than my arm. We needed six of these cables long enough to stretch across the canyon and tie through the carved rock anchors. Four of the straw cables made the bridge floor, and the other two went above to be handrails. I knew from the story of Tangara that we had learned this way of building the bridge from the men of the Inca.

We women were still braiding coyo when the teachers came to see. The pieces we were working on went into the bridge as a kind of woven wall that linked the floor of the bridge and the hand ropes, a cage that kept children or animals or drunk people from falling out between the big ropes. Working, about twenty of us sat on a little patch of grass just at the edge of the rocks.

I was happy. When the teachers came, it made me even happier, because sitting in this group, I could watch their faces and listen to them without showing more interest than anyone else. By then, I could understand Spanish. I wouldn't speak it to anyone but Lazario or Alejandro, but I could listen as much as I wanted.

Alejandro caught my eyes once, but I looked away. He sat near me on a rock. Reynaldo joined him. They were talking about a man named Guzmán in Ayacucho, a teacher who, Reynaldo said, would save this country from itself. I thought to myself that Reynaldo ought to remember what had happened to José Gabriel Tupac Amaru, another man who would save this country. They cut him into pieces.

In time, Reynaldo began to frighten me.

"Violence is the only way we can clean out the gangrene," he spoke vehemently, as if cursing. "Guzmán says we must completely destroy the state apparatus, cut out all the dead flesh before we can start again, and then we start with cadres that are pure. If you leave any of the cancer behind, it grows again." Reynaldo's snowy cold eyes went over me, but they did not see me watching and listening. Around that iciness, the skin of his face was slick and sweating.

"You're talking about killing people?" Alejandro asked him.

I looked at Alejandro's face. I didn't know the words to say it, but I knew from my stories the kind of answer that would come from Reynaldo.

"The corruption is worse than death. We will kill those who are killing us."

"Who would you kill in Wasi?" Alejandro was intent.

"There will be executions. There have to be executions. We can't have a revolution without the violence that scours—"

"But for whom? If you kill the people, who is this for?"

Reynaldo smiled a father's smile. "We won't kill the people. This is a revolution of the people. It will be for the Indians, the peasants. Guzmán says—"

"Well, who?" Alejandro interrupted again. "Who will you kill in Wasi?" Alejandro looked around at our working people.

"The question is, Alejandro, who will you kill? You must be part of our revolution. This isn't a matter of watching. You participate. Every-one participates. Indians. Women. They will be warriors and execu-tioners, too. There is no neutrality. Not only will you see executions, you must be willing to do it, too. To kill people for the revolution."

"Who is the enemy?" Alejandro stood. "In Wasi, who is the enemy?"

"Wasi is the same as everywhere. Those who don't participate are the enemy. If you mean which people are first to change or go, then there are those like the hacendado and the priest, of course. But they are only representations. It's the system inside everyone that must change. That's what will be cut out."

I stopped braiding. This, I did not understand. Always the peeled ones wanted the Runa to do those things that the peeled ones told them to do. First, it was the Inca and then all the different kinds of peeled ones. But now, here was this Reynaldo, a peeled one himself, a misti—our word for mestizo—saying that the first enemies were two other peeled ones, the priest and the hacendado. A peeled one leading the Runa against other peeled ones? Reynaldo leading the brutes?

"Pilar!"

I jerked. My fingers ran into themselves trying to braid again.

"Pilar." It was Lazario. He ran up into this nest of women. "We need more coca for the offering," he demanded.

I dug into my coca bag. Seeing him, I felt better. Lazario was so diligent. He would be the camayoc, the bridge builder, his father was. It was the calling of a son, something like what I felt being the daugh-ter of twenty-three mothers. All the purpose filling his face made it shine. His body stood in front of me, but his face was already running back with the coca.

"There's the boy with all the stories. His great-grandmother was a sweetheart of the Inca." It was Reynaldo. He laughed at his own joke.

Lazario regarded him curiously. I dropped some of the coca leaves and picked them up again.

"So tell us a story," Reynaldo told Lazario.

"What story?"

"Don't be insolent. One of those stories that are supposed to go all the way back to the Incas, the stories you bragged about."

Lazario looked at me. I warned him with my eyes.

"She's the one?" Reynaldo asked him, looking at me.

"Yes. She's the one. Tupa Inca used to chase her in the savage place, but he could never catch her," Lazario joked. "Pilar runs fast."

Alejandro grinned. I put my hand over my mouth. I did not want Reynaldo to know that I could understand his language.

Reynaldo stared at Lazario. I could see the danger in Reynaldo's eyes. "The coca," Reynaldo tipped his head at the leaves in my hand, "is this an offering to the spirits?" He asked this with a lowered voice.

Lazario was puzzled. I was, too. Lazario nodded.

"There are no spirits," said Reynaldo, "only science."

"Are there any naqaq in your science?" Lazario asked. A naqaq is an evil spirit that steals fat from the bodies of people, or castrates men, or eats little children.

Reynaldo cackled. "The naqaq steals the fat of the people and uses it to grease the mining machines. Ha ha. That's what the brutes believe." His laughter was ugly. "Only a brute would believe that." His laughter was loud in the canyon, even with the sound of the river there. "And Wamanis, the good spirits, are white men with beards who counsel the president in Lima." Reynaldo shrieked like a bird.

All the women quit braiding to watch him.

"You better watch out for the naqaq," Lazario said.

"The naqaq wants my balls." Reynaldo clutched at his groin. The women giggled at him. "The naqaq is a pinnacle of stupidity." Reynaldo scowled. "Your superstitions are stupid. There are no superstitions in science, and soon, there will be no room for them in Wasi. We will take the idiot out of the brute."

Lazario took the coca and started away. Over his shoulder, he said again, "You better watch out for the naqaq."

The next day when Alejandro met me in the savage place, I wanted to know about this science thing, about why peeled ones would ever want to lead the Runa against other peeled ones.

"The science thing I don't understand. It's something about man coming from animals before history, and now in the time of history, it will go on past man, not past us, I guess, but to something different, something better. Reynaldo says . . . or this man, Guzmán, says that it has to be done with killing, so that everyone knows that the revolt will stop at nothing. Guzmán says something about a river overflowing its banks to do the killing and then slipping back into the channel, so that everyone knows they can't stop it any more than they can stop a river."

"But who will do this killing? You asked Reynaldo that. I don't understand. No peeled ones will lead the Runa against other peeled ones." I didn't want him to answer that. I wanted to believe I could live without being chased. I wanted to believe that although most of my mothers had to live in the times of chasing, it wasn't going to happen to me. My stomach twisted to think that many years from now some mother would tell her daughter the story of how Pilar had been chased. I did not want to escape life; I only wanted to do the nice things that people did. I wanted a husband and children. I wanted to plant corn in the fields of my helper families and watch it grow in our fields. I wanted to shepherd and weave in the savage place and watch the condor soar overhead.

"Don't forget that Manco fought for conquistadors," Alejandro said. "Before he saw what all they had in mind. There are, and always will be, those who will help the outsider. But it's more than that. These people of Reynaldo's want to get power by using the Runa to overthrow the mistis, which would be fine with the Runa except that they don't understand that, after the mistis, the Runa are next."

"What did he say about the priest and the hacendado? It's the other peeled ones who would have to do it. The Runa have no power."

"You've heard the grumbling," he said. "Every summer there's the argument about who has to give up a year of their life to herd the church's cattle and llamas. No one wants to plow the church's fields either, or do the harvesting. The church has the largest fields and the largest herds, and the priest charges too much money for every marriage and burial and baptism. He's at every fiesta where he eats and drinks more than anyone else. He—"

"But there's always been grumbling about the priest and the church."

"But there's more to it now. You watch what happens. Reynaldo says they will move on the priest first and then the hacendado."

This idea stopped me. I wanted to believe bad things would happen to the hacendado. I hated him. He had raped women of Wasi. He was a drunkard. He was rich. If we said anything about him, he would tell the soldiers that we were stealing from him, and the soldiers would take us to Ayacucho and put us in jail.

"How can we do anything to him?" I asked.

"There have been some changes in Lima, a government that rules for the villages. Sometimes. The Runa who go back and forth from Wasi to Lima, to Little Wasi—the barrio there in Lima—they know about the papers and the court and how the village can do things to take their land back from the hacendados who stole it from them. The village has papers three hundred years old—"

"Yes, I know about these things. In the story of Genera, my great-grandmother, Mother Twenty-one, the judges didn't care about those papers, the ones that said the land was ours. It was the great-grandfather of this hacendado who stole the land from Wasi. They were all wicked men, and I wish for this one that his soul burns and cries forever inside the peaks of the savage place he stole." I could feel my voice changing, my face turning into a mask. I felt like Reynaldo inside.

Drawing his head back, Alejandro watched me as if I were a mad dog. "You know that story, too?" he asked, shaking his head. "That was at the end of the last century, and you know that story?"

I nodded.

"If the Wasi migrants take the matter to court, they would want you there to tell what you know."

"No," I said, "those are my stories."

"They're—"

"No," I said.

He watched me for a while. "Why do you hate the hacendado so much? It doesn't seem like you to hate anyone like that."

"I saw him do a terrible thing."

Alejandro waited, but I waited, too. I could not tell if this was something I would say in words, out loud. Talking changes things, and I had to be careful.

"It was my mother, Hilario," I said.

"Your mother? How would the hacendado have known her?"

"I was with her. And Lazario, too, on her back. He was just a baby. It was in the savage place, near the Wamani's monument, down on the other side where the hacendado's big field comes up to Wasi's land." I didn't want to remember that day. I was six years old then.

I looked at Alejandro's face. "This isn't my mother's story. And it's not my story. This is a story about an evil man. This isn't about us or Wasi. Do you understand what I mean?"

"Yes, I do."

I untied one of my braids and then tied it again. "There had been a storm," I began. "Lightning and rain, wind. We hid in the rocks in the little hut my mother had made in that rocky island next to the monument for the Wamani. Then the storm went away, and the sun came out, but there was still mist in places. One of our llamas was gone. We went to look for it. The mist wouldn't leave, but all the time there would be holes in it where the sun came through. We went onto the land of the hacendado. We called and whistled and looked, and finally, back on the edge of the canyon where it drops off to the plowed fields of the hacendado's, we found the llama. Mama scolded it and started back.

"We were hurrying. Mama didn't want to be there. When a clearing came in the mist, we saw the hacendado mounted on a horse. He galloped up in front of us and stared. His cheeks made knobs around the bones of his skull. His lips were thin. He said a few words, some in our language, others in his. I didn't understand. My mother told him no, that we had only found our lost animal." I swallowed and fidgeted with my braid again.

"He got off his horse and told her something I didn't understand. Mama said no, and he hit her face. I started crying. She scooted me away. She pulled Lazario off her back and gave him to me. He was still wrapped in the shawl. She told me to quit crying and sent us behind a little rise of ground. But the hacendado came over to us and ripped the shawl off of Lazario. He went back over the rise with my mother. I couldn't quiet Lazario's wailing.

"I waited a time before peeking over the rise. They were both on the ground, the hacendado on top of Mama. Her skirts were pulled up over her face. He had laid the shawl below her, down where his knees and feet went. Mama's back was in the mud. He was hunched over her and grunted like a monster. Nothing could be so ugly. I wasn't crying, I remember, because Lazario was crying for everybody. I tried to hush him. Between Lazario's sobs, I listened for the man to quit grunting. When I looked again, the man was getting on the horse. Mama had pulled her skirts down, but she was still lying there. She pulled the muddy shawl over her breasts and cried until she saw me. Then she got up and became like Mama again.

"Back in the canyon, Mama washed herself for a long time. She put the leaves of the lina plant inside her and said it would kill the seed of the monster."

I had been telling this to the ground. I looked at Alejandro. He was crooked in the water of my eyes.

"What happened to Hilario?" he asked quietly. "Why did she die?"

"That was two years later. I was eight. It was her breathing. There was blood that came with her coughing. It had nothing to do with him. Always, her breathing had made a sound that wasn't right." I cleared my throat and blew my nose in the hem of my skirt. I could feel myself coming back. Mama Hilario was dead, and I could understand that better than I could understand the man who would hurt her after covering her face with her skirts.

7

i AM PAYITA, the twelfth mother, but in this story, the one I pass
on, I think of myself as a twelfth daughter instead. My grandmother, Puylla, had three sons and a daughter named Tiki, but when
the corregidor of Huamanga—that is what they called the governor of
our district—sent for servants, they took Tiki and two other girls from
the lower barrio. Those girls never came back. Grandmother Puylla
had passed her moon cycles before any of her sons had married. She
could have no more children, and at the time, she still had no daugh-
ters-in-law. She went to her friend and comadre, Layqa, and asked her
if she would learn the stories, so that Layqa could pass them on to the
wives or daughters of Puylla's sons. Layqa taught them to me after
Puylla died. There were three of us then: Layqa and her daughter,
Yauri—who was blind—and me.

The Inca empire stole our people, but they did not steal as many as
the pink ones did. They took my father and my mother, but they left
Yauri, Layqa, and me. My father did not have to go to Huancavelica,
where many died mining quicksilver, but both he and Mother had to
work in Huamanga at the cloth machines. After a long time, my father
came back. He told me how the machines roared like a storm and ate
the wool. But Mother never came back. Father never even got to see

her body. On the day she died they made him work at the machines. And he was working when they buried her.

Sometimes, when we pastured the llamas and alpacas near the Wamani's monument, the place of the mountain spirit, we looked for the magic place and the lost illas. These illas were supposed to call the Wamanis to protect our animals, to make them fertile and healthy, but when Puylla died, we didn't know where to find them. We didn't know the magic place. Layqa had hunted with us many times, but we found nothing. Puylla had planned to show the place to Layqa, but she never had. Puylla had avoided it, not because she wanted this secret to die with her, but because she had shown it to her lost daughter, Tiki, and she had never given up hope that maybe, someday, Tiki would return. Showing this last secret to anyone else might have made it seem that she had given up on Tiki. Then, Puylla died suddenly; she was sick one night and gone the next morning.

From the stories, Layqa, Yauri, and I knew that there were at least four illas hidden somewhere in the savage place: the little condor and the deer that Soona had brought from Pomba one hundred and fifty years before, a llama that Karu had put in the bundle, and then a ram from Iphu, Puylla's own mother. From the story of Askha, we knew that the bundle was near the Wamani's monument, but that's all we knew.

When Yauri and I went to shepherd the llamas and alpacas, I led her. The llamas and alpacas went in front of me, and Yauri came behind, using two canes. Through a hole in each end of one cane, we tied a sling strap; one strap went around her waist, the other around mine. We each kept one hand on our own end of the cane, so she didn't run into my back. She could tell from the angle of the cane whether I was stepping up or down on the trail. In her other hand, she tapped the cane that wasn't tied to us.

The rock spires there in the savage place stood in groups. Among these islands of stone clusters the grasses grew in yellow belts. At the borders of the grass and these forests of black stone sticking out of the ground, two dark mounds of llama and alpaca dung marked the places where Yauri and I spent our days in golden light. That high plain of rocky islands and grass was empty of everything else except for a few small ponds of blue water where a pair of geese came now and then. Sometimes a condor crossed over above us. Yauri would hear it, often before I saw the shadow.

That's how it started.

"The father of birds comes to see us. He comes." Yauri pointed to the rocks behind us. In a moment the giant bird appeared, and then I heard the feathers whining, too. He passed quite close by, and I could see his head turn beneath to watch as he floated away. A shadow covered us, and Yauri shivered. "Tell me," she said.

"He *is* a father," I told her, "with a crest, and a collar of white. And he looked at us kindly." I watched the giant float away like a cloud.

"I heard him before you saw him," Yauri said.

"You always do."

"Maybe I can see with my ears, like you see with your eyes."

I thought about this. "Maybe," I said.

"No, I mean really see. Just like you do with your eyes."

I looked at her. She had been talking like this for a few days, and I didn't understand. The week before she had wet her blankets when she was sleeping, and she cried telling me about it. I waved my hand in front of her face.

"I hear you moving," she said.

"What was I doing?"

"I know," she said.

"Tell me then."

"No," she said, sounding angry, "but I know."

"All right."

"You don't believe me," she wailed. The llamas and alpacas all looked up at us.

"Yauri!"

"You don't believe me," she wailed again. "I know you don't."

"Tell me what I was doing."

"I won't tell you." Yauri started to cry.

"Don't be stupid, Yauri. You could hear me moving, just like you can hear the condor before I can. You heard me moving, but you didn't know what I was doing."

"I can *see. Just like you.* Only it's different," Yauri screamed at me.

I stood up. "Yauri."

"Say you don't believe me."

"No. You'll yell at me."

"I don't like you anymore."

"I don't like you either." I got up and walked around the island of rocks. I heard her crying and went back. "Yauri, quit crying. I like you. But why are you starting fights?"

"I'm not starting fights," Yauri hollered. "You're starting fights."

I walked around the big island of rocks across from us. When I got back I found Yauri walking around, tapping with her canes, and saying quiet little words to herself. "Yauri . . ."

"What?" She was still yelling.

"I'll say whatever you want me to say."

Yauri ran at me and swung her canes to hit me. I backed off and she tripped and sprawled.

"If you could see like I can see, you wouldn't have fallen," I yelled back at her. "If you can see, you can walk back down into the canyon by yourself." I left her sobbing and walked around three islands this time.

Returning, I told her that I didn't want to talk about seeing anymore. She sat with her face lying sideways atop her propped-up knees. She didn't say anything, and I knew it was over. We didn't say much the rest of that day, and in the evening I led her back down into the canyon to Wasi.

The next day when we went back up, we didn't say much then either. When the sun was highest, I gave her some boiled beans and corn from my bag, and she started all over again.

I was thinking to run away up into the rocks and watch her and the llamas and alpacas from up there. But then I realized that she wasn't asking me any questions. I quit chewing and listened.

"I can hear the Wamani," she began and paused to hear if I was listening. "I can see the mountain spirit with my ears, just like I see condors."

I wanted to tell her that if she could see the condor just like I did then I wouldn't have to tell her whether it was a mother or a father condor. But I did not say anything.

"The Wamani tells me that I can see through my eyelids and that I can see at night as well as you can see in the day."

Throw away your canes, I wanted to say. Yauri was getting to be worse than no company at all.

"The Wamani says I can learn the stories faster and better than you can, because my inside eyes are better than yours."

I jumped up. "Well, let me bust your canes into little pieces, and we'll just see how good your inside eyes are."

Yauri smiled her mean smile. "The Wamani didn't say that. I just wanted to make you mad. Because you make me mad when you don't believe that I can see with inside eyes."

"Quit talking. I don't like your talk anymore."

"Do you know what a Wamani looks like?"

"No."

"He is a tall white man with long hair and a long beard."

"Everybody knows that," I told her. "His eyes are what color? Tell me that. You don't even know what a color is."

Yauri turned quiet. She looked hurt. I got mad just looking at her.

"I don't want to talk to you," she said. "I'll talk with the Wamani."

"Good. He is better company for you than I am." I went off around some of the rock islands and one of the ponds and told myself the story of Askha, because I sometimes forgot parts of it. I was thinking Askha may have been a little like Yauri.

When I came back, Yauri was standing, listening hard, her head thrust forward. She looked tight and strange. I was worried. "Yauri," I whispered, wishing things could be as they had been before all this seeing talk.

"Payita, look!"

"Look?" I glanced around. There was no condor. I couldn't hear anything. "Look at what?"

"There are three men in the rocks."

I looked around, but there was nobody. "Yauri, no one's there. I hate this game. I don't want to fight anymore."

"The three men are in the rocks. I mean they are rocks that look like three men. See them. See!"

See? I looked to see where she was pointing, but she was only listening, her head and lips stuck out.

"Find them," she whispered. "Look at all the rocks. Take me with you. Bring the llamas and alpacas. Look at all the rocks until you find the three men."

"Yauri . . ."

"Do it," she cried, "please do it. And then I won't make you mad anymore. Please do it."

I gathered the llamas and alpacas, and we wandered among the islands of rock. Tired and sad with this strange obsession, I didn't look hard. But then I saw the three men. I saw them from behind, and I recognized them at once. I knew all the rock islands in the savage place, but I had never thought to look at them as if they were men. Seeing them frightened me.

"You see them?" Yauri squealed. "You do. You do see them." Her hands ran all over my face. She felt me watching the backs of these three stone men. I didn't know what to say, what to do.

"In the hands," Yauri cried, "in the hands of the second man, the middle man—"

"We're behind them," I told Yauri. "How do you know they're there when you can't even see that we're behind them?"

"Go around," she demanded. Banging at the ground with her canes, Yauri started off in the wrong direction.

I left the llamas and alpacas where they grazed and took Yauri around to face the three men of stone. They only looked halfway like men, but on the second one, I could see hands, rocks that looked like hands, and in the hands, a rock that looked like a stone box. "The box?"

"The box in his hands," Yauri shrieked joyfully.

I felt dizzy. "I don't know how to get up there."

Yauri's face darkened. "I don't know. I can't see, I mean I can't see a way. Isn't there a way?" Off she went again banging her canes.

I stopped her. "Wait, Yauri. I'll go up there. Maybe there's a path I can't see from here."

"Hurry!" Her hands went all over my face. She was laughing, enjoying my confusion.

I threw her hands away. And then I caught and squeezed them.

I climbed the steps in the leg and back and came out around the neck. The box at the end of the arm was a square stone almost as big as I was. A round stone fit the top of it like a cork in a hole. I shook. I was afraid to take out the cork. Maybe the Wamani would reach out and pull me in.

"Payita," Yauri called from below. Her voice was far away. "You can look inside. The Wamani won't hurt you."

I watched Yauri. Then I took a breath and pulled the rock out of the hole, and there in a carved basin were four illas. I picked them up one at a time and returned them, the condor last. It was a she-condor, one wing partly out. A stone bird no larger than my fist, the same stone that Phuyu had wanted to give her son, Huaman, but could not.

My heart hit against my ribs. I put the stone back over the hole and went back down to Yauri.

"Yauri, the illas were there. I'm afraid."

"You saw them. You did. I told you," she whooped. Her hands flickered across my face.

The next day, we brought Layqa up to the savage place and showed her the illas. We brought them down so that Yauri could feel them, and then we put them back. I could tell that Layqa was afraid of her own daughter. We both tried to be like we had always been, but we couldn't hide our feelings from each other or from Yauri. She didn't seem to care, as long as we believed she had eyes inside.

⁓

That year, after the rainy season, the priest and a woman priest came and took Yauri from us. Layqa cried and screamed, but they wouldn't leave Yauri in her home. They said that Yauri should become a peeled one, another black-robed woman like a priest, and that if Layqa didn't quiet herself about it, they would send her to the cloth factory in Huamanga and send Yauri off to cook food for the miners.

We knew from the stories that we would never see Yauri again, and we did not. Yauri knew the stories better than I did, and I will always wonder if she lived to be a woman, if she taught them to another girl somewhere else, maybe to a daughter of her own—if she ever escaped the priests. Maybe, in some other village, there is another family of story-women whose first twelve stories are the same as ours.

8

W E TOOK BACK the church's field and the herd. The priest
fled to the church in Huinga. He would not come back to
Wasi. People had to go to Huinga to be married or baptized, or to die,
if they wanted to do it with a priest. We waited for the soldiers to
come, but they did not. The peeled ones from Little Wasi celebrated
with the Runa. But, inside, the Runa remembered the danger. They remembered that it was never good to let themselves be seen by the
peeled ones, nor was it good to follow them or do their bidding. Even
though we were on our way to take back what was ours—this time
from the hacendado—it did not feel right to be doing it with peeled
ones. We had never trusted them.

I was walking with Alejandro. "You're afraid?" he asked me.

"Yes," I said, "but I'm almost finished with it. Whenever I get
scared enough that I'm no better than dead, I quit being scared."

Alejandro smiled. His teeth showed in the light that was coming.
All around us stood the fingers of dark rock. We arrived at the edge of
the stolen land at dawn. We took down the marker cairns. We flattened
the rock fences around the plowed field below. We put up another
stone wall in the middle of the field where the old boundary had been.

The hacendado's herders came up with their cows and llamas.

They stopped when they saw us. "Go back," Mayor Chunca yelled. "Tell the hacendado that Wasi has reclaimed its land. The government in Lima will back us up. Go tell him."

The herders ran away. We were three or four hundred and we had all the llamas with us, too. We had come to take back what was ours.

When the hacendado came, he brought three other peeled ones with him. All rode horses, and all had guns. I pushed up to look at the hacendado's face, now old and withered, his neck like the straw ropes of the bridge after they'd rotted and needed to be replaced.

They stopped across the new wall and pointed guns at us, but we did not move. There were too many Runa, and they knew it. One of the Runa, a crippled man named Marcos, climbed to sit on the wall. He had the reins of his horse in his hand. It was the only horse we had brought.

"Get off that wall," one of the hacendado's men yelled at Marcos. Marcos waved a fist at the man, and the peeled one shot the horse in the head. The horse dropped and did not move.

The Runa roared and started for that peeled one. He backed his horse away, his face paling, but the hacendado spurred his horse in front of the man. He threw his gun to the man behind and waved his arms and yelled, "Stop." The Runa stopped.

"If you hurt him, the army will come, and you know what happens when the army comes."

"We aren't leaving," Mayor Chunca answered. "This land was stolen from us."

"I've got papers," the hacendado said.

Mayor Chunca signaled José to speak. José came from Little Wasi, which was the barrio in Lima where those from Wasi went. José stepped forward. "Wasi has papers, too. You bring your papers and a judge, and we'll bring ours. Here," he pointed to the ground. "We will bring everything here to the place we're arguing over, and we will settle it. Until then our animals will stay."

The hacendado whispered to his men then turned back to us. "No judge will let you do this."

"Maybe, maybe not," José said. "But we will do what the judge says. And there's nothing to be done about it until then. We are not moving."

"I'll bring the soldiers before I bring any judge."

"Then they will have to shoot us."

"This is crazy," the hacendado shouted. "Get out of here."

The Runa said nothing. Swearing, he spurred his horse, and they left.

We kept our animals there for two months. Then word came that a judge would rule. The judge was an older peeled one who came with a young man. The young one wrote down what everybody said. I had nothing to say. When the judge left, he said he would send back word of his decision. I would never know what he decided.

Explosions went off in the plaza when Wasi met Sendero Luminoso, Shining Path. There were seven of them waiting for us to gather there: Reynaldo and José and five other mistis I had never seen before. They had exploded dynamite caps, one in each corner of the plaza, then gone through the streets calling the people and telling them that we were all to go to the plaza. As we walked, I listened to the Runa, to their words about what Wasi would do next for itself. The Runa were excited that José was with them, for he was a peeled one who was an enemy of other peeled ones.

All of Wasi gathered around the little crowd of mistis. They stood above us on the stone and looked down at us as the priest once looked down at us from his place in the church. When the Runa saw that two of the mistis were women, their chatter turned to questions, all of them asking what women were doing there.

Then came another surprise, because one of the women spoke for them all. She was a tall woman, younger than I, light skinned with a thin face and the eyes of a spider. She yelled at us in Runasimi, "You are free now. Sendero Luminoso has come to free you. We will teach you how to keep your freedom. No one will take your land or your animals again. Or any of your food or anything else that's yours."

Several from the upper barrio called out and waved their hats.

"My name is Marina." And then she named the others, Reynaldo and José, last. A few from the upper barrio cheered again.

Marina called out in her strong voice, "The soldiers might come, and if they do, you say nothing of this meeting." The people quieted. "Reynaldo and José will leave with us when we go. But we will be back. We're staying in this district until the soldiers are wiped out."

At this, the plaza was still.

"In the meantime, we will come regularly to teach you the rules and ways of Sendero. It will be like a school, and you will learn how to read and write and how to fight, too, how to take back your land and your lives. There will be no choice about who does it. We will kill anyone who refuses." She paused, apparently to let the weight of this settle. We moved our eyes away from hers.

She called out as loudly again, "Eventually there will be no rulers and no one ruled. All people will obey the same laws with the same things happening to everybody. There will be no thieves, no adultery, no drunkenness. No priests. No whores. Sendero punishment will be swift, public, and terrible.

"We will decide what to do with the church land and herds," Marina said, "after Sendero has taught you how to be the people. I have two more things. Listen carefully. First, Wasi must practice its courage. You must prove your willingness to be free. You've taken your land back from the hacendado. Now you must go back and take his cattle."

The Runa murmured. A woman in front of me shook her head.

"There will be no hacendados in Peru," Marina said. "There will be no rich people and no judges and governors and soldiers to protect them. We take from them the freedom they've stolen from us. We start now and go up from the bottom. Other villages are already free. We will go to one village at a time, one department at a time, and Peru will be delivered back to its people."

The plaza was silent. Reynaldo grinned as though he were at a fiesta.

"You will do as I tell you," she went on. "I bring you the message of Abimael Guzmán, who we call President Gonzalo. Everyone will do as he has instructed. Those who don't will be killed in this plaza, and you will watch them die. We've freed other villages. We kill those who try to stop us, because we won't be stopped." Once again she paused, and her spider eyes fanned over us. "That's all I have to say for now," she said, and she stepped down. The others followed.

The other woman and the three mistis we did not know strode to the corners of the plaza and fired four blasting caps. Then, they joined Marina at the street leaving Wasi, and without talking to each other, they walked out of town in two lines. Marina was in front. They did not look back at us. All of Wasi stood in the plaza facing the road out of town and watched the backs of the seven people as they disappeared around the first bend below.

In the plaza no one looked anyone in the eye. No one talked. Not even the peeled ones. Most of the Runa went back to their homes. Wasi was still. Not even the dogs barked.

Alejandro found me in the plaza. "What will they do?" Meaning the Runa of the lower barrio.

"They won't do it. The Runa won't steal the hacendado's cattle. They will only try to become unseen, to be little and of no matter to anyone. That's what they will always try to do."

"And those of the upper barrio?" His eyes showed no light.

"I don't know. The women will listen. Some of the men in the upper barrio work for the mistis. They're not in their fields or home as much, and there's talk of these men doing things with other women, and more drinking. With their husbands gone, the women do most of the work in the fields. They will like the Senderista's words, but I don't know if they can make the barrio do what they want."

"Pilar, it won't work this time! These people will kill anyone who doesn't obey. I know they will do that. They've killed so many in other villages."

"Don't yell at me, Alejandro. You asked me what they would do, not what you wanted them to do." I turned and left him. He wanted to be mad and scared, and he wanted me to change it for him. I was mad and scared, too, but there was nothing to be done. Alejandro called after me, but I wouldn't listen. I wouldn't wait. I didn't want to believe that the killing would come back.

I went to the savage place the next day and sent Lazario back down to help Oqoruro with the quinua field. I brought food and stayed in the little hut near the illas. I wanted to fill myself with their power.

I felt the power, nothing to tell me exactly what to do, only the power to know what was coming. I'd walked into the shadow of a mountain. The power of the illas breathed in me, but I knew that I would be hurt. Our world would be hurt.

After four days up there, I saw a figure coming up out of the canyon. Isidro. The thought that once I had had him inside me made me smile. But I knew that day was over. I knew why he was coming to see me.

"Pilar, the sorceress," he called when he reached me, "she hides above us."

"Hello Isidro, lover of women," I said, thinking that he used rhymes to give himself more time to keep from saying the wrong thing.

Smiling gently, he approached and sat by me. "Once, that loveliness was all that filled my mind." His eyes softened. He looked inside for words. "Now that idle peace, that good game . . . neither can I find."

"And what do you find now?" Quickly, I put my finger on his lips and nodded. "I know what you find."

He looked down toward Wasi. "Your friend, Alejandro, is talking in the upper barrio. He wants them to join with those below."

I dropped to my knees. "No, Isidro. No, he's not." But even as I was saying it, I knew I was wrong. "Tell him no, Isidro. He can't do that. If they find out, they will kill him. They will do that now. They want to kill somebody who tries to stop them. They want Wasi to see somebody killed."

"Yes," Isidro said, his face gray. "Maybe he believes they can't win, if all of Wasi won't let them in."

"But that won't happen, will it?"

Isidro would not answer.

"And what do you see?"

Isidro would not look at me. He shook his head.

"You don't know, or you won't tell?"

Isidro would only shake his head.

9

i AM TITU MARÍA, mother seventeen. My father died in the quicksilver mine at Huancavelica. My mother, Ninakuru, was alone with me. My older brothers were taken to the factory in Huamanga and never returned. This happened to many families, so there weren't many men left in Wasi. The women could not care for the children, plow all the fields, shepherd the animals, and sow the seed, so the fields went to weeds, and many animals died. People starved. Those that lived were often sick.

I was eleven when I found the little purse between my legs and learned how many coins I could get when I let men do what they wanted with it and when I did to them what they wanted. When the peeled ones came to Wasi, I learned how to show them enough of my leg, perhaps a glimpse of the purse—I would lift my dress and wash my legs in the canal in the street—so they knew what I had in mind. Always the women of our blood, the blood of Soona and Warkari and Puylla, had something that made men lick their lips, their necks swell, eyes narrow. I took them to the savage place and showed them how hungry flesh could be and to see how many reales they had in their pouches. When I knew how many they had, I did all that was needed to get every last coin. Soon the peeled ones came to Wasi for nothing more than to give their coins to this wild animal up in the savage place, this Titu María.

At fifteen, I was pregnant with Leonor. She must have seen a hundred snakes lunging up my burrow at her. After she was born, the only thing I did for her was to keep her on my breast, so as to keep the sticky milk of men from starting another child. In the savage place, sitting on my shawl, Leonor watched all the snakes coming at her mother, but I never let any of those men touch her.

Then in one rainy season I sickened, my milk dried up, and afterward my moon cycles did not return. There would be no more children inside me. I gave Leonor to Ninakuru along with the reales the men gave me, and I spent another six years working the bodies of men until they had nothing left inside them or their pockets. In time, they knew not to bring all their money, but I played them like the quena flute, and they returned with enough money to have Titu María play all their songs and devour them.

I became a peeled one. Even as I lived in the lower barrio and went to all the baptisms and marriages and funerals and fiestas—the few that were then—the Runa of Wasi knew that I wasn't among them, that I was made of rutting flesh and musks made for the peeled ones to buy. I could speak Spanish. After all, they were the ones who talked to me, who whispered and grunted in my ear.

~

Melchor, the tax collector, was a hated man in Wasi. In the lower barrio, we hated Calisaya, our cacique, but not as much as we hated fat Melchor. Because Calisaya was a simple man in a position of power, he did what simple men will do. As much as we hated Melchor, there was one we hated even more, Gregorio Morales, the corregidor of Huamanga and our district. Even though none of us had ever seen him, Morales was our master, the hated Spaniard, who took our young men and women, who counted us and taxed and fined us and made us buy the things he sold. And Melchor was the man he sent out to the villages to see that it was done. In Wasi, Melchor's only friend was Calisaya. Calisaya, the Runa leader, and Melchor, the Creole tax collector, plowed Wasi like a field, but they didn't give us—who were their seeds—enough sun and water. They took too much. I didn't know then that it was the same in all of the world, that there were fifty of these corregidores and in all the corregimientos they took too much from the Runa. It had gone on since Phuyu. Ten generations: Rumi Pachak, Karu, Askha, Iphu, Puylla, Layqa, Payita, Araullu, Kusi, Isabel, Ninakuru. I, Titu María, would be the last.

But about Melchor. In Huamanga, he had heard of me. The fierce Runa woman in Wasi who would take a man to the savage place and exhaust every wish, most of them ones a man didn't even know he had. So the next time Melchor came to Wasi, he asked Calisaya to see me. That day I left all the other men and went with Melchor.

The fat man surprised me. He had blue eyes, and they were like little birds on a wall. He took time with eating and lovemaking and drinking and sleeping and listening and watching and talking. Those eyes like little birds were never careless. He was a big man who walked with the grace of a boy. He ate delicately. And always he watched me like I was somebody who tasted very good. He was a good tax collector and would listen to no whining or complaining. He did everything completely and perfectly and always on time, and he expected the same from everyone else. For Melchor, a complaint was rude. It was an excuse, an admission of one's own failure. Living for him was a kind of tax collection. Everybody had to pay their way, and it wasn't to be questioned. "Pay nothing, and you have nothing," he said. "The world passes through us like time, and from it we take our labor and our pleasures. Tributes and freedom are the same thing. We must work to eat, but eating is more than surviving. It's tasting." Then he would lean over and touch me with his tongue. That was fat Melchor, a talker, a taster, the hated tax collector, the only man I ever loved, the one who took me from Wasi.

The year was 1781. The Runa rebellion raged. What did the Runa have to lose in war? Their lives that made others rich? I found out from Melchor that the corregidores had two registers, one that said how much the people were supposed to pay and another that said we must pay more. The corregidor kept for himself the difference between the two lists. The corregidores wouldn't let us grow our own tobacco, because they wanted us to pay a tax on their tobacco. If people had no money to pay their tribute or their taxes or fines, they became servants or workers for the governors. For life.

Of the Runa men sent to the mines in assignments of forced labor, only one of five returned. Those who refused to go were beheaded. The villages became communities of women, poor women. When the corregidor was given money to make buildings and plazas in our towns, he kept the money for himself and made us bring the lime, the rock, the wood, and do all the work. He gave us coca leaves to chew while we worked.

In the villages, the priests took the best fields and the best animals and the best seed and made all the Runa work for the church. They invented fiestas and made the people pay for them. Whenever they wanted more money they thought of another saint the people had to honor. They would call the people to services and hold them there until they had paid all of their fees. People couldn't pay what it cost for baptisms or burials or marriages.

The corregidores made the Runa men buy razors when they had no beards. They made us buy books when we couldn't read. They made us buy blue powders for our hair and silk stockings for our legs. The people hated this repartimiento, this forced buying of things they could not use, more than they hated the taxes or tributes.

A few of the ruling caciques objected to how the Runa were being treated. They wrote letters to the governors and viceroys and asked that the repartimiento be forbidden, that the mita—the assignment of labor—end after the eighteen weeks it was supposed to last, instead of a whole life. They asked that the tributes and the taxes be shared by all people instead of only the poorest. One of these caciques, José Gabriel Condorcanqui, the great-great grandson of Tupac Amaru, wrote many letters to the governing powers, but no one answered them. His wife, Micaela, even though she was pure-blood Spanish, was as angry as her husband about the mistreatment of the people. The Runa called her Micaco. When these two saw that no one listened and nothing would change, they captured the corregidor of their district and hanged him. José Gabriel Condorcanqui took the name of Tupac Amaru, and the Runa rebellion began.

The Runa had no guns, no horses, no armor or cannons, which they didn't know how to use anyway. They died by the thousands. Tupac Amaru and his family were caught, tortured, and killed in the plaza at Cuzco.

Many Runa believed that those of them who had died fighting could come back to life if the Runa won. Melchor laughed at the idea, so I didn't believe it either. In Choquetapa, I saw a man under the gallows who was waiting to be hanged. He must have thought he would soon come back to life, because he was eating. He sat on his folded poncho under the gallows and calmly ate a roasted guinea pig. Even without the threat of a final death, I would have feared the pain of my neck snapping or the pain of strangling by my own weight. He threw the clean bones of the guinea pig to a little dog hiding under the scaffold.

I was scared. Before, I had looked after my life as if it were a deer others wanted to kill. I had used the little purse between my legs as others used money. But the day came when I looked upon what I had worked so hard to keep, and I saw there was nothing left to have. I tried to live, but everything that happened took my life away in pieces. When people can kill anything, they have already killed everything.

My heart, although it was still beating inside me, had been stopped by what I had seen, what I knew.

Melchor, who found me and took me from my home in Wasi, was a man I would have never chosen to join. Not from what I knew. He took the money from our village. Maybe at first he thought to sell some of me to others, then discovered he didn't want to share it. He could never devour all the corn Wasi grew, but maybe he thought he could devour all of me.

The first time Melchor laid down with me, he brought a robe of vicuña for us to lie upon. He found me in the savage place. Calisaya had sent him where I was herding. In the times of Soona and Tangara, only the Inca had anything made from the fine wool of the wild vicuña. I put it against my face and then my neck. It was soft as air. I took off my dress and put the vicuña against my breasts and belly. Melchor laughed a catchy little laugh, as if he couldn't get his breath.

In a way I had forgotten about him. What I was doing with the blanket made him hot and hungry inside. I took off his clothes, laid him on my poncho, and glided around his fat body, touched him, teased him with the vicuña wrapped around my fingers. The lighter I touched him, the harder and tighter he got. It made me excited, too. We were alike inside. More lightly, more lightly, more lightly, I teased the stretching shiny skin of Melchor until, gasping, panting, he could hold it no longer, and jerking, banging like the beat of his heart, he splashed all over himself. I laughed and laughed. I hadn't even let him touch me yet. I let him catch his breath, and then I took my own fill.

That was how I met Melchor of the enemy race, the hated tax collector, the outsider whose body I could play better than any body I had ever touched. To go from Wasi to Huamanga takes two days, but because of all our playing, we took three.

~

Melchor took me to Cuzco. I couldn't keep my mouth closed. Gawking at the hugeness of it all, I almost fell off my horse. Melchor had to yell at me to follow. The buildings, the plazas, the streets, the churches—all built of perfectly cut stone—widened, towered, covered all the land as if it had been built for giants. We went by a church that was like a mountain peak, it went so high. At the bottom, the stones had been cut square and tight, and yet they made a wall that was round, a wall that held up the mountain of a church.

"That's the church of Santo Domingo," Melchor said. "Once it was the temple of gold, the Coricancha. The foundation is Inca. The church is ours."

Stretching my neck, tipping my head back, I got dizzy.

"Come on," Melchor yelled. "We aren't staying here." He slapped my horse with his reins. The horse jumped, and I fell off.

I scrambled to my feet and pulled down my skirt. It was a short skirt, not an Indian skirt. "You're acting like a foolish Indian," he hissed. His face was red. Three people hurried by on the street. "She's a stupid yanacona," he said to them. Yanacona is a name for servant.

Then we came out of a high-walled street into a plaza, and I held my breath. That plaza was almost as big as all of Wasi. It was like a canyon of stone with all the cliff-faced churches and walls of stone. I knew what it was. Melchor had told me about it—the Plaza de Armas. The plaza of the Inca palaces, the plaza where they killed the Incas, the plaza where they had just killed the family of José Gabriel Tupac Amaru. Everybody knew about this terrible place. I put my hand over my mouth.

It was here where they tried to cut out Micaco's tongue before garroting her, but they couldn't get her mouth open. Her neck was so slender the garrot wouldn't tighten enough to kill her. So they beat her to death, then cut out her tongue. They cut out Tupac Amaru's tongue and then tied each hand and leg to the girths of four horses. Four men drove the horses in four directions, but the horses couldn't tear the Inca apart, so they cut off his head to kill him.

"This is the killing place," I said.

"What's happening?" Melchor called to three soldiers. I waited behind, looking around. My nostrils searched the air for the smell of death. Across the plaza, I could see the wooden floor and the beams for hanging people. Melchor came back. "The rebellion is worse. I have to see what I'm supposed to do. But we won't be here tonight." He dug in his pouch and gave me ten pesos and two reales. "Go to the market. It's straight down that street. You will come to an arch. Just beyond. Get what you can of dried meat and bread. I'll meet you here."

"Not here," I said. "Somewhere else." The place smelled of demons, of naqaq, of hatred, of many dead Runa. Cuzco was a city everybody wanted to see, but I knew from the stories that it made people crazy with an evil hunger for power and metal, as if one could eat silver or gold. I looked at Melchor and feared him for the first time. Here he was made, born of this place.

Maybe he could see it in my face. "If you can't get enough meat or bread, meet me here. If you do, go back to the church of Santo Domingo where you fell off your horse, but go the other way on the road, to the south . . ." He saw my eyes jumping. "Away from the sun." I nodded. "That street will take you out of Cuzco. Wait for me at the river." He turned and left.

I went to the market. I stopped to look at the stone condors carved in a wall and felt a little better at the sight of them. The Spaniards' bird, the one on their shields and buttons and helmets, was an eagle with sharp claws. The Runa's bird was the condor, a bird that does not have sharp claws for killing. It was a bird made out of wings. The soul of our people was made out of wings, condor wings. The Incas and the Spaniards wore gold and sparkling stones. The Runa wore the chilligua, a little badge of ichu grass. That was the difference.

In the market, once more I was breathless. It was another city, a whole city of Runa markets. I got off my horse. I had to think of what I was doing, or I couldn't move. I wouldn't listen to my mind. I would only let my eyes guide me to the bread and meat, and then later, when I was away from this overwhelming place, I would let myself think.

I tied my horse. There were lines and lines of Runa women sitting behind piles of potatoes and corn and beans. And there were kinds and colors of foods and grains that I had never seen. I hunted for bread and meat. The women were all dressed as Runa, long skirts and shawls, but their hats were different, black round ones, tall white ones. They could see that I was an Indian with the clothing of white people, but it didn't seem to matter to them. Yanacona, that's what they must have thought. Just another servant.

I found bread. The woman and I bargained. It was the same as in the market at Wasi, except that we didn't know each other. We spoke Runasimi. I had never spoken Runasimi before with someone who didn't even seem to know I was there. We spoke to each other as if we were dead people. I hurried on and found the meat, bought it in the same way, and then rushed back to the horse to get far away.

Later, at the river, I met Melchor. "It's bad, very bad," he said. "The Runa want to die. They don't care that Tupac Amaru is dead."

"Maybe they don't know he's dead."

But Melchor wasn't listening. "They don't want any more Runa joining the fight." He shook his head. "I'm not a tax collector right now. They want me to deliver a message to an army in Riojuy, a village south of here."

"So now you're in the war, too."

"The war's everywhere, so it doesn't matter," he said bravely.

We traveled six days to get to Riojuy. I didn't know the world could be so big. We went into the mountains where villages were dead and flattened. The fields and gardens were empty. Sometimes we saw children or a few women. Even though we were no more than two people and three horses, they ran from us and hid. Some of the villages still burned. Along the road there were sticks with heads on them, and legs and arms hanging from posts. Everywhere was the stench of rotting flesh. The vultures and caracaras ate the eyes out of the heads. Some of the heads fell off the sticks and our horses kicked them when we went by. The hands at the end of the dangling arms still looked alive to me. They were always half open, and I could see dirt under the nails. Melchor and I didn't talk. At night we slept pulled tightly together, not because our bodies were cold, but because our hearts could find no warmth. It was the first time I had ever slept with a man who didn't want my body. There was nothing of that feeling left. We were in the land of the dead. The world I knew would never come back.

Near Riojuy, we came onto a little girl carrying a baby. She ran to hide when she saw us, but we could hear her in the rocks crying. We followed the sound and found the two. She was streaked with dirt and smears of charcoal, her dress ripped, her nose running. The baby's eyes were red and empty. Melchor told the girl we wouldn't hurt her. He gave her a piece of bread from his pocket. She gulped it down. He gave her another for the baby, but the sick baby wouldn't take it.

"Where is your family?" I asked her. She turned her head away.

"How far is it to Riojuy?" Melchor tried.

"Not far, but they're all dead," she said.

Melchor drew back. "Who?" Leaning then, he touched the girl's shoulder.

"All of the women. My mother. They're all dead. The soldiers came and the men went with them. Then the Runa from the other villages came. They were mad that the men went with the soldiers, so they killed the women. Give me some more bread."

Melchor gave her more bread. "Where did the soldiers go? Are there any authorities in Riojuy—cacique, priest, anybody like that?"

The little girl shook her head. It wasn't an answer. She didn't want to talk.

We left her and the baby in the rocks.

In a while, we came to a head on the road, a woman's head with one braid still connected and tied, the braid on the other side chopped and half unraveled. Another head waited around the next corner. And then another and another. I counted ninety heads, all women's.

The town seemed empty. In the plaza, we found another five

heads. It was the place of the dead. Melchor was pale, his lips tight. I ached to see the living, except that anyone alive in Riojuy was probably a killer. "Melchor, we should go before somebody comes back. Whoever has killed these women will kill us."

"But where are the soldiers, the men of this village? We have to find them before the Indians find us."

"We didn't see them on the road. If we go back—" Then I heard something that tightened my throat. A drum, flutes.

"My God!" Melchor cried.

It was a Runa band, and they were probably marching with a Runa army, perhaps the ones who had killed the women.

"The church," I cried, darting away, "run to the church." The church was across the plaza. I left the horse and ran on foot. The marching music grew louder. They were coming to the edge of town. Melchor ran behind me. The church door was closed. I banged at the handle, but the door was locked. Melchor hammered at the great wooden door with his fists. We were trapped.

Suddenly, silently, the big door opened a crack and two pairs of arms reached out to snatch us into the darkness. The doors shut. I could hear the sound of the locking bolt. "Be quiet," a voice said in Spanish. "The Indians are coming back. Not the soldiers."

"We know," Melchor said. "Who are you? When's the army coming back? I have a message for Captain Carrera."

"We don't know. Listen. They're almost to the plaza. They'll see your horses and look for you."

My eyes were opening to the darkness, and I could see that the man speaking was the priest. The person standing beside him, the one who pulled me in, was dressed in the clothing of a woman priest. But I knew it wasn't a woman. I had felt the strength of a man.

"Who will they kill?" Melchor asked. "Women?"

"They'll kill anybody who is Spanish," the priest said, "or who looks like they're Spanish, or even dresses like the Spaniards. They'll kill them all and all their dependents. That's what they said. They'll kill anybody who doesn't join with them." His voice wobbled, and he looked over his shoulder. "We came over the mountains from Omayos," he went on. "We didn't come by road. The army had already gone. We hid in the church when they came. We heard them in the plaza when they said they were going to kill everybody, when they found out that all the men had gone off with the soldiers. We heard the screaming when they took all the women."

"Why?" I asked. "Why kill women?"

"Because their men went with the Spanish. In Omayos, the soldiers found Indian women and their babies in a field above a lake. They attacked those women. The women jumped off the cliff into the lake and drowned. The soldiers killed all their babies. When we heard that, we ran. All the Indians gathered to fight. We came to Riojuy to escape. To find the soldiers. But the Indians came here to fight the soldiers. But now there are no soldiers. Only us. They'll kill us."

"Where did they kill them?" I asked. I was thinking of what I would have to do to stay alive.

"By the river. We could hear them down there. It took a long time to kill them all."

"They won't come in the church," Melchor said. "They're afraid of the church."

The priest said nothing. Nor did the man in the woman-priest clothing. He didn't want us to know he was a man.

"Who's this?" I asked the quiet one.

He turned away. Melchor and I looked at the priest. The priest looked away, too. "Come to the back, so they don't hear us. The others are there."

"Others?" Melchor blurted. There was hope in numbers. Others to hide among. Others to belong to.

"A few," the priest said sadly.

We followed him through the darkness of many colors. Outside the sun was going down. The falling light showed through stained glass. The Runa band started another song. Maybe they wouldn't think about the horses. Maybe they would think the horses had always been there. In the room behind the altar, there were four other people, two men and two women, all dressed in black and white as women priests. They were Spanish or Creole, not mestizo. Like Melchor, they were the people the Runa outside would like to kill. The people inside knew it, too. Their white faces were whiter with fear.

"I am Melchor. I am a tax collector. If they catch me before Captain Carrera returns with the soldiers, they'll kill me. I have a message for the captain."

The others only looked at him. They had nothing to say. Whoever they were, they wanted no one to know. Hacendados, I was thinking. The priest said, "There's no Captain Carrera that I know. And maybe those soldiers won't return. But the Indians won't profane the church." He said this firmly.

"But what about the men of this town?" Melchor asked. "They'll return to find their families gone."

"Everybody will fight until they're all dead," I said bitterly. The others looked at me like I was a devil. I didn't care. I believed that those outside would profane the church if they knew we were inside. I was Runa in a Spanish woman's dress. I knew how close we were to death. As soon as someone discovered that the church door was locked, the drunken ones would know there was more blood to spill. Revenge is a circle.

"Where's another door?" I asked the priest. It was almost dark.

"You can't go outside. They'll kill you." The priest held up both hands.

"I'm going."

"Titu!" Melchor cried. I could see in his face that he knew he was going to die that night. He knew that I knew, and that I was right. He was the only man I had ever loved. He was the hated tax collector, a man my people hated and should have hated. I realized then that maybe everybody was like that, even myself, Titu María who had forsaken her own daughter, her mother, her people, all the stories that were over now. I knew that I loved Melchor and that he loved me—no matter what other people thought or did or said. We drank as much of this life as anybody ever would.

"Take me to the door behind and let me out," I told the priest. "I won't die here in this dress."

"Let her go," Melchor said. "She won't betray us."

The priest looked at Melchor, then at me, and Melchor again. "Come then," the priest said. He pushed me in front of him. I thrust my hand back and touched Melchor's hand. In the gray light I saw Melchor's wan smile. A piece of one tooth, a glimmer in one eye.

When the priest let me out behind the church and bolted the door, it was dark except for the light of flames bouncing off the walls. In the plaza, the Runa were burning something. The sounds were drunken, even the music from the band sounded drunk and angry. I ran into the darkest street toward the river.

In a big field at the edge of town, I found the bodies of all the women. They were beginning to smell bad. I felt sick feeling around with my feet and my hands to find a body with a dress that wasn't bloody. My feet and hands were sticky with blood. Every headless body lay in its own swamp of blood. Finally, I found one woman atop another, one whose dress seemed dry. I pulled it off her. She was stiff as wood. I ran to the river, slipped off my own dress, and threw it out into the water. I washed my hands and feet and the bottom hem of the dress where I had stained it with my bloody fingers. Then I put it on. They could kill me like the other women, but I wasn't going to die in the clothes of the other race. I would be Titu María.

I went back to the church, but I couldn't get in. I knocked lightly, but they couldn't hear. Then I heard the Runa banging on the front doors of the church. The ones inside had been found. The Runa were hollering louder than ever. I went around to the street and circled the plaza. Our horses were still there. There were a hundred people, maybe more, crowded in front of the church. The flames I had seen were from all the torches they carried. Still, the quenas and the drums and the panpipes and the cow-horn trumpets were playing. Under one torch I could see one of the giant wakrapuku, the cow-horn trumpet. It was bigger than any I had ever seen, maybe ten cow horns nested together in two, almost three, coils. It made a faraway sound that came through all of the other noise and went into my bones.

In the blackness behind them I crept nearer to watch. I saw women among them. I didn't think anyone would notice me. They were like vultures at a horse with no skin. All could eat at once.

⁓

"Open the doors, Father," one of the men yells.

There is a sound beyond the doors, and the crowd hushes to hear. I can't hear the words coming from inside.

"No, Father," the man outside calls back. "It isn't a sanctuary. Under the face of any god, those people have killed us and killed us and killed us. We will make this world a sanctuary. We will kill the beasts. If you don't leave them, we will kill you, too. We will tear down the doors."

Again, there is a voice inside.

"No," the Runa man calls back. "What's this . . . 'blasphemy'? I don't know that word. Those are your words, their words. Your statues are no more than paint and wood. You have no magic. Under the face of any god, they must die. It's their own doing. And yours, if you don't leave them."

Again, the voice inside.

"No, Father—" the man interrupts, "we are through talking. We talk with spears and knives. It's too late now. You wish to die. We don't talk anymore." A roar rises from the Runa. The light of the torches changes, waves as the mob charges the door.

But they do not break it open. When they step back to charge again, it opens, and the priest comes out carrying the golden pot with the little breads in it. Behind the door slams and is latched. The priest lifts the golden pot up above his head.

"No, Father," the Runa leader says. "You don't understand." He shakes his head and turns to the crowd. "Bring Chachingo up here," he calls.

The mob quiets. They part to make a path. Out of the crowd they bring a bandaged man. His arms and head are covered with cloths. "See, Father," the Runa leader points, "see Chachingo. He was taking a message to Azanviri, and the soldiers caught him. But they didn't kill him. Instead, they cut off his hands. They cut off Chachingo's nose, and they cut off his ears. You see, Father, they didn't just want to kill him. They wanted him to bring back another message. Do you understand Chachingo's message, Father? Do you understand it?"

The priest has said nothing. Still, he holds the pot high above himself. A man with a lance runs at the priest and puts the lance through the priest's chest. The golden pot clatters down the steps. The little breads spill out. The priest backs toward the wall of the church. He puts his hands back to brace himself there, but the point of the spear hits the wall and stops him. Blood comes out of his mouth. He falls forward. The spear throws him to his side.

Again all the Runa charge the doors. This time the doors break open. The torches light it up with orange and yellow colors and long black shadows. Everything is moving, and I hear the screaming of someone who sees death coming.

I do not go into the church, but I watch from the place of the broken doors. There is a roar of surprise. The Runa are shouting, but it sounds like glad surprise. "Quevado! Quevado!" they are chanting. "Corregidor Quevado!"

I can't believe that it's true, that they have found a corregidor. This is a demon I have never seen. They are dragging them all to the altar, four of them dressed like women priests and then Melchor. I can't see Melchor's eyes very well. I'm sick with the fear of death.

The men are hollering about the corregidor, about how to kill them all. They argue and yell, but there is a terrible rushing as if they fear they might lose their chance if it isn't done at once. It's as if they can't believe it will happen.

Then the women scream. "Kill the wife first," they call out. "Let Quevado watch her die as Tupac Amaru watched Micaco," one woman yells from the back. She waves a knife. "And let me do it. Let me cut out her tongue first." She pushes her way through the others. With a crowd of men around her, the Runa woman shoves up into the face of the Spanish woman.

Maybe the wife faints, because the men and the woman bend to do their work. I can't see her, but I hear the scream turn to a gurgling. Still, they keep working and the sound goes away. I can see the Runa woman's elbows working still, and I don't know what she can be doing. The people in the church become quiet as if something is wrong. Then, with a shriek, the Runa woman turns and lifts her arms high, in one hand the head of the Spanish woman, in the other the knife. She holds the head by the hair. The front of her dress is slick with blood.

They drag out one of the men and rip off the black robes and white collar. I can't see Melchor behind them. "Kill the corregidor," the people chant. The corregidor is the man who was at the door with the priest when Melchor and I first came. He is almost naked. Maybe he is white with fear, but I have never seen such whiteness of flesh. The woman killer dangles the head of the corregidor's wife in the face of the man.

"Wait," another calls from the back of the mob. The man rushes past me out onto the steps. I hear him kick the golden pot. He picks it up, runs by me back into the church, and pushes his way up to the altar.

Two men start at the corregidor, and he screams. I can see one cutting in his mouth at his tongue, and the other slices at the poor man's throat. They thrust the pot under his neck to catch the blood. There is blood going everywhere. Then they have another head to wave about. The pot goes from one person to another. Some drink. Some don't. Those that have drunk wipe the blood from their lips and teeth. They grin, and the blood makes black lines in the darkness of their mouths.

They bring Melchor forward. Two men hold each arm. They ask one another who he is. Melchor is crying quietly. I can see the light of his tears. "He is one of them. Look at the color of his skin, his eyes. Kill him," one says. Another rushes forward with a spear, and Melchor collapses.

Quickly, they bring out the other three, spear or knife them, and cut off their heads. They let the woman Runa kill the other woman captive. I can't see if they cut off Melchor's head. When they come out to get the priest's body, I back away into the darkness. I sneak around to the horses and take mine. From across the plaza I see them put their torches to the church. Inside, the altar is piled with bodies. The fire burns up around them.

The god of those people has done nothing to save them or his church. On the road, I can see the orange light of the burning church over my shoulder all night long.

10

*i*SIDRO FOUND ME in the savage place. This time I didn't see him coming. The llamas had wandered into the rock spires not far from the illas. I herded them on over to the three stone men, and then beneath them, I pounded in my loom stakes and began to weave. Because he didn't call or speak, Isidro startled me. His face was like a fist; the muscles of his jaws seemed ready to break his teeth. "They're coming," he said. "I see someone falling." Isidro did not sit. Blocking the sun, he stood over me and made a shadow across my face.

"Who?"

He shook his head. "Yesterday, in Huinga, a man in the wrong bed got fifty lashes on the back and head. A woman falling-down drunk didn't think anyone would hear. Those peeled ones cut off her ear." Isidro swallowed and looked away.

"What else, Isidro?"

"A woman who spoke to others against them . . . didn't think she'd risked her life. They stabbed her . . . they . . . killed her with a knife."

"And the people did nothing?" I heard myself yelling. Behind me were the illas, the three stone men.

"Punish if you will, they said, but don't kill. Who will care for the

97

children? You can't kill the women. We will learn these ways of yours, but you don't kill the mothers."

"And still they killed her?"

"You must leave Wasi, Pilar." Isidro looked at me with his face shaking. "Soon. Now. And far."

I untied the loom from around my back and dropped it. "I have to tell Alejandro," I said, standing. "Where will I go, Isidro?" Inside, I searched for the illas, but I could not find their power.

"Pilar, don't go back. You can't go back. Here, take this. Here." His hands were shaking, his rhyming was only repeating.

I looked in the cloth bag at the beans and corn and dried meat. "Thank you, Isidro. I don't know where to go, but I will leave. First, I have to tell Alejandro."

"I'll tell him, Pilar. And I'll tell him to run, too. You must go, Pilar." His lips kept moving, but there were no more words. I never thought I would see sly Isidro like this.

"Come," I said. "I will go. But first I have to tell Alejandro, and Lazario, and Oqoruro. I can't leave Wasi without seeing it again. I don't know where to go. I'm afraid, Isidro, but I'm going back down to say goodbye. They won't come yet." I started to run. Isidro came along behind me. I left the loom and the llamas, but I had Isidro's sack of food. The sun was in its highest place.

I knew that Isidro was right, that Alejandro and I were in the greatest danger. But only if anyone in the upper barrio told the Senderistas that Alejandro and I had been the ones talking there. We had been the only ones in Wasi to show ourselves. The others said that they would go on and live as they had, without stealing, without making more trouble with the hacendado or with the soldiers. They would do as we asked, but that was all.

"If anybody says anything, they'll come for you," I had told Alejandro. We had met at night in the cemetery.

"What else is there to do? If the barrios split, then the Senderistas will kill those from the lower barrio. Our only chance is to keep Wasi together. It only works for the Senderistas when they can divide us into sides."

"But if anyone says anything about you, the Senderistas will kill *you*," I pushed my face up toward his. "And, besides, the Runa won't listen to you, a peeled one."

He didn't say anything. He kissed me. He put his lips against mine and then took them away. "It's what I'm going to do," he said. "Now, I must leave. I need to think about all these things so that I can make myself stronger." He climbed over the stone fence and was gone. I had wanted him to kiss me again, to put his hands on me.

That night I decided to join him. They might listen to me.

I went into the upper barrio the next day, and I talked to the Runa. One of these was Mayor Chunca. He had already heard what I had been telling others. I could tell he didn't want to see me. He was sorting potatoes.

"Wasi doesn't dare steal the cattle of the hacendado and make war with the soldiers," I said. "The Senderistas won't kill all of us, but the soldiers might. Or put us all in jail."

"Maybe the Senderistas won't kill us all," he said, "but they're looking for a place to start. You're crazy and so is that Alejandro. You're the two crazy ones the Senderistas will kill first."

"But what if we tell them that no one, not one person, in Wasi will steal those cattle? Maybe then they'll give up and go somewhere else. To Huinga . . ." Remembering Marina's spider eyes, I knew it probably would not happen. Mayor Chunca shook his head at me. It was that way with all the Runa I had talked to that day.

Isidro and I hurried down toward Wasi, but when we were almost there—when we could see the first edge of the village below—we heard the blasting caps fire.

I whirled around. "Get away from me," I told Isidro. "I'm going down."

"No." Isidro was shaking his head. "Go!" He pointed back up at the savage place.

"I'm going down. Stay up here. You've got to stay away from me." I ran away from him. When I looked back, he was still standing where I had left him.

When I got to the plaza, across and through the crowd, the first thing I saw was Reynaldo and another misti dragging Alejandro toward the Inca stone. Marina was standing above it and yelling. I pulled my shawl around my face and tried to leave, but I couldn't make myself stop watching. No one seemed to notice me. So I moved closer into the people. Maybe, I thought, they would only yell at Alejandro, or cut off his ear.

Marina had a long knife. "Tell me," she yelled at the people, "tell me, what do we do when we have a part that's diseased?"

No one answered. The crowd quieted. I drew the shawl more tightly over my face. I could see Alejandro's face as they pulled him onto the rock. It was the face of a little boy. I saw him whisper to Reynaldo. Please, his lips said. But Reynaldo would not look at him.

"What do we do with gangrene?" Marina screamed at us.

Alejandro looked at me.

"We won't listen to him," a man called. "Nobody listens to that teacher. He doesn't matter."

"Punish him," another man cried, "but don't kill him."

Marina made the smile of a mad woman. "But you don't see. You don't understand. Everybody must be part of this revolution. And what we must do and what we will do in this revolution is kill anything and everything that stands in our way."

She turned to Alejandro as if to say something or look at him. But, instead, she drove the knife into his chest and then took it back out. I screamed. Others made a big sound as if many people had been hit. Marina watched him die before turning back to look at us. The people in the plaza made sounds like those of angry people, but it was a sound of pretending, a sound of the snarling dog that won't bite, the one that squeals when you kick at it.

"You'll come to believe us," she said in a low voice.

Reynaldo and the other Senderista dropped Alejandro's body behind Marina. With a handkerchief, Reynaldo wiped the blood from his shoes. Then they stepped down from the stone.

I backed out of the crowd. I couldn't see Lazario or Oqoruro. I went up the little back street to the upper edge of Wasi, and still with my shawl clutched around my face and with the bag of food, I climbed back up toward the savage place. I ran, stumbled, walked until I had my breath, and then ran again.

I was at the top of the canyon, when the mother of condors came and spoke to me with her watching, saw me recognize her, saw me understand. Straight up she went then, until as a speck, she broke off the rising into an arrow of flight, the arrow that pointed toward Cuzco. Cuzco was the only place I knew that lay in that direction.

When I got to the little hut near the illas, the sun was only one hand from the edge of the earth. I sat in the hut and rocked back and forth on my crossed legs and cried.

At dark, there was a half moon. It would be out only half the night. There wasn't enough time to go back to Wasi, to return to the savage place, and then get very far across toward the canyon of the hacendado. If I went to Wasi, I would get only to the hut by the time the moon had set.

But I had to say goodbye to Lazario and Oqoruro. I had to warn them to leave Wasi. I had to see them, touch them once more. This time, I left Isidro's bag of food in the hut. If I didn't come back, I wouldn't need it.

When I got to Wasi most of the fires in the houses were burning low. I stayed in the shadows at the edges of the street and out of the moonlight. I wondered where the body of Alejandro was, if anyone had taken him yet from the plaza.

I could hear angry voices. One of those voices was Marina's. I ran ahead a little, already knowing where it was coming from. Oqoruro was saying, ". . . was, but gone . . ." Then another voice. And then Marina's. I heard her say my name.

I turned and ran. I didn't stop until the tile roofs of Wasi were tiny beneath me. At the hut, the moon was off one shoulder. I dashed into the hut and took the blanket and my bag of food. I could see the three men in the moonlight. I wanted the illas, but their power could not be taken from the savage place of Wasi. What would they do there without me? Only Pilar and the dead knew they were there.

When the moon set, I kept my eyes on the cross of stars and went more slowly. When the first light came, I had dropped from the savage place into the canyon of the hacendado's wide land and big house. I circled below his house and path and went along the stream for another hour. Then I found a little hole under the roots of a river tree. I ate some of the beans, drank some water from the stream, and curled myself into the hole.

When I woke the sun was high. I ate a little more, some of the meat this time, and then I went on, staying out of sight along the trees and brush of the stream bottom. I didn't look for any paths. I followed the stream until dark. And then I slept under some bushes. I slept all night.

The next day I felt safe enough to look for a path to another village —just as long as that trail kept me with the sun at my back. I knew from the stories which way to go on the paths, and that on the Inca Road, it would take five, six, or seven days. But I didn't know where to find the Inca Road. I crossed a high place that day, and the sun was starting down when I came to the first Runa who gave me food. They were hilling up their potato plants. One family. The man called, "Where are you going, sister?"

"To Cuzco?"

"To Cuzco!" He grunted and said something to the woman. They rose from their work and sat on a rock fence around their plot. "You have a long way to go. Where are your people?"

"I have no people."

He nodded as if he understood everything. "Come, sister. Then you must eat with us."

I went over and sat with them. The woman poured me a squash cup of chicha and the man gave me roasted corn and beans and handfuls of boiled corn. We ate without talking. They knew that I would tell them whatever I wanted to tell them. I was silent. When I had my fill, I started to leave.

"Sister, your bag," the man said.

I took it from my shoulder, opened it, and held it out. He put in three handfuls of boiled corn. "May you go well, sister."

II

*t*HE DOG didn't bark. Like a hunter he came to get me. I heard the corn rustle. I grabbed my walking stick and backed up against the wall. I heard him again coming through the row in front of me. "Hayiii!" I screamed and swung the stick, just far enough to knock down a few corn plants and make some noise. He stopped and growled a low sound. It was a noise like something about to break, a roof ready to fall.

"Hayiii!" I screamed again, but I kept the stick in front of me. The dog was too quiet. I yelled, smacked a few more corn stalks with the stick, and turned to jump up on the wall. The dog caught my leg. Falling, I turned back to hit him with my stick. I heard the grunt of a man. "Thief!" he cried. His voice rattled with the job of pulling back on his dog.

"I'll pay you," I cried. I felt the weight of the dog moving off me. I could hear the animal gasping. My leg didn't hurt, but I could feel the wet, running blood.

"Who are you?" he asked. "What's a woman doing out here stealing at night?"

"My name is Pilar. I have been walking for eight days. There's fighting in my village. I don't have any food. But I'll pay you with work."

"Come into the house," he said. "I have the dog."

⌒

Alberto and Dorinda let me stay for three days. Dorinda was old enough to be near the end of her moon cycles. They dressed my wounds and fed me. The corn I had stolen wasn't ready. I had eaten three tiny ears, cob and all. Those plants would bear more. The plants I had hit with the stick, we tied back up with string and stakes. I worked those three days weeding their barley patch. When that weeding was done, Dorinda came out to talk to me. I knew that I had to leave, but for those three days, I let myself make it into a dream, pretending that I had always lived here. When I saw Dorinda on the path, I knew the time had come for me to wake.

"We don't have enough for three," she said.

"I know," I said. "I thank you for what you've done."

"Here." From the inside of her blouse she took a tiny roll of money.

"No," I said.

She unrolled the dirty, tattered bills. She took two of them. Three remained. "You will walk to Nayle tomorrow morning. You must leave here before it's light. Nayle is two and a half hours. In the plaza there will be a truck that goes to Cuzco. Give the driver one of these bills. You will be in Cuzco tomorrow afternoon. There's a village not far from Cuzco, down in the Sacred Valley, a village near the end of the road along the river. It's called Ollantaytambo. I have a cousin who lives there. Her name is Orfelia Diaz. If you can find nothing in Cuzco, go to her, and tell her Dorinda has sent you."

"You can't—"

"Orfelia Diaz is her name. And the village is Ollantaytambo. Remember that, and keep your legs out of the mouths of dogs."

⌒

When the truck entered Cuzco, I stood on a bag of corn to see over the truck rack and cab. I thought about Titu María. Somewhere near here she had been looking at all the high stone buildings and had fallen off her horse. There were so many cars and trucks and carts and bicycles. People in different kinds of clothes were going everywhere and fast, not looking; even those who were waiting for busses or trucks had no eyes for seeing anything. There was a smell of truck smoke and mixed in, from the food carts on the corner, the smell of cooking meat. We passed a crowd of shoeshine boys, each carrying his stool box. Another cart was covered with newspapers and magazines. A line of Runa women sat against one wall behind mounds of sweaters, gloves, stockings, hats. Everywhere there were the flashing, flying lines of legs. What would I do in this city? I had followed the line flown by the condor. What would I do now?

Our truck stopped at a kind of plaza where three roads crossed, and all the Runa and mistis in the back of the truck got out with their loads of potatoes and onions and beans and chickens. We jumped from the truck, and I watched them all rush away into the different streets.

I had my shawl, a blanket, and my little bag with the corn and beans Dorinda had given me. I began walking. I walked through many streets and looked into the windows of stores to see all the books and pictures and food and clothes for the mistis. I listened to white people speaking in languages I didn't know. I watched them taking pictures with their cameras, and I watched them buying sweaters from the Runa women. These women sitting on the street spoke Runasimi with one another and Spanish to the white people who wanted to buy their things.

I asked one of the Runa where the Coricancha was. She called it the Cathedral of Santo Domingo. When I found the big church, I looked at the round wall Titu María had told of in her story. It made me dizzy, too, gazing up at the high walls overhead.

I asked another Runa woman where the market was. She told me directions. I went through many streets. I tried to look like the others, somebody with no eyes who walked in straight lines and turned sharp corners.

The market! My mouth fell open. It was so big, so many colors and smells. I wandered down long streets. I went along the tracks of the railroad. I went under giant roofs. I roamed among tents and carts and lines and lines of people selling food, all kinds of fruits and vegetables and grains and juices and spices and meats and cooking stoves and pots and ropes and blankets and dyes and seeds, so many things. One street was nothing but lines of men who fixed shoes.

In time, the people and all of their carts and tents began to leave. Others took down their stalls. The sun was falling. Soon it would be night.

I found my way back out of the market into the city of stone walls, of bus and car noises and bad smells, and the crowds of hurrying people. I didn't know where I would sleep. Up on the hills above town, I could see some trees, so I walked toward them. When I reached the edge of the city, I climbed high up into the hills to find a place where no one would see me, a place where there were no dogs. When darkness came I was in the trees in a little place shaped like a cup of the hand. I folded myself into my shawl and blanket and tried to sleep.

Before dawn it started to rain. I went back down into Cuzco and walked. In one large plaza, I stood under the roof over the sidewalk. There was no one else, so I sat on a step in the doorway of a store. I wrapped myself in the wet blanket and shawl.

I woke to the sound of voices and early daylight. It had quit raining. Soon the sun was going to rise. A truck rumbled on the other side of the plaza. Crookedly, I stood. My body felt like the square-cut stones I had been sleeping upon. I went out into the plaza and waited for the sun. I sat on a bench and ate a little of the corn Dorinda had given me.

A bus arrived. I had never seen a bus like it before. It was yellow, but most of it was glass, curved glass. I could see all the way through it. The bus stopped at the corner, and ten or fifteen people came out. They walked near where I was sitting. Most of the bus people were white-skinned and dressed in thin pants and jackets with little color.

The woman who led them was different. She had the black hair and eyes of the Runa, but the shapes of her lips and eyes were thinner and sharper. Her dress seemed to be one long piece of heavy shining cloth that wrapped around her body and went over one shoulder. She had gold rings in her ears. She spoke to the others in Spanish, in a voice loud enough for all to hear.

"This is the famous Plaza de Armas," she said, "the square the Incas called Haucaypata. It was more than twice as large then and extended toward the market. The foundation of this cathedral before us," she swung her arm and the cloth of her dress shimmered, "was once the foundation for the palace of Viracocha, one of the early Incas. It was in this plaza," her voice became sharp, almost angry, and she pointed at the ground, "where the last Inca was beheaded by the Spanish in 1572. Then, two hundred years later, the Indians rose up again under the leadership of another Inca descendant. They killed him here, too."

So this was the plaza where the Incas were killed, the plaza that scared Titu María. When she was here, the gallows were still up. I listened for the voice of Tupac Amaru's little boy, the one they did not kill. After the soldiers had killed his family, they made the boy walk beneath the gallows. Some say that you can still hear his screams, but I heard only the sound of car and trucks. I did not want to hear his voice.

"In the world of the Inca, no one starved," the woman was saying. "All were cared for."

Yes, I thought, it's a fine time to live if The One Who Sees All doesn't come to your home to find what he will take from your life.

She took the people past me, so that I couldn't hear what she was saying. The bus they came in was empty and I could see the cathedral doors through its sides.

I didn't know what else to do in Cuzco. I began to feel the lost souls of headless Incas in that plaza, so I rose to leave. I knew that I would need to use the last bill of money Dorinda had given me to find her friend in Ollantaytambo. I had little food. I knew no one. There was nothing left for me to do here.

One of the Runa women on the sidewalk told me where to find the trucks that went to the Sacred Valley. The truck this time was a small one, and we all stood in the back with our heads in the wind over the cab. At another town we changed trucks. The road went along a river of brown water, and through a warm, green valley where there were many large fields of corn and onions and fava beans. I had never seen fields so large.

Ollantaytambo was a small village, not much larger than Wasi. It lay at the edge of a river where another canyon came in. Inca terraces and ruins looked down from above. The city itself was mostly stone. Houses, streets, canals, walls—all stone. On each street, a stream of clear water ran in a stone canal at the foot of every doorway. I found out later from Orfelia that the village had been designed and built by the Incas, and that it was one of only a few that hadn't changed much.

Orfelia lived on a street called Chaupi. A woman on the last truck told me where to go. The truck stopped in the plaza. "Just around that corner," she pointed across the plaza and up two blocks. "The lintel stone of her doorway is the largest on that street."

I looked at all the lintel stones when I went up the street. I didn't think anybody would cut rocks of that size just to put over the door of their house. Some of those stones were almost as big as the doorway beneath and would have taken many men to lift. In Wasi, we had only used pieces of driftwood found along the river.

Orfelia surprised me. She wasn't much older than I. Yet her face was hard with the work of living. She was thin and suspicious.

Walking with her from the doorway into the little courtyard beyond where she had been sewing, I knew that it would not be good to be disliked by her, that it would be important not to chance it. Also, that pretending to be somebody I wasn't would put me on her wrong side fast. I knew she would either like me or she wouldn't. All I could do about that had already been done. "Yes?" she had said at the door.

"I am Pilar, and I've been sent by Dorinda. I'm looking for a place to work and to live."

"Why did you leave the place where you worked and lived?" she asked.

"They are fighting in my village. The peeled ones who came would have killed me. They wanted to kill people to teach us a lesson."

"You didn't come from Dorinda's village?"

"No, I come from Wasi, a village many days from here. I was stealing corn from Dorinda and Alberto. She gave me money to come in a truck."

Orfelia's eyes widened. "So you're a thief?"

"I hadn't eaten for a few days."

"You have no husband?"

"No," I said, frowning. Maybe I wanted help too badly.

Orfelia must have seen a change in my face. "Come in," she said. I followed her into the courtyard. "Would you like some beans?" I nodded. She went into the little room and brought out a bowl.

"So you're a very pretty woman with no husband. No family."

"The men think I'm a sorceress."

"Are you?"

"Not in the way they think."

Orfelia smiled for the first time. "What will you do now?"

"I will eat these beans."

"And wait to see if I will help you?"

"I won't beg." I could always go back to Cuzco. I could go anywhere. And I could still beg, if I had to, but I didn't have to yet, and I would never have to do it in front of people like Orfelia. I could eat her beans and then leave.

"I can help you . . . probably," Orfelia said, as if it was something she had just decided, "even if you are too pretty."

12

I WAS AT THE EDGE of the river washing clothes when I saw a man waving a long stick. He waved it the way one cracks a whip, but instead of a rope with a frayed end, he was throwing out and drawing back a long string. He threw it out into the river and waited. Then he whipped it back in and over his head behind him in a long arching curve and flung it back out again. The string went almost all the way across the river. It was pretty the way it looped and landed on the water. He walked along the opposite shore toward me. I put my eyes down when he glanced at me. I beat and rinsed and soaped the clothes.

Then, when he was past me, a fish caught itself at the end of the long string. I saw the man smiling. The stick bent almost to a circle. The fish ran up and down the river, and the man walked along with it, first going one way and then another. Finally, the fish came to the shore where the man waited. He squatted down, and the fish went into his hand. He took the string away from the fish, and then, still with a happy face, he held the fish up and showed it to me.

There I was, up on my knees watching like a vizcacha perched on a rock. I slammed my mouth shut and snatched myself back to my work. I scrubbed. From the top of my eyes, I could see the man throw the fish back into the river. Everything he was doing was surprising me, but I kept from looking up. Then, he came down across from me again. I saw him from the edge of my eyes. He stopped as if he were waiting for me to see him. But I wouldn't do it. I had gotten caught once watching him.

The man went back up the river. He waved his stick and string upstream so that mostly his back was turned toward me. So I watched him again. It was like a condor flying the way he moved; it was so smooth, the string rolling and looping with the long, thin stick drawing and curving in and out of those loops. He seemed to be one of those people from another land, one of those with another language who came to Ollantaytambo to see the Inca fortress. His hair was brown and his skin pale, and like most of those who visited here, his lips and nose were thin and straight and seemed not quite finished. He was taller than most Runa men, but he moved well; he walked across the rocks with the smoothness and balance of those who walk all the time.

I had been living with Orfelia and Romero Diaz for two cycles of the moon. The dry season came, and all of the green had turned to gold as it always had done in Wasi. The river, once brown and heavy with currents that tore and swallowed, had become blue and calm as clear sky. It was warmer in the day and colder at night. Courtyards and corrals were yellow with the drying cobs of unshucked corn. Burros went around and around tromping the stalks and pods of fava beans. People flailed shocks of grain with short whips. The papaya and granadilla and cherries were ripe. I had never seen so much food.

Romero drove a truck loaded with beer and potatoes and flour from Cuzco over the pass at Abra Malaga down into the jungle and brought back sugar and pineapples and mangos and chirimoyas. He was gone most of the week. Often, the first day he was home, I heard them together at night. It made me ache. But I wasn't in a place to be wanting more. I was lucky to have something to eat and a place to live.

My Spanish got to be as good as theirs because that was all I was speaking. When I dreamt of Ollantaytambo, I dreamt in Spanish. When I dreamt of Wasi and of my mothers, the words were Runasimi.

Orfelia took in the washing from the two hotels and two hostels in Ollantaytambo. I did that wash, Orfelia and Romero's clothing, and mine, too. I liked being outside, and I liked the river and the walk down when the bag wasn't so heavy. The only thing I didn't like was doing the same work every day, something that didn't change with the season. Romero always drove the same truck on the same road with the same loads. Always, Orfelia had washed the same bedding. How different it was for those who planted and weeded and hilled and harvested and shucked, who herded and sheared and butchered, who spun and wove and sewed.

Romero drank canazo all the time. And Orfelia watched everything too much and complained about everybody. She said Romero drank too much, and he had a loose eye for women. And me, I was willing to let men look at me. She said the neighbors had no shame about raising their voices, sharing their failures with everyone. And Ollantaytambo paid too little respect to the priest. People let their children shit in the streets, and the streets in the plaza weren't swept often enough. She never said anything about my being childless, although once she asked me if I was interested in having children.

"Yes," I said, "I want to have children. Especially a daughter."

"A daughter!" Her eyes widened. It was a surprising thing to say. Even with the Runa, it was better to have a son. But for mistis, wanting a daughter was like being crazy.

"Yes, I'd like a son. But I want a daughter first, sometime. I have to have a daughter. In the line of my family, daughters are important."

She laughed. "There is no such thing as a daughter who can be important. How were you important, Pilar-with-no-family?"

"Not in any way except to us, to ourselves. The women in my family have always been close to one another."

"So where's your mother? And your sisters?"

"I have no sisters, and my mother is dead."

"How can you say that the women in your family are close, when there are no women?" Orfelia spoke to me as if I were a lost child who didn't know she was lost.

"I remember, that's all. That's all I have to say about my family. I want to have a daughter. That's what you asked me, and that's what I want."

When I came back from the river on the day that I had seen the man catching the fish with the flying string, I told her about it.

"Some of the foreign people catch fish that way. They have a little hook at the end of the string. The hook has bits of colored thread sewed and tied on it so it looks like an insect."

"He put the fish back in the river and let it go."

"Those people do strange things. Did he see you staring at him?"

"No!" I snapped.

The next day I went to the river and washed in the same place. It was a good place for washing; the rocks were cleaner there for spreading the laundry; the water was deep at the edge and had a current for carrying away the soap and dirt. I had a sandy place for my knees. I hadn't done much when I stopped from scrubbing to push at my hair with the back of my hand. And there was that man again, only this time, he was approaching on my side of the river. He was waving the string, but I could tell he had his eye on me.

Maybe, I thought, I should gather up my wash and leave until he was gone. No, I thought. If I did that, it would be for Orfelia. I wouldn't do that for her. Besides, he can go right on by me. I am Runa, a brute Indian, and this man shouldn't be looking at my kind. The closer he came, the harder I scrubbed. By the time he got up to me, I had worked up a good sweat.

"Hello," he said in Spanish.

I looked at him. He was smiling. His skin was so light, his clothes very fine—clean and smooth with a fine weave. I could see he wanted more than to just say hello. He had nice square teeth and, behind his glasses, blue eyes. I said hello and went back to my washing.

"It's a fine day," he said.

"Yes, it is." I wouldn't look up.

"Do you live here?" He squatted.

"Yes," I said, still without looking at him. It alarmed me that he was squatting there beside me. I didn't know why I should be alarmed, except that he was a peeled one.

"If I can catch another fish here, would you like to have it? I have no way to cook them."

I could hear Orfelia answering no, so I said yes. I looked at him. He smiled. "Good," he said. He went around me and began throwing out the string again. The pants I had been washing were so clean that the suds were white as clouds. I rinsed them and laid them on the rocks. From the top of my eye, I watched the man move on up the river.

Here, Orfelia take this fish and cook it for me. A man gave it to me. I gave him a good smile. You know what kind of smile I mean? Ha!

There I was, washing a sheet, talking to Orfelia, while a white man was trying to catch a fish for me. When I saw him get a fish on the end of the string, my heart jumped with the fish. I quit washing. I had to see what he would do with my fish.

The fish went up the river, and he followed along behind, not seeming to care that the fish was going farther and farther away. I didn't know why he didn't stop the fish and bring it back. The fish jumped again. A big one. If Orfelia didn't want to cook it, I could sell it to the restaurant. I wanted to believe these things so that if he didn't bring me the fish as he said he would, I could feel bad about it.

The fish turned and the man drew it in. He stooped down and took the fish in his hand. He untied it from the string and then struck the fish's head against a rock. The fish slipped away from him, but he caught it in the rocks and struck it again. Then he held it up to show me. I didn't move. He would have to bring it to me. I picked up the pants I had already washed and soaped them. He brought the fish and laid it on a rock beside my finished clothes.

I stopped working. "Thank you," I said.

"You're welcome," he said. "My name is Arnie."

I nodded and went back to my washing.

"What is your name?"

"Pilar," I said. I stopped to look at him. I had given him my name. I looked at his face, at this man who had my name. It seemed gentle enough, but who could tell with a face where all the parts are so small? He had a moustache and glasses and two little holes on the sides of his nose where the glasses pushed in. Jerking, I smacked the pants on a rock and scrubbed. "I have to work now," I said.

"Yes, well . . . goodbye then, Pilar."

"Goodbye." I didn't watch him go.

"Here," I said to Orfelia. I gave her the fish. I had hidden the fish, carried the wash back to the house, and then I went back down to the river to get the fish. I didn't want to get any of the slime or smell on the laundry. I had walked down and back with my eyes on the cobblestone. I was confused about what I had done. But I knew when I gave that fish to Orfelia, I would say something that would make it clearer.

This time Orfelia's mouth was open. But I spoke before she could. "The white man at the river gave it to me. Tomorrow I'll do wash on the Patacancha." The Patacancha is a little river that runs through the village. "You don't need to tell me about men." I went out before she could answer. I went to the Patacancha to find a place for the next day's work.

We ate fish for dinner, Orfelia and I. It wouldn't keep until Romero was home.

"I didn't ask for it," I told her.

She nodded. She seemed to trust that I would take care of this business.

"But I told him my name."

Again, she nodded.

"And his name is Arnie."

"Arnie," she said.

I looked at her to see what she was thinking. She made me nervous, that mind of hers stirring a little stew inside.

"Arnie," she said again, "oh dear Arnie." She smiled, giggled, and made little kissing shapes with her lips. "Oh, Arnie, Arnie," she teased. We laughed like girls.

13

*T*HREE OF MY MOTHERS fell in love with white men. Both Iphu and Kusi tell of a love of another kind, of a different spirit. I knew it was different not simply because of the color of the skin and hair or of the eyes, or in the shape of the nostrils and lips, but because of something inside. The ways men eat and sleep and wake and touch the women they marry are different because each past is of a different shape, something fashioned by the hands and words of another hundred mothers, all of it under a sun that crosses a different part of the sky. They have come from a place where nights are darker and hotter or colder and shorter, where the blossoms of trees might be blue or green, and the wind is the color of starlight.

It was something that I thought I could know more about.

I taught Runasimi to Arnie Wolcott, and he taught me English, an agreement like the one I had had with Alejandro. When Arnie was in Ollantaytambo, he came three days a week, in the afternoon after I was done with the wash. We went for walks, sometimes back down to the river, or up the Patacancha canyon to the Pumamarca ruins, or along the road past the Tired Stone, which was the big cut stone the Incas left on the road when the Spaniards came. The people of the Ollanta Valley stared at us: the foreign man with the Indian woman.

Orfelia said nobody in that valley had seen such a thing before. I didn't care who stared. Arnie didn't seem to notice. Maybe they had always stared at this tall, pale man.

At first, Arnie and I told each other words and greetings in the two languages. In time, we went back to Spanish and talked of other things. It was impossible to talk very long in languages we didn't understand. We wanted to know about each other.

"Why have you never married?" he asked on the first day. Arnie wasn't cautious about his questions. If he wanted to know something, he asked.

"That's a question that takes too long to answer," I told him.

"This is a long walk. We have enough time for long answers."

"Why have you never married?" I asked back.

"I have," he said, "but it lasted only a year."

"How does one get unmarried in your country?"

"If it's easy—that is, if you both agree and have little to split up—you just fill out a few papers and talk to the judge. Then you shake hands and say goodbye."

"I don't understand people who would get married for only a year. Here, we live together for a year before we get married. The Runa do. Not the mistis. The priest won't let the mistis. He wouldn't let the Runa either, but we don't tell him. You wouldn't have to fill out any papers or see a judge if you did it the Runa way and just tried it for a year."

Arnie smiled at me. "I imagine there's plenty your people could teach mine."

I frowned. "No, I don't mean that. I don't want to be like a priest, who always has the right way. But I'd think anybody would know better than to marry someone before they know each other."

"What do you mean by 'know'?"

"Everything," I said. "That's what I mean by 'know.' I mean everything."

"I don't think I'd want anybody to know everything about me," he said.

"No. That's not what I mean. There are two kinds of everything."

Arnie laughed. "Yes. There are." He stopped to watch across a field at a man plowing with two oxen. "When Sendero came to your village, did others leave with you? Are there others somewhere else?"

I shrugged. "I don't know." It hurt to think about Wasi. "Are there mountains where you're from?" I asked Arnie.

"Yes. It's a little like this valley, but the seasons are different. In the winter the nights are long, and everything is frozen, all snow and ice. But in the summer it's like here. There are more trees there, but they are mostly alike."

"What would your people think if they knew you went walking with a Runa woman?" I watched to see if he thought too long about his answer.

"Nothing much, I don't think, not any more than what they would ask about any woman who was my teacher."

"Woman," I said. "So what would they ask about the woman who was your teacher?"

"They would want to know if I liked her. If she was interesting. They would want to know, but probably wouldn't ask, if she was pretty."

I looked at him, at his waiting face. He *was* a teaser, this Arnie. "You can't tease me. I won't listen."

"And Orfelia, does she ask about your teacher? What do you tell her?"

"She asks if he tries to touch me, and if I let him."

Arnie whistled and looked away. This time I had stopped him. He hadn't ever tried to touch me, and neither of us knew what I would have done if he had. Arnie looked off across the canyon. Orfelia has told me that I tell the truth too quickly and without any clothes on it.

We looked at the Pumamarca ruins and started back. We practiced our words, first a few Runasimi ones, and then a few English words. I liked the word "silver." I liked the way it curved off my tongue. I asked him if there were any words in Runasimi that he like the sound of. Yauriviri, he said. I laughed. It was the name of a lake. Sacred fat, it meant.

⁓

For three days every week, Arnie went on the train to the Machu Picchu Park to study a bear he had never seen. In his own country he had studied another bear, a bigger one. In Peru, the bear he wanted to know lived in the mountain jungle. The spectacled bear. It had white circles around its eyes. I had never seen such an animal, this bear, nor had I seen the forest Arnie described.

"What can you find out about a bear you never see?"

"I talk to some of the people who live there, who have seen the bear, and they tell me things I want to know. The train engineer has seen a few bears swimming across the Urubamba River along the railroad tracks."

"He tells you that they swim across the river. Now you know that? What else do you want to know?"

"Plenty. I find the bear's droppings and from them I can tell what he is eating, which trees, which plants. Then I count those plants and trees to see how many bears can live there."

"You study caca." I made a face at him.

He laughed and caught my wrist. He had never touched me before. Two Runa men came up behind us, and Arnie dropped my arm. We were on the road to Abra Malaga.

"Hello papita, mamita," each one said, and they hurried by.

Arnie watched their backsides. "Do they speak Spanish?" he asked.

I shook my head. "They're Runa. The ones who can speak Spanish are called cholos. The ones who chew coca like the Runa but not so anyone can see. That's cholo."

"So Orfelia and Romero are cholos?"

"No, they're mozos. Mozos live in town. They can read and write. A mozo man won't wear a poncho unless it's raining. Sometimes he hires an Indian or cholo to work for him. Orfelia and Romero are mozos, and I'm the brute Indian they've hired."

"You can't read or write anything?"

"No. But they've been good to me. I was only joking."

"I know," Arnie said. "So who's next after mozos?"

"Next are mistis, the mestizos who own everything, the land and businesses. Everybody else works for them. Mistis send their children to school in Cuzco."

"And they speak only Spanish?"

"Most of the mistis here can speak Runasimi, too, but they do it only when they want to talk to an Indian or when they want to make a cholo or a mozo feel bad."

"Humiliate them?"

"It's a way to tell them they're like the other brutes. Like me." I lifted my chin, and I looked at him out of the corner of my eye. When I walked with Arnie, my clothes were always just washed, and my body, too, and my hair just brushed. Orfelia noticed, but we didn't talk about it.

"So, is everybody trying to climb higher? Do the Runa try to be cholos, and cholos try to be mozos, and so on?"

"Sometimes, but mostly it doesn't work."

"Why?"

"Too many reasons," I said.

"Then tell me some. We're doing our lessons, and this is a lesson." That was true. I sighed. "Mostly money, that's what it is."

"When you get more money, you move up?"

"I guess. If it worked that way, but it doesn't."

"Why?"

"Why? Why? Why? You have a hungry mind."

"So do you," Arnie said. "Tell me why."

"There is faena, the work you must do for the town, which makes a way the rich can own the poor. It's complicated." I waved my hands. "Yes, yes." I touched his wrist. "The ones above own the ones below, and the Runa are owned by everyone. On this road, the alcanzador waits every Sunday to cheat the Runa who are on their way to the market."

"Alcanzador?" Arnie's brow wrinkled.

"The alcanzador on the road is a cholo who buys the Runa's eggs and beans with things like salt or kerosene, things the Runa don't have. But they always cheat the Runa. The mozo alcanzador goes with his money to the Runa's home and makes them sell whatever they're growing, sell it before harvest. They pay them hardly anything. In town, the storekeepers divide the Runa among themselves so that there's only one place that will sell to each family. That way they can charge what they like. If the Runa refuse any of these vultures, they get beaten or jailed, because those with money pay the judges. That's how it is."

Arnie watched the ground. As bad as he felt, it made me feel better. I liked seeing a peeled one feel that way about the Runa. I went on. "And there's the enganchadores. They buy men to work in Quincemil and other places in the jungle on coffee or coca plantations. The Runa can't read the writing that tells how much work they must do and how little money they get. Once they get there, they can't leave. One enganchador who comes here is a misti woman from Cuzco. She buys girls to go to the city. They call them maids, but everybody knows what they'll have to do."

"So if the Runa can't read contracts, why don't they learn how to read? I know there are schools."

"Most of the teachers are mistis. Just like everyone else, they take all they can get from the Runa. Manuela—who sells vegetables to Orfelia—she doesn't send her child to school anymore. Her boy was sick once and didn't go for a few days. When he went back, the teacher beat him until he was bleeding. Manuela sent a chicken the next day to pay the fine for missing school. The teacher came to Manuela's and said that it wasn't enough, so he took one of her sheep."

We had stopped. Arnie stared at me. His face was pale, his blue eyes thin with color, thin as morning sky. "It's always been this way," I said. "Since the Incas."

"How do you know that?"

I started walking. "People are like that. They haven't changed."

"Pilar?"

"No. That's my lesson. Talk English now."

~

Arnie loved chocolate, and his favorite was a paper-wrapped bar called Sublime. Once, on our lesson walk, he bought two bars. I had never had Sublime before, and Arnie laughed to watch me eat it. I took only little bites so it would last. I shut my eyes and let the sweetness fill me. Arnie said that the only thing better than eating a Sublime was watching me eat one.

One evening he came to see if I would go with him to the plaza for chocolate. He told Orfelia that he had a sudden craving that night for watching Pilar eat a Sublime.

From the plaza, we walked in the dark down to the ruins and then toward the Patacancha to the Baths of the Chosen Women. It made me a little sad that I couldn't tell Arnie about Phuyu, mother five, who had almost been forced to become one of the chosen women, who might even have had to live here, had the girl Mayu not drowned, had Phuyu's mother been somebody other than the fierce Tangara. We were standing by the bath where the water fell from the spout and splashed on the stone slab below. The moon was almost full, and I watched Arnie's face. His face was kind but a little mischievous. His chocolate was gone. He was folding up the wrapper and putting it in his shirt pocket. I could feel the cool mist of Inca water on my legs. I still had my last piece of chocolate. I always made it last longer than he did. Inside my mouth, that last piece was slick and smooth and rich.

"Hey, Arnie," I whispered, "put your head down here."

"Ummm?" He was thinking far away. But he dropped his head a little. I put my hand on the back of his neck and pulled his face into mine. When his lips touched mine, I pushed the slick, warm piece of chocolate from my mouth into his. He jerked back, as if I had poked him in the stomach.

"Whohoo," I laughed.

He took the chocolate, messy and melted, out of his mouth, looked at it, put it back in, and licked his fingers. "Will you take it back?"

"No."

"If I give it back the way I got it?"

"Yes."

~

The next day when I was washing sheets at the river I lost myself in thought. When I looked up to see where I was, I found my work already done. But I knew what I had been doing. I had been searching for courage. I knew that I was letting crazy things happen, things that would hurt me. And anyone who can remember twenty-three stories ought to remember how much hurt is possible.

Arnie and I had no lesson that day. He had to go to Cuzco for something to do with his study. But he came at night. "Sublime?" he asked and wiggled his eyebrows. He leaned against the doorway.

We went with our chocolate back to the ruins, to the baths. The moon sat on the skyline of ruins. I stood near the water to feel the spray again. Arnie stood behind me. He put his arms around my waist. I put my hands over his hands. I didn't know what we would do. I didn't know what I wanted us to do. He didn't move his hand. And he didn't press himself against me. I was about to move his hand onto a better place when he spoke: "Pilar, there is a town named Cotas in the Apurimac Canyon, and they have a fiesta there next week. I found out about it today in Cuzco."

"I don't care about a town named Cotas that has a fiesta."

"In this fiesta, they tie a condor on the back of a bull and watch them fight."

"I don't care about a condor and a bull fighting." I took my hands off his.

"The fiesta takes four days."

"I don't—"

"I want to go see it. Will you come with me?"

"For four days, you mean?"

"Yes."

I put my hands back onto his. He waited for me to answer. I was sick of all the different Pilars inside me.

"Yes," I said. "I'll go with you."

"For all four days?"

"Yes, for all four days."

I put one of his hands on my breast. I unbuttoned my blouse, and I slid it in. My nipple was hard as a bean. "In your country," I asked, my breath starting to come quickly, "do you do these things with words? With talking?"

Arnie

 **I**

*M*Y NAME IS ARNIE Wolcott. According to my visa, I'm a thirty-three-year-old gringo working on a field study in Peru for a master's degree in wildlife biology. My research subject is the spectacled bear, an animal I have not yet seen. I *have* seen a fair amount of spectacled bear feces, and although the nature of my investigation abstracts to bear populations, habitats, carrying capacity, and other contrivances of the mind, I am tempted to title my thesis, "Ordure of *Tremarctos ornatus*." Which is to say that the essence of my work is the stink of shit.

I love bears, grizzly bears in particular. The first time I worked on grizzlies, I saw a car drive between a sow and her cubs. The sow charged the car and struck the front fender with her head. She knocked the car a little to the side and fell dead with a broken neck. I had read stories about animal loyalty and sacrifice, but that was the first time I witnessed it so clearly.

I saw that during my first summer out of high school. I was working in Yellowstone National Park for Dr. Goro Ikeda, a Japanese-American who was a school chum of my father's. At the end of that summer, Ikeda and I tranquilized a two-year-old sow that had gotten a tin can stuck on her front foot after a visit to the dump. We removed the can and half the torn pad of her foot. Then we fitted her with a radio collar and followed her all fall in hopes of finding her den. We called her Celeste.

One day, toward the end of fall, I happened onto her in a sunny meadow. She saw me and moved away toward the timber. But her hurrying seemed arrested, as if she were so tired that she forgot what she was doing, where she was going. She sat, and as she watched me at a distance, she fell asleep. Her head wobbled, and she tipped over onto her nose. I left her there sleeping with her head tucked between her front legs.

On Halloween, a big storm came in, and she started for her den. We followed her for three days before she holed up. Her den tunneled in under a big lodgepole on a steep northern face. We could see the entrance fast filling with snow. Flagging the trees, we marked our way out so that we could return in the spring to inspect the den.

I never saw Celeste's den. I persisted with my original intention of majoring in English, so I didn't return the next spring. Years later, I did find a den; its small, tunneled entrance descended through tree roots into a chamber containing a bed of conifer boughs, moss, and grass. I lay on my side on the small shelf, tucked my head against my chest, and tried to dream bear dreams.

I stuck with English for three years, but the bears called me back. I tried to jimmy myself into an inconspicuous corner of one of Ikeda's projects where nobody would notice me. Considering it temporary, Ikeda suffered the indulgence. In the winter I worked up bear data, repaired equipment, ordered replacement gear, made lists—the sort of work I hoped would make me if not indispensable, at least painful to replace. I maintained no pretenses about studies. I was the only one on the department payroll who was not en route to a degree. I clung to my self-made niche for four years. In the meantime, I followed Celeste's life. In all, I saw her with four different sets of cubs.

Ikeda knew I'd leave if the university tried to force a master's program on me. So the good professor came up with a scheme of his own. He offered me the spectacled-bear study as a thesis project.

"Spectacled bear?" I asked him politely.

"They live in the Andes."

"Umm."

"The project would be in Peru."

"Peru?"

"Yes, and there will be no Park Service, no Forest Service or Fish and Wildlife Department overseeing anything. You would be on your own."

My palms were sweating. "And money here is getting tight?"

"You've never been to Peru. You're single, and you're getting on, Arnie."

"Yep."

I left for Peru in the fall of 1982. I was thirty-two. Celeste was seventeen. We were both getting on.

⌒

Where I expected quaint diversion in Peru, I found instead a place of raw harmony, a place ancient, spectral, and scoured with light. You can step off a jet in Cuzco and, just walking for an hour or two, go back a thousand years or more. When you leave the tarmac and walk into the city, you find yourself standing beneath walls of stone hewn to obsessive perfection. There is no mortar. There is no space between the stones.

Keep walking this path of time, a little more slowly perhaps, because the air here at almost twelve thousand feet is low in octane. In these high prairies of ichu grass, little girls shepherd flocks of llamas and alpacas. There are no fences—only rock and adobe walls. Beyond are some of the homes. The strip of color on the knoll is a woman sitting, weaving with a backstrap loom. The homes are small with sides of stone or adobe; some of the roofs are thatched with grass. The animal and plant fibers and the weave of cloth have not changed for a thousand years. Their food is the same: corn, beans, squash, potatoes, the guinea pigs that scurry over the floor. And the words, the songs, the flutes and panpipes and drums. The same, all the same.

Another part is the light. It can't be just a thinness of air. A welder's arclight cuts the sky and fuses everything in all of its essential connectedness. In that assault of light, there is too much to see.

Even the nights are luminous.

I am in the Plaza de Armas of Cuzco where I wander beneath the colonnades that ring the plaza. It's a cloudless July night, bright with a starry chill. Vendors line the walkway, their crafts spread on blankets. A girl, six or seven years old, confronts me with a fistful of postcards.

"Buy these, mister," she says in Spanish.

"No thank you," I tell her. She has an almost frightening brightness about her. I keep on walking. She joins me with a manner entirely calm, as if she were my daughter. At one corner of the colonnade, a woman cooks a shish kabob of potatoes and chunks of heart meat. The smell of cooking meat and potatoes is powerful in the thin night air. The woman asks if I want aji, hot sauce. I do. She paints it on, using an onion as baster—the roots are the brush. The shish kabob stick is a splinter of bamboo, and the napkin she wraps it in is a corn sheath.

The girl following sees another gringo and rushes off. An hour later, I recognize a sleeping figure in the alcove of a closed shop. She has squatted down upon her legs, her postcards spilt across her lap, and her head thrown back enough so that her sleep-formless face points straight up. Her open mouth makes a small black oval. She is propped against great carved stones.

A little band is playing across the plaza. I cross to watch and listen. The music they play is a quicksilver weave of pure clean notes and a windlike huffing that puts in the ear what standing in the mountains puts in the eye.

In this Peru, I met Pilar Achahuanco.

2

*O*UR TRUCK drops into the enormous canyon of the Apurimac, and it takes four hours to cross. I can't see much through the rack except for the flowing colors of green, gray, and tan, the fleeting blend of earth and shrubs alongside the road, and the singularity of blue overhead. At Nuno, the end of the road, we get off the truck. We walk for two hours before the sun begins to set. The others who are walking to Cotas go on ahead. The town is only another hour away, but Pilar and I have nowhere to stay there, so we stop to make our camp while there's still light. We find a flat room-sized sward of grass alongside a spring not far from the trail. She putters with the cooking, while I put up the tent. I watch her out of the corner of my eye for some indication or guidance.

From inside the tent, I watch her again. She stirs the soup. She doesn't seem to anticipate anything. I crawl out and sit on a rock. She pours the soup into our cups, hands me a cup, and smiles.

"It's getting cold," she says.

"Yes," I say, "we'll have to get in our bags soon." In Cuzco, I'd rented a sleeping bag for Pilar. Also, a sleeping pad, backpack, and water bottle. She said that she must be the first Runa woman to have ever worn a gringo backpack. The mistis at the rental place gawked at us.

After dinner, I wash the dishes in the spring. When I go back to the tent, Pilar is in her bag. Her dress and her sweater are not on her. From the pack's side pocket, I slip out a condom, and then in the tent, I put it under my pants, which I have rolled up to make a pillow. Pilar watches quietly. Her eyes are enigmatic. I don't think she knows what a condom is. I flick out the light, and for want of anything to say, of anything else to do, I undress and then slip into my own bag.

"Pilar?"

"Yes."

"Can I ask you a question?"

"Yes."

"Is there anything you want me to do, or is there anything you want me not to do?"

"Not to do?" She giggles at my bungled syntax.

I feel the heat of my own blushing. She has an upper hand I suddenly resent. I must seem like a coward to her. I lunge over and kiss her. She answers back with her lips. I touch her breast. She doesn't resist. She gropes, finds the zipper to her bag, and unzips it. Then she unzips mine. I slide to meet her. She does the same, and we lie shivering on the tent floor. Panting, laughing, I feel around trying to get her bag beneath us and mine over us. Pilar pulls me at her.

"Wait," I mumble. I grope for the condom and fumble with it.

"What're you doing?" she cries. "What is this?"

"So we don't make a baby."

She feels it. "It's so thin and weak. It won't break?"

"No."

"Hurry," she says.

Later, we're still together when she moves to rearrange the sleeping bags. Her motion arouses me. "You can keep moving like that," I say.

"Ho," she answers, pulling me against her. She makes a deep chuckling sound. "I will. I won't let you out. I'll keep you right here, you and your shovel with that little poncho on it." Rising, pressing with strong hands, she chuckles again.

~

The next morning we meet the boy, Santos. He pokes at our tent with a cane. "Who lives in this bladder-skin house? Come out and talk to Santos."

"Who is Santos?" Pilar asks. She sits, finds her sweater at the other end of the tent, and slips it on.

"*I* am Santos. Me. Here I am outside your skin house. Come out."

I pull on my underclothes, my shirt and pants. Pilar pulls on her skirt, unzips the tent door, and crawls out. I follow. Santos wears a ragged red poncho, a sweater with holes in the elbows, and pants with holes in the knees. A shawl filled with something like potatoes is tied around his shoulders. His hat is thick, stained felt in the shape of a safari hat. His face is wide and gently, almost femininely, shaped. His eyes are dark, teeth white, each round cheek arches over a deep line cleft from his nostril to the corner of his smile.

"Hello Santos. I'm Arnie, and this is Pilar."

Pilar has squatted at the edge of the grassy park. We can hear the unbridled rush of her urination. She gazes in our direction but doesn't seem to see us.

Santos seems unperturbed with everything. "You're going to Yawar Fiesta?"

"Yes," I say. "And you?"

"I'll wait for you."

~

Cotas sits like an eyrie on the steep side of the Apurimac Canyon. Below the edge of the village, cliffs shoot down into the ravine. The houses, the streets, and the plaza are spread out on separate knolls, shelved at the edge of a green-gold void. Some of the ravines between the knolls are terraced and planted with corn and fava beans.

At the edge of town, Santos points at tile-roofed houses across the gully and speaks authoritatively to Pilar. She nods and translates for me. "He said that we might get to be guests of Don Manuel. He is one of the 'owners in charge.' "

"And what does he own?"

"Every year there are two 'owners in charge.' They put on the fiesta. They pay for everything. They try to outdo each other. Today, Don Manuel is butchering a cow and four pigs. His condor comes today. The condor for Don Hernando, the other owner, comes tomorrow. Each owner has to hire a team of Runa to capture a condor."

"And the owners are different every year?"

"Yes. Santos says that Don Manuel sold his field and house to pay for it. He'll be a poor man after this year, but everyone will respect him."

"That's a lot to pay for respect."

"What else is there to want?"

"You can't eat respect for dinner. What's he do for a home now? And his land? How does he grow anything now?"

"On shares. Unless he has other fields. But others will help him if there isn't enough. That's what respect is for."

Santos appears across the way and signals us to come. We go up the road. A man, neatly dressed in slacks and sweater, follows Santos. I judge him to be in his fifties. He shakes my hand and bows stiffly at Pilar. He seems a little uncertain; our relationship is a mystery. "Please," he says, pushing through his puzzlement, "be my guest at the fiesta. I would be honored. We haven't had gringos visit us before." He glances uncertainly at Pilar. Don Manuel has a thin moustache and small eyes. We accept. He invites us to stay in the Council Building, a single room sheltering a large wooden table and chairs.

Later in the day, when the condor comes, we're in front of the church, a huge, adobe structure with a swaybacked tile roof. We watch people empty from the surrounding houses. In a few moments, the trail is a glittering zigzag of movement. High up on the mountain, we can see the flecks of color toward which the villagers race. Pilar and I join those walking at the end of the line.

I'm gasping when we get there. My throat's raw and scorched. Don Manuel arrives just behind us; he doesn't seem winded at all. He wears a blue satin cape and carries another smaller one and a gourd of chicha. A native band plays, and some Runa dance in a circle on a wide spot in the trail. At the lip of the trail, where it breaks out into the widest view of Cotas below, two Runa men hold the spread-out wings of an enormous bird. The condor is black and white with a naked head and a soft white collar. Its eyes are red. The beak is tied shut with a strip of leather threaded through its nostrils. The men flanking the standing bird hold the feathers at the tip of the wings. I guess the wingspan at about ten feet.

"She's a female," Pilar says. Pilar seems unusually somber. She steps between the dancers toward the bird.

"How do you know?" I call after her.

Pilar doesn't seem to hear. She approaches and squats to face the magnificent bird, then brushes the condor's breast with the back of her hand. The condor bumps her hand with its tied beak. One of the men holding the wings says something to Pilar, enjoins her in some way, for Pilar, still squatting, shuffles a little to the side. I can see her talking to the bird.

Don Manuel approaches the condor with an open gourd shell filled with chicha. Pilar moves aside. Even with her beak tied shut, the condor leans toward the cup, immerses her beak, and sucks. Others press forward to watch. Pilar returns to stand beside me. "The male has a crest, like a rooster with a comb," she says grimly. I look into her troubled face, but she won't look at me.

I'm about to ask her what it is about the bird that bothers her, when abruptly, I sense someone's eyes. A man standing behind the condor stares at me with apparent alarm. He's a middle-aged Indian dressed in an old poncho and wearing a brimless felt hat. His head has little flesh in the cheeks or around the eyes and looks like a skull.

I avert my eyes to watch the band. Two of the men in the band are blowing enormous curled horns. In sound and profile, the instruments resemble French horns. Each is made from ten to fifteen cow horns bored out and fit one into the other, sealed with a black pitchlike tar, and wrapped with laces of rawhide. Their resonant cry is an eerie backdrop for the panpipe, flutes, drums, and the one battered trumpet.

"What are those big instruments called?" I ask Santos, who stands with us. The man with the skull-like face has not stopped staring at me.

"Wakawakara," Santos says.

"In Wasi we call them wakrapukus," Pilar says. "Why is that Runa man staring at Arnie?"

Santos looks uncomfortable. "He is a sorcerer. He is Don Manuel's sorcerer."

I look at the sorcerer. His eyes break off for a moment, and he moves off to the side toward Don Manuel. Again, he stares at me. I notice then that Pilar has left and is circling the crowd toward the sorcerer. Without taking his eyes off me, the sorcerer says something to Don Manuel. Don Manuel has maneuvered himself behind the condor where he is tying the blue satin cape to the bird's back. The bird moves her head at his hand, and Don Manuel jerks back. The sorcerer takes the cape from him and ties it on. Then, talking to Don Manuel, he looks at me again, points with his chin. I can see Pilar listening to them.

His scrutiny unsettles me. "Does each owner have his own sorcerer?" I ask Santos.

"Oh yes," Santos says. "Without a sorcerer to bless the bait and the trappers, there'd be no condor. It's very hard to catch a condor. The sorcerer has to swear to the mountain spirits that the bird will not be harmed and that the condor will be honored. Whatever happens to the condor happens to us. And to the sorcerer first."

Some of this I knew. From reading, I'd learned that the condor-bull encounter was thought to represent the Indian and the European. After the condor had ridden the bull, the bull — this outsider — was killed. One of the guides who worked at Machu Picchu told me that in his hometown of Paruro when they released the condor, they fitted the bird with a necklace of three little bottles, one filled with chicha, another with cane liquor, and the last with wine. These allowed the condor to share drinks with other condors as the owner had shared what he had with his neighbors. The village, then, would fare as well that year as the ritual condor prospered after departing the fiesta.

I asked Santos how they caught the condor.

"I've never seen it. Only the sons of condor trappers are there. But I've heard that the sorcerer blesses the ground and the sheep or whatever they've killed for bait. They put the bait in a little hollow and all the trappers hide back over the edge. Maybe they wait for days. If the sorcerer does a good job and he's worthy and if the mountain spirits are pleased, a condor comes and feeds. When the bird is full, it can't fly very well. At the sorcerer's signal, the trappers run over the edge of the hollow and throw bolos and blankets at the condor."

"What else does this sorcerer do?"

"He makes offerings to the mountain spirits, gifts that he burns at night. In caves. The smoke goes to the spirit. Sometimes in this fiesta, when one of the owners isn't doing so well, his sorcerer helps him. Maybe the other owner's band is better, or his fireworks, or his bull fights better, something like that, then the sorcerer sits in one corner of the plaza and scrapes the beak of a dead condor, or the claw of a puma. He tries to put a hex on the other owner. Or on his band or the fireworks or his bull."

Pilar makes her way back around the ring of dancers.

Don Manuel leads the parade down the mountain. Behind him,

the two men, carrying the condor by the wingtips, swing her forward, then walk past her and swing her forward again. Her head and neck make long arching motions to compensate for the sweeping cadence of their descent. Behind the condor, the band and the dancing villagers follow. Many have stuffed bunches of ichu grass under their hatbands.

"The sorcerer had a dream that an outsider will put a hex on Don Manuel's fiesta," Pilar whispers. We are pulled into the ring of dancers. The women sing in high wails that sound like Oriental music.

"So I'm a threat to our host?"

"You could be," Pilar says. She looks worried.

The other dancers in the circle call us to join. Pilar sings with them, and I give over to the dancing. We go down into Cotas. Up and down the streets and around the plazas and fields. When we get to Don Manuel's, everyone has gathered on the gentle slope behind his house.

Twenty or so long tables festoon the field, all set with white table-cloths and covered with bowls and platters and bottles of wine and liquor. Some of the tables have plastic tent roofs tied overhead. From them hang paper decorations and ribbons. Bowls of beans and shelled corn and platters of creamed potatoes and slabs of roasted meat are the centerpieces. On the longest table, the roasted head of a pig is garnished with long red and green peppers; the peppers stick out of its eye sockets, ears, and mouth. Boxes of Cuzqueño beer, twelve big bottles to a box, await in stacks at the foot and head of each table.

The villagers rush to sit. We are guided to a table near the middle. Beers are opened and passed around, plates filled. Sessions of toasting intersperse the feasting. The toasts are in Spanish, so that I understand some of what I can hear above the din of celebration. Most of the tributes go to the present owners in charge and to ones past. I hear a few intimations about who will serve next year.

By the time it's dark, Pilar and I are both drunk, and so, it seems, is everybody else. Torches are lit, and once more we follow the band to dance through the streets. For awhile we go house to house, where we down shot glasses of cane liquor. Gradually, everything seems to blur. I find myself standing in the doorway of the Council Building asking Pilar why she is not as drunk as I am. Then I'm on the floor in my sleeping bag and the floor buckles and rolls. I hear the band far off.

For the three days we are in Cotas, the celebrations go on. Night and day, the processions, the music and dancing and drinking do not end. On the morning of the condor-bull confrontation, they take a statue of the Virgin from the church and carry her on a litter through the streets and around the plaza. At each crossroad, in a gesture both Christian and heathen, the litter is tipped so that the Virgin bows in each of the four sacred directions. Offerings of chicha are spilled onto the ground, a splash for each of the sacred peaks on the distant skyline. When the Virgin returns to the church, the wakawakaras begin the final call at the small plaza. The bull and condor are about to meet.

Across the plaza I can see the sorcerer for Don Manuel. He paces. In a balcony, Don Manuel waves at us, beckons us to come.

"What should we do?" I ask Pilar. "I don't want him to get mad at us if something goes wrong."

"Come," Pilar says, as she takes my hand, "we can't insult him. He's a mozo. Maybe he doesn't believe in the things the sorcerer has dreamed." We go into the building under the balcony and mount the stairs. Don Manuel meets us at the top with two cups of cane liquor. We toast him and down the liquor. He is swaying a little. Some of his people drag him out onto the balcony. We follow and stand in one corner. Below I see Santos. He grins and waves at me. He whispers in a man's ear and points to us. The man puts Santos on his shoulders. Santos stands and beckons to me with one hand. I glance down the balcony at Don Manuel. He shrugs, so I lean over, grasp Santos's hand, and haul him up.

A roar goes up, and we look out just as a bull trots into the plaza. A half dozen Indians, all of them apparently drunk and all of them waving their ponchos, rush out to provoke the animal. The bull rushes one man. I gasp involuntarily at the man's languid, ineffectual feint to one side. The bull knocks him over, gores and tramples him. All the Indians are laughing. Several run out and drag him back to the fence. In the meantime, the bull has knocked over and trampled another.

The people in our balcony are cheering more loudly than the others, and I realize that this bull is Don Manuel's. The wakawakaras sound again, forlornly. Three men on horses chase the bull and rope him. They wind the ropes around a lone tree in the plaza and pull the bull to the trunk. They tie his head against it, and then they tie his feet. His balls are swinging in the effort at escape.

Another roar erupts, and we see a crew of men marching out with Don Manuel's condor. Behind them, in the corner of the plaza, a squabble breaks out. Three men are restraining the sorcerer, who is yelling.

I stoop. "What is it, Santos?"

"He's afraid about the condor."

The skull-faced man seems honestly terrified. "What is he afraid of? What can happen?"

"He is the one that brought her. If she's hurt or dies, maybe he'll die, too." Santos says this with bleak flatness.

The bull bellows and struggles mightily when they pierce his hide with a large curved needle. After threading a cord through the bull's hide just above his flanks, they lift the female condor onto the bull's back and lash her legs to the cords on each side of the bull.

Pilar puts her head down and doesn't watch.

"Are you all right?" I ask.

"I can't watch this part." She shakes her head.

"Because of the bird or bull or just everything?"

"I'm afraid for the condor."

Everyone yells. They've released the bull. He bucks across the plaza. The immense wings of the condor rise and fall like sails. Once, as the bull turns to hook his horn at the bird, the condor bites at his ear and rips it. Blood runs down the bull's head. The bull twists and leaps, throws the condor from one side to the other. When the condor's wings hang down, they nearly obscure the bull behind a wide mantle of black and white feathers.

An Indian runs in front of the bull, and the bull chases him. The Indian leaps onto the pole barricade and flings himself over. The bull crashes into the barricade with such force that it breaks loose from one wall. A tide of men rush to push it back, but the bull charges them. He vaults through the opening against the wall of the building. We see the bull's hind legs and hoofs and the condor's wings disappear down the little street.

A hush fills the plaza.

Santos pulls my hand. "Come," he whispers, "you must come."

I look at Pilar's stricken face. She mouths the words, "We go." Santos leads us down the stairs. In the plaza, a mob rushes toward the corner where the bull and the condor disappeared. Santos pulls us toward another corner. He runs. We run behind him. Soon, I realize he's taking us to the Council Building.

At the door, he waits for me. "Your key," he says. "You must hurry. You must leave Cotas. Probably this condor will die. The sorcerer is a dangerous man, and he'll look for you. I know another path into the canyon. But you must hurry."

I fumble with the lock. We stuff our bags and packs and hurry out. I leave the key on the table. Santos takes us to the far edge of town. We drop into a ravine, down to a narrow trail that skirts terraces planted with corn. For half an hour we descend, all the time under the cover of brush and small trees.

Santos stops at one opening where the spur of a ridge comes down into the gully. "We can see from here," he says. "This is the last place. But keep your heads down."

We don't speak. Stealthily, Santos climbs the ridge spur. We follow. At the top, he crawls behind a low hedge of shrubs, parts them, and peers through. We hear him murmur. He beckons to us. Pilar and I crawl up alongside and look through the brush.

The ravines and cliffs beneath Cotas form an amphitheater. We stare across the open void. Beneath the cliffs, on a small slide of talus, lie the bull and the condor. The condor's wings are spread and motionless. The bull is still, his legs outstretched as if in death he still leaps to rid himself of the winged curse tied to his back. At the top of the cliffs, the villagers move in droves like brightly colored insects. We hear nothing but the sound of wind.

We move on down the trail. No one speaks for almost an hour. Then Santos stops.

"Santos?" I look up.

The sorcerer stands on the trail in front of us.

"Oh," Pilar cries. She pushes up around me. The sorcerer watches only me.

Santos says something to the man, but he doesn't seem to hear. Then Pilar speaks. Again he doesn't answer, nor does he look at her, but something I can't describe changes in his expression. He pulls his eyes away from mine and looks at Pilar. He says something to her, his voice low, rich with threat.

Pilar speaks to the sorcerer again. Once more the man drags his eyes away from mine and, nearly whispering, answers her again. Santos stands with his head bowed. The sorcerer wears a machete in a scabbard.

Pilar seems reluctant to stop watching him. "Santos told him that you meant no harm," she says to me. "The sorcerer said you brought harm, harm to him and to Cotas. I told him that you're leaving Cotas and won't come back. I said you did nothing to cause what happened. He said that you brought bad luck without doing anything."

"What does he want to do?"

Pilar doesn't answer. There is another exchange between Santos and the sorcerer. This time the sorcerer looks at the boy. Pilar watches intently as they speak. Finally, the sorcerer shakes his head. He puts his hand on the handle of the machete.

Pilar interrupts, still speaking in Runasimi to the man. He shakes his head and draws out the machete. Santos and Pilar both speak at once, obviously making some plea. Santos waves his hands.

"Wait," I yell. "Let me talk. Ask him if I can speak for myself. Let me talk to him. You translate. I'm the one he wants."

The sorcerer tests the sharp edge of the machete blade with three fingers. He nods at her words.

Her eyes fixed on the sorcerer, Pilar answers me in Spanish, her tone level, the cadence deliberate. "Santos told him that the army will come if he hurts you. I told him that there would be more harm coming to him and to Cotas if he did anything to you. He said that was all tomorrow, and that now, there was only what had to be done today."

"Tell him I'm sorry I came, that I didn't know what would happen. Tell him that if he does anything to me, he'll have to contend with the spirit I've brought with me. If he'll let us go, I'll take that spirit with me."

Pilar looks at me doubtfully and then translates. The sorcerer answers. He watches me with interest as Pilar turns with his reply. But she doesn't give me his reply. She says, "I'm not going to tell you what he said. You know he's dangerous."

I swallow. "What can I tell him?" I ask Pilar. "What do you know about the magic? What about the condor? Can you tell him anything about the condor so that we . . . I . . . am no threat? Do you know anything to say?" I find myself waving my hands and yelling. The sorcerer seems disgusted with my outburst. He frowns. He steps closer, pokes at my chest with the blunt tip of the machete, and asks Pilar something.

Shaking her head, she retorts vehemently.

"Wait—" I yell.

"He wants a finger first. He wants to bury one of your fingers in the plaza."

"Do I get to keep the rest of me?"

"I don't trust him," Pilar says. "I don't think a finger will be enough. I think he wants to play with you. Maybe he's a little off in the head. There's something bad about him."

"What do we do?" I can hear the whine in my voice.

Santos says something to the sorcerer. Toying with the blade, the man listens to the boy. Pilar says something. The sorcerer looks at me. The sweat trickles down my sides. The sorcerer's eyes remain implacable. Despair wells up in me. "Tell him that I can send him a lot of money," I cry.

"He doesn't care about tomorrow. Maybe today he'll die. That's what he believes. Because of you."

Slipping into hysteria, I suddenly feel as if I'm losing Pilar and Santos. "You believe him, don't you?" I accuse her.

"Stop it, Arnie. Don't say crazy things."

Impatiently, the sorcerer slaps his leg with the side of the machete. Pilar blurts something. Her expression changes, the tone of her voice, too. I sense something taunting, some oblique aim. The sorcerer looks at her with interest. Pilar steps into the grass, squats, and urinates. Beneath the wide concealment of her skirt comes the rushing sound. When she stands, she catches part of her dress, and her leg shows to the thigh. With her chin, she beckons at the sorcerer.

"No," I tell her. "Don't do that—"

Santos bumps me with his shoulder. When I glance at him, he shakes his head grimly, signals me to shut up. Pilar and the sorcerer exchange short questionlike phrases.

"No—" I protest.

"You go with Santos," Pilar says. "The road is another half an hour away. Wait for me there. I'll be all right."

"I don't want—" I say.

Again Santos bumps me. Pilar and the sorcerer exchange words again. I hear the word "condor" spoken several times. "Go!" Pilar says fiercely. "Now!"

Santos pulls at my hand. I resist. "Go!" she yells. "I'll come soon." She pushes me hard. I stumble back. I can see that the sorcerer doesn't want to look at me again, as if he'll change his mind. Santos pulls me down the trail. We make long, crashing strides. I'm sick with a tangle of tension and relief. Sick with shame.

———

When Pilar comes out of the trees at the road, I can tell from the pallor of her face and flatness of her gaze that she's had to pay more than she had expected. She clutches one hand in the hem of her dress. A shiny patch of blood glistens in the material.

I'm yelling.

"It's all right. It's just my little finger, and only the last joint."

"Why?" I go on yelling. "Why would he do that?"

"He needed something to bury in the plaza, some sacrifice to free the spirit of the dead condor, to protect himself from the condor's anger. Because of how she was treated."

"But he wanted *my* finger." I can't stop yelling.

"I told him some things about condors, things that made him think I could argue for him with that spirit. He wanted part of my finger for the offering."

"After he raped you?"

"It's all right. I didn't let myself care. I knew he was scared. And it was something to take away that fear. It didn't hurt so much when he whacked my finger with the machete. It hurts more now, but I think it's stopped bleeding. So," she manages a smile, "everything's all right again."

Santos taps me on the back. "Goodbye, gringo," he says, "and mamita." He bows a little toward Pilar and then starts away. Everything is in chaos. I'm overwhelmed with enormous debts.

"Santos," I call him back. I rummage around in my pack until I find my flashlight. "Here." I hand it to him and then dig in my pocket for money.

"No," he says at my groping. "I'll take this." He holds up the flashlight. "I like this little torch."

Pilar chucks him on the chin with her good hand. He starts away again.

"Will you be all right? Will he do anything to you?" I ask the boy.

"No," Santos calls back. "I am Santos, son of Benigno. My father is apukuna, rich with friends who owe him much. If the condor lets the sorcerer live, maybe he won't talk to me anymore. That's all right because the condor has already made him crazy. Everybody knows that."

The boy waves.

3

*i*N OLLANTAYTAMBO, Pilar seems changed for a while. She tells me that she's all right, that it's not the chopped finger or the memory of lying with that man. When we returned through Cuzco, I took her to a doctor. He bandaged it and gave her a prescription for antibiotics. She'd never taken antibiotics before, and it amused her that the contents of a red capsule could do anything better for her than her own body. When we got back to Ollantaytambo, she removed the bandage and wrapped the stub with the leaves of a plant she found by the river. The finger had healed quickly.

Still, I sense a sadness inside her, something deep and remote. I know it is something about the condor. And I know that the experience of having been made to flee her home and family and village so recently must have flown up again at her when we fled Cotas. Maybe, I think, she feels there's nowhere she belongs.

Helplessly, I go on trying to fill one part of her life and mine with Sublime bars and fresh-squeezed orange juice at the ruins, and sojourns in my bed or along the Patacancha.

When I'm gone for four days to work on my study in the park, she's all I think about. Wandering around in thickets of laurel, I collect bags of bear shit and measure claw marks on trees, all the time making love to Pilar, this lovely, profound, elegant woman who laughingly calls herself a brute. I'm haunted by her loyalty to me and to everything she loves, and by all she did to protect me.

In my bear study, I set out sampling plots, step out the corners, drive stakes, count the various plants, and collect specimens of those I don't recognize, all the time perfectly mindless as to what I'm doing.

In three weeks I'm supposed to leave Peru. I don't know what to do.

One morning Pilar and I buy mangos, oranges, cheese, and bread, load it in my daypack, and climb up into the canyon of the Abra Malaga. Our destination is Tastayoc, a village high among bronze and gold cliffs and smooth green canyons that merge with the snows of the pass. Pilar has chosen this route. We climb for three hours. Then we sit by a waterfall to eat lunch. Giant green hummingbirds probe at a cactus flower just above Pilar's head.

At Tastayoc, we meet a grandmother named Manuela and a little boy, Andrés. They live in a stone-walled house thatched with grass. They don't speak Spanish, and I can only watch as Pilar chats with them, making what I assume is small talk. Both are wearing red ponchos. Andrés grins at me and puts out his hand. There is a pebble in it. I take it. He waits for me to put it in my pocket. I have half a Sublime bar in my daypack, which I give to him. He rolls his eyes as if to say, "Oh my." Manuela is pointing at the mountain behind us. Pilar and I turn and crane our heads, but I can see nothing except the cliffs at the top. Pilar thanks her, and we depart.

We start back down the mountain. "So what's up there?" I ask Pilar.

"You'll see," she says.

"Is whatever's there the reason we came to Tastayoc?"

She doesn't answer, but her eyes gleam. I'm elated to see her this way again.

"You say that in your village a couple lives together for a year before they let the church marry them?" I hear myself ask. It's like the one who lives in me, the one I haven't been able to hear for so long, has just broken out of a cage.

Pilar doesn't notice. "They get married in the village by the old ways, but unless the priest finds out, they don't get married in the church for at least a year."

"So they don't really have to be married, not in the eyes of the people. They can just try it out."

Pilar stops and looks at me. Her eyes seem to go back and forth over me, yet they never leave my eyes.

I wonder which one of me she is seeing, which one of me I am. "Just thinking about the Runa, that's all," I say and start down the trail again, then stop. "Would you want to try it? Would you want to come to the United States with me and try a year of that? You know, just something to try?"

She drops her gaze. She stands on the trail above, and her face seems as confused as I've ever seen it. We stand there. I've said it. It's on the table, and I'm leaving it there. Slowly, she turns back to watch the mountain Manuela had pointed toward. "Come over here and sit beside me," she says. "We must watch this mountain for a while. Then we'll think about these other things."

She sits on a rock at the edge of the trail. I go back up to sit beside her. There must be a question on my face. "No," she says, "you just watch." We watch. Nothing happens. "Which way is your home?" she asks, "I mean, from here, which direction?"

I point to the north. "Toward the middle of the sun's path," I tell her.

For a while, Pilar stares off to the north. I wait quietly, wonderingly. "Look," Pilar says. She points up at Manuela's mountain.

I see the condor circling there. Very slowly, in immense circles, the great bird rises and rises. Then the condor sweeps its wings once, returns them to a half-folded position, and shoots away, gliding. We watch until the speck it becomes in the endless distance vanishes entirely. The line of the condor's flight is north.

"Yes, Arnie. I will go with you," Pilar says. "It's what I want to do, and it's what the condor wants me to do."

Serenely, she watches the empty sky.

4

WHEN WE LEAVE Ollantaytambo, Orfelia and Romero come to the plaza to see us off. I have a full backpack and two trunks of gear and specimens. Pilar has only a string bag, and most of the things in it are mine: a journal, two measuring tapes, and a small tape recorder. She has an extra blouse from Orfelia and an over-sized sweater that I gave her.

Orfelia and Romero both shake my hand without warmth. Orfelia's eyes spill over when she hugs Pilar. The truck starts, and we have to scramble over the tailgate. The vehicle hammers off across the plaza cobblestones. Pilar stands leaning over the steel canopy railing and watches behind long after Orfelia and Romero have disappeared around the first corner. She doesn't turn back until we get to Calca, where we transfer to a bus. She smiles bravely at me. Her eyes are dry, but I can tell she dares not speak. I look at her hands. Her finger is nearly healed, but the skin there is translucent and thin.

In Cuzco, we take a taxi to the Santo Domingo Convent where the sisters run a school and a small hostel. The bathroom is shared and a little gruesome in the morning, but the rooms and beds are clean. When the taxi turns down Calle Ahuacpinta, behind the Santo Domingo cathedral, Pilar's eyes begin to dart. "Arnie, that's the Coricancha!"

"Yes, it is. The cathedral was built on the foundation and lower part of the sun temple. The convent we're staying at is on part of the church's grounds."

The taxi stops in front of the steel gate. Pilar stares up at the cathedral and on down Ahuacpinta at the old Inca walls. I ring the bell at the gate. She seems possessed. "Is there something about the Coricancha?" I ask. "Something you know?"

"Only things I know from my family," Pilar murmurs. "Nothing that matters."

"Your family has something to do with the Coricancha?"

"No," she laughs and looks at me finally. "No, nothing like you're thinking."

"Nothing you'll tell me, you mean?"

Pilar's answer is a bland look. A boy opens the gate. We ask for a room. He takes us to a nun, a bespectacled, middle-aged woman whose view of our alliance is clear from the frown hidden beneath her skin. She gives the boy a key, and we follow him upstairs and down a hallway with a glossy parquet floor. At the other end of the hall we can see another boy polishing the floor with pillowlike brushes tied to his feet. Up and down the hall he skates.

That afternoon we go shopping. I ask Pilar what she wants to do about clothes, whether she wants to wear her traditional skirts and blouses—in which case, we should buy another set or two before leaving Cuzco—or if she wants to wear what gringas or Peruvian mestizas wear.

She doesn't hesitate. "I want to learn English. I want to learn how to hold knives and forks like your people hold them. I want to live like they do and learn those things. I'll wear underclothing. I'll wear whatever you think makes me look nice."

"Not for me," I say. "This is for you."

She shrugs. "For me, for you, it's no different."

The mestiza clerk at the dress shop is shocked. She stands with her head tipped back, as if somebody has a knife at her throat. Pilar tries on several skirts and several blouses. First, we buy her a brassiere and other underclothing. The clerk looks away. Pilar is not insulted. At first, she is amused then provocative. "Which of these two blouses is nice with my color?" she asks the clerk. The clerk's face falls. *She* is insulted. Pilar laughs a high, happy sound and squeezes the mestiza's hand. "I'm making a joke, because this is such a nice day for me." The clerk eyes Pilar darkly.

Pilar wants to give away her old dress and blouse to somebody in the market. Bravely, she puts the old life behind her. Watching her in her new cream blouse and slate blue skirt, her new sandals, I can see that her life has been circumscribed by events that will not let her waste anything.

Pilar is like her lovemaking, her appetite enormous and guileless. Mine, by comparison, seems enormous and tactical.

We head to the Chifa Los Angeles for a Chinese dinner. The restaurant is on the Plaza de Armas, and Pilar asks if we can walk around the plaza first. It's late afternoon with a breeze, and the light is wonderful —long and cool and clear as water. She holds tightly to my arm. We haven't made it halfway around under the colonnades when I realize that our pairing seems of no consequence to any of the vendors or anybody else strolling there. With Pilar no longer dressed as an Indian, we are no longer an oddity.

"Are there rich Indians?" I ask.

"Yes, some, seed of the Inca. Others with noble blood who helped the first Spaniards. They were given land and servants. But that blood must be mixing. Maybe they are mistis now with Indian names."

"How do you know all this history?"

"It's the story of my country. We tell the stories of our past."

"So being an Indian doesn't mean you have to be at the bottom of the pile?"

"No, the difference between a rich Indian and a poor Indian is greater than the difference between you and me."

"You're exaggerating." I stop.

Pilar is standing in front of a doorway. She's looking at the stones there. I can tell she's not listening.

She points down. "The first night I came to Cuzco, I slept for a while in that doorway. It was raining. A little memory, only. Come on." She pulls at my hand. "Tonight, when we eat, we speak only English."

The next day we board a jet. We stay in Lima for five days. I have the marriage license from the priest in Ollantaytambo. Orfelia and Romero had stood up for us in a ceremony there that made no pretensions beyond our need for a paper that would let Pilar leave Peru.

In Lima, Pilar and I go through several Peruvian bureaus to get written recognition of Pilar's existence. She has no birth certificate nor any papers of identification. We have to go to the American Embassy to find out what paperwork regarding our marriage has to be supplied from Peruvian agencies. After four days' collecting papers and stamps, Pilar gets her passport, and we're free to leave.

The night before we depart, I take her to a movie. *The Return of the Jedi*, the last of the Star Wars trilogy, is playing.

Pilar is horrified. "Naqaq!" she cries and shudders.

I put my arm around her and feel her muscles working. "It's just a movie, just pictures," I whisper.

She looks at me unbelievingly. Her eyes spin, and she can't seem to get her breath. She shakes her head. "Naqaq," she says again.

"No," I whisper and hug her. "They're machines made for the movie. They're not real. Nothing about them is real."

"They're naqaq," she persists.

"The movies these days are very good at seeming real," I say bouncily when we're walking back to the hotel. "But it's all made up, the story, the characters, the monsters. They're just something somebody thought up."

"Yes," she answers, "I know what you're saying. I'll try to be better at these things." She looks a little haggard. "It was all made up," she says as if reciting, and then with renegade conviction shakes her head. "Those were naqaq." Her face is hard as crystal. "And qhepqe," she says, "a giant qhepqe."

"What are qhepqe?" Naqaq, the demons who steal body fat and castrate men, she'd described to me before.

"The qhepqe are flying heads. They leave the body when you sleep. They go to the burning place where we make the llipta ash to chew with coca. That's where they meet at night to make their plans. They decide when the people they belong to will die. And how. It can happen to anyone's head. If the woman is married and has lain with another man, her head—after it leaves at night—gets tangled in the thorns and brambles. It can't return. That's why it's dangerous for another woman to be out after midnight. The qhepqe might find her and leave her with two heads."

"Whew." I shudder thinking of my disembodied head tangled in thorns. "That's worse than anything we saw in the movie."

She stops and looks at me with grim, grasping eyes. "That Jabba Hutt is qhepqe. A giant qhepqe."

I feel the heat rising from her face.

~

The next day, after a two-hour delay in Lima by AeroPeru, we must wait another two hours in the Miami airport. I call my friend Clyde Goligoski in Missoula. He will meet us at the airport. Then I find Pilar again. She wanders along the row of stores and bars where she is dazzled by glitz. When she sees me, I ape her gawking. She comes at me, swinging.

Laughing, I duck into a chair and pull her down beside me. "Here, calm down, Indian. I have to tell you what's next."

"You speak English," she says defiantly.

"When we get to Montana . . ." I wait to see if she follows. She does. "We will be met at the airport by my friend Clyde."

"Yes, Clyde," she says.

"Clyde Goligoski. He's a veterinarian. You will like—" I rush to confuse her, so we can revert to Spanish. But she has raised a finger, so I speak slowly in English. "Doctor of animals. You will like him. Shelly, wife, you may not like at first. You must let me describe Shelly in Spanish."

"No."

I take a breath and throw myself back in the chair with obvious annoyance. Pilar does not relent. "Quick thinker . . . cynical—"

"What is cynical?"

"She sees the bad things first," I say in Spanish. "And she uses them for her sport."

Pilar frowns in puzzlement.

"You'll see what I mean."

"I understand," Pilar says. "One of the old people I know was like that." She smiles. Her eyes lose their focus. "A Runa mother, long time ago. She was always thinking everything was wrong."

"A long time ago? How long ago?"

"A long time. A relative only. So this Shelly, she'll meet us at the airplane, too?

"I don't know." I puzzle a moment. "You know, I couldn't tell Clyde about you. You are your own explanation. At least for me."

"You're not ashamed of me?"

The question catches me off guard. "No, of course not. I'd never be ashamed of you. But I might be a little ashamed of how everything might seem."

"That you've bought someone to take home for your bed?" Pilar ventures.

"Do you believe that?" I ask her.

"Maybe a little."

I swallow and look away. When I turn back, she's grinning. "And what have I bought?" she taunts. "A man with a bed in a place I haven't seen. We've bought each other. But tell me what about this hair?" She twirls a braid, shows it to me. "Look at all these funny ways they make hair go." She points at the crowd in a ticket line. "It looks like a mess of spider webs. Is that what you gringos like? It must feel stiff and stickery like sisal twine."

I tell her they are upper-class qhepqe—loose heads with some of the brambles still attached—and she giggles herself into a fit of smothered laughter.

~

Somewhere over the Midwest, I awake once. The inside of the airplane is gloomy, and the air is warm and stagnant and feels like flannel. I glance at Pilar. Eyes closed, she sits upright, head erect, composed and alert somehow, even in sleep.

5

*I*N Missoula, Clyde and his ten-year-old daughter Jeff meet us at the airport. As Pilar and I walk toward them, I can see Clyde's eyes deciphering the space between Pilar and me. I shake his hand. "Hi, Jeff," I say to the girl standing behind him. I turn to Pilar, who smiles grandly. "This is Pilar, my friend from Peru. Pilar, Jeff Goligoski, and her father, Clyde."

"Hello, Pilar," Clyde says, taking her hand. He nods once at her and then glances warily at me. Clyde is a man of generous size, barrel-chested with a heavy belly that does not sag, coarse, splotchy skin, and hair the color of new rust. He has a freckled nose, also generous in size, and crooked teeth, and although there is something disheveled about him, his movements are lithe. Looking at the floor, he laughs to himself and wags his head disbelievingly. He tells us that Shelly couldn't come because she's sick.

"Hi," Jeff says. Jeff Goligoski is slender, all legs and neck with a pixie face. She has a pug nose, round, dark eyes and deeply arched, almost puckered lips.

"How you do," Pilar says firmly.

"Pilar is my friend from Peru. There was guerrilla fighting in her village, and she had to leave. She came to the town where I was staying. I asked her if she wanted to come to the U.S. and see what it's like here. To do that, we had to get married." The last part I deliver with pointed insouciance. I tell Pilar in Spanish what I've just said.

"I understand most," she says. "No more Spanish. You put me on horse, I hold to ride."

Clyde laughs.

I'm encouraged, hopeful that he won't misunderstand. "Pilar is trilingual. She speaks three languages," I tell Jeff.

"Three?" Jeff lifts on her toes. "What three? Will you say something."

Pilar pushes her head toward me. Her eyes spark with frustration because I have to translate the last exchange.

"Not three. Two and a piece, this English," Pilar says to Jeff. "I say to you in Runasimi:

> *Munankichu willanayta*
> *Maymantachus kanichayta?*
> *Haqay orqo qhepanmanta,*
> *Clavelinas chawpinmanta,*
> *Ausinas chawpinmanta.*

From where do I come? Other side of mountain come I . . . a place with flowers . . . two flowers . . . kinds . . . the names I don't know . . . not in English." Pilar laughs. In Spanish, she tells me where the flowers grow in Ollantaytambo.

"She comes from beyond the mountain, in a place where lilies and carnations grow," I tell Jeff.

Jeff is charmed. "What was your town like? I mean how many—"

"Hold it, Jeff," her father interrupts. "Let's head for the luggage while we chat. I'm in a ten-minute parking slot."

Following us to the luggage conveyor and then out to the van, Jeff and Pilar work at conversation. They fill in the gaps with gesticulations.

In the van, Clyde says, "Like I told you on the phone, we finished doing the downstairs apartment. It's got its own side entrance. The kitchen isn't much—it's part of the living room—and then a bathroom and a bedroom, but you're welcome to it till you find something better. If you want to rent it yourself, that's fine, too. Whatever. With housing the way it is in Missoula, we'll have no problem finding university students next month."

"Thanks, Clyde. I'll probably do some looking around."

"Yeah." He looks at me from the edge of his eye. "I'm sick of the place, working to get it done by fall. Shelly was on my ass to contract it out, but I couldn't do it. I can't hire somebody to work in my own house, doing the same work I can do."

"Ass?" Pilar asks from the back seat.

Jeff snorts. Rear end, I tell Pilar. "It means Shelly was complaining, and I don't know why it means that."

"I can teach you English that even Arnie doesn't understand," Clyde says to Pilar over his shoulder.

"You haven't told them about mom," Jeff says.

"No."

"Can I?" she chirps.

"Yes."

"Mom's going to have a baby."

Startled, I stare at the side of Clyde's head. He shrugs. "Two months along. We just found out a couple of weeks ago. A little surprise."

"And Shelly? Is she happy?"

"Sickeningly. And sick. That's what she's got, knocked-up nausea."

"So are you. Happy, I mean. I can tell."

"You couldn't tell if it was raining."

At the edge of town, Pilar asks about the white letters on the big hills. In Spanish I tell her that the M is for the University of Montana and that the L is for Loyola High School.

Clyde lives on the north side, Missoula's version of the wrong side of the tracks. The Goligoskis have more education than the rest of their block combined, but they're more at home with people who have garlic on their breath and lodgepole tripods with engines hanging in their backyards than they are with doctors, lawyers, professors, Rotarians, and Unitarians. Nonetheless, the Goligoski home is more like those of the campus area, two-story with a large front and back porch, white and well kept. Clyde keeps it disguised behind an untended thicket of spreading lilac, leggy locust trees, several cottonwoods, an unpruned apple tree that looks like a giant magpie nest, and vines that spill out from every purchase on the porches and sides of the house. The new entryway to the downstairs apartment is cut through the center of a magnificent Virginia creeper. It looks like the entrance to a bower.

Clyde and Jeff help us carry the luggage down to the apartment. Shelly is napping. She asked Clyde to invite me to dinner, and Clyde extends the invitation to Pilar. "Relax and settle in. Take a nap of your own," he says. I try to read the intent of that comment, but he turns away. He points at the bed. "You can put the mattress on the floor if the bed is too soft."

The apartment is simple: a small formica table, particle-board cupboards, a rummage-sale sofa—legless—that looks like a loaf of bread folded lengthwise, chairs of chrome-plated pipe, and a small electric range and a refrigerator that huddle together in the corner.

When I go back to the bedroom, Pilar is undressing. I pull the shade over the little window at the top of the wall and lie down with her. Face to face on the pillow, we touch each other lightly on the arms and shoulders and back. Her breath brushes against my lips. Our hands wander. One thing leads to another.

Afterwards, we are still lying together, slick with sweat. I am in her. She nuzzles and nibbles at my neck under my ear. She begins thrusting her hips.

"Sorry, Pilar, I'm out of bullets."

She doesn't seem to hear; her thrusting is like the suck of a river. "Can't do it again this soon," I tell her. "Sorry, Pilar."

"You just . . . I . . . this one," she murmurs, her eyes milky.

I feel like a clam in the grip of a starfish. There's something deliciously predatory about it. I can't resist that tyrant of synchrony, and at length, we gallop together.

Later, when she returns from the bathroom, she sits straddled across my thighs. "Tell me what your once wife was like?"

I frown.

"No, not like here." She points at the bed. "I mean . . . was like."

"Ann, ummm, Spanish or English answer?"

"I not speak Spanish, no understand." She slides back, partly on top of me.

I take a breath and shift my legs, but Pilar will not get off. "Ann is somebody who wanted to do something important. Maybe she's going to law school now, I don't know. She went back to Seattle where she's from. Seattle is a big city like Lima. Do you understand?"

Pilar listens. "Most. You sad she left?" she asks.

"Yes, then, but it was good that we split up. I think she considered marriage to be something one did, like being born or getting a job. An achievement. Number nineteen. Most people got married at that age, so she did, too. It was the same for me. We acted like we were married, pretended to do things together with pleasure, but it wasn't true."

Pilar is perplexed. "No other man or woman?" She nods at the bed.

"No."

"What you like of her?"

"What did I like about her?" I shift my legs, but Pilar won't move. "I liked the way she worked. I liked the way she got mad at injustice."

"Injustice?"

"When somebody does something bad to somebody else. I liked the way Ann told the truth. I liked the way she felt about things. But that means I have to tell you some of the things I didn't like. She didn't care about grizzly bears. And I didn't care that much about women's issues. She was too angry for me, too rigid." I swing a straightened arm. "She wanted what little we did do together to be like a model, or a lesson on how marriage should be. I think marriage should celebrate differences — certain differences — fit them to feed each other, instead of denying them. She may have been the angry one, but it's also true that she worked harder than I did to make the marriage last."

"You, she, not want children?" Pilar asks.

I sigh. "I don't know, Pilar. In white America, it's not usually the first thing you do."

"Shelly with baby."

"Yes, and they have Jeff."

"I like that Jeff. She tell that her name Jeff is name of boy."

"Yes. It is a boy's name. Her real name is Chandler, a family name, but Clyde always thought it sounded pompous, so he called her Jeff after an old-time movie star named Jeff Chandler. Jeff stuck. Everybody called her that name. Shelly tried to keep it Chandler, but Jeff teamed up with her dad." I smile at the recollection and then realize Pilar doesn't understand. I explain again in Spanish.

She rises from my legs and begins to dress. "So wife first not care about bears. I like bears."

"Pooh," I say. "You've never even seen a bear."

Pilar's eyes flash. "No, but animal I like, know." Frustrated, she shifts into Spanish. "I like animals, and I know them better than you. I've grown up with animals, llamas and alpacas. I've made them work, loaded and unloaded them. I cut the wool. I helped them give birth. I fixed their wounds. I knew when they needed water or new pasture. I can see things about animals that you don't see. I saw you with mean dogs — on that day we went to Tastayoc — and you didn't know what to do. When we met burros and horses and oxen on the trails, you always watched to see what I did. I can like a bear I haven't seen, because I'm a woman of animals."

For a moment I am at a loss. "Yes," I say finally, "I believe that. But I know some bears better than I know most people. Maybe you'd like bears, but you've no sense of my feeling for them."

"You never said much about the bear in Peru."

"I never had much of that bear, not even glimpses. I never got to know them, the individuals or the families. All I did was science. I measured everything that remained—tracks, claw marks, shit; I sampled and counted all the plants that grew where they live—and now I'll let the computer and statistics, instead of my eyes and my heart, make sense out of all the numbers." Staring at the shaded window, I consider again how many second thoughts I have about this business of mine. "Scientists aren't supposed to let their hearts get in the way of the job. But the truth is that most scientists suffer that deprivation all their lives just for the rare chance they get once in a while to let their hearts peek through the keyhole."

"I don't understand, but I don't care about this science anyway. Tell me about the bear, the one here." She is buttoning her dress. I pause to watch her. She is turned sideways to me, and I can see the muscles of her arm, her back, and her neck. They are smooth and womanly, yet with a lovely hardness, too. "Tell me," she says again. She puts on her blouse. Elbows out, she confronts me straight on.

"All right, but we don't have time for much."

Pilar sits on the floor to listen. I tell her about my first experience with bears. I describe the night when a station wagon of onlookers drove between a sow and her cubs, how she attacked the car and killed herself.

Pilar is silent for a while; she sits folded and cross-legged, looking away from me. "And what happened to the cubs?" she asks.

"We left them. Later, another sow adopted them."

She straightens. "Another bear took those babies, the babies of a different mama?" she asks, disbelief crackling.

"Yes, it's not uncommon with grizzlies."

"Ah, they are different from many animals. They're more like people."

"Well, yes and no. We worried about the cubs, because sometimes a boar will kill them. They're bears, not people."

"No, I know, Arnie. That's why that mama killed herself. She's the mother who watches for anything that will hurt her children." She stands in one motion. "Now we go meet Shelly."

⌒

Jeff meets us at the door. Clyde follows behind. Shelly stands in the living room where she waits to be introduced. The introduction throws me off balance. Shelly takes Pilar's hand, nods perfunctorily, almost icily, and says hello. Then she turns on me. "You surprise me, Arnie. I didn't think you would raid the treasures of another country."

"Back off, Shelly," Clyde groans.

"I'm no raider, but you're right about Pilar. She's a treasure," I say. I look to see what Pilar is making of all this. Oblivious to the exchange, she winks at Jeff.

"Sit down," Shelly says. She gestures at the sofa and two soft chairs. Clyde asks about drinks: whiskey, beer, juice? Juice for Shelly, whiskey for the other three adults. Pilar wants to try it.

"Strong," Shelly warns. "Very strong." She squints and shivers.

Pilar shrugs. "I try what Arnie drink."

"That could be a dangerous philosophy," Shelly says to me.

"You . . . with baby," Pilar says. She is sitting on the sofa bent forward with her legs a little apart, her arms crossed, her elbows propped on her thighs. The position approximates a peasant squat, something I wouldn't notice except that she's perched on an American sofa. I wait uneasily for Shelly's response.

"Yes," Shelly says. "In March."

"Want boy or girl?"

"A boy would be nice, but it doesn't matter." Shelly says this to me as if Pilar wouldn't understand.

I don't meet Shelly's eyes. I watch Pilar.

"In Peru, is better boy. Everybody wants boy. For me, no, I want girl . . . to teach."

"And what does your husband, Arnie, want?" Shelly asks, watching me. "What's on his agenda?" She makes no effort to exaggerate her enunciation.

"I have a thesis on my agenda," I say, and then I translate the last exchange for Pilar. She protests, but I do it anyway to make a point to Shelly.

Clyde and Jeff bring out the drinks. Shelly and Jeff have cranberry juice in a wine glass. Clyde toasts our return. Pilar draws her head back at the taste. Clyde has served the whiskey undiluted on ice.

"See what I mean?" Shelly crows.

"Is what Arnie, Clyde like. I try. I come here for . . . come to learn."

"Well, don't let them teach you too much. Don't lose yourself," Shelly says to me.

"Shelly, cut the shit," Clyde says vacantly.

Jeff rises from her chair, leans torward Pilar, and asks slowly, "Can I show you my tree house, house in tree?"

Puzzled, Pilar tips her head. Jeff offers her a hand. "Yes," Pilar says, "I think yes." They go out through the kitchen. I can hear Pilar tinkling the ice in her glass. I have been nervously swirling and banging the ice in my own drink. "Shelly—" I start.

"Arnie, I don't approve of going to another country and getting a cheap lay for your own pleasure by dangling a standard of living seventy times higher than hers—" Her voice is shrill.

"I didn't do that! And you quit treating her—"

"Fuckslave." Shelly says this like she's driving in a rapier.

"What?"

She draws back and plunges again. "Fuckslave."

"Jesus Christ, Shelly," Clyde says wearily.

I'm shaking. "I'm sorry," I say to Clyde, "but I don't think I can sit down to eat with anyone, with anyone who would . . ."

"Say it," Shelly snaps, "with anyone who would say it. Don't say think. Don't say with anyone who would think it, because everyone but you would think it. And why wouldn't they, Arnie? You knew it, or you would've had the courage to tell us. You wouldn't have just shown up."

I feel the skin stretching across my face. I set my drink on the sofa cushion. My heart is beating at the inside of my ears. I storm outside and find myself in the back yard under a huge ramada of tangled tree canopies. I don't see Pilar or Jeff anywhere.

Clyde finds me. "You know how Shelly can get. Ignore it." He leads me to the corner of the yard, to an apple tree. Midway up the tree is a box with a roof and a little balcony. I see a small door and two open windows. A rope ladder leads to a trapdoor in the center of the floor. Pilar, in her tight skirt, is up in the tree house. They're laughing. "Pilar, we have to go," I yell. A perplexed face appears in each window.

"Shelly's on the prod," Clyde says and wags his head.

"Prod?" Pilar asks. They disappear from the windows. I can hear Jeff telling Pilar what prod means.

Pilar descends the ladder. On the ground, she shifts her skirt, and through her blouse, tugs at her brassiere.

"Let's go," I tell her. Suddenly, she seems like an enormous burden.

"No," she says, "drink whiskey." She finds her drink on the fence railing, downs it, and squints. "Shelly? Why prod?"

"No," I tell her. "She likes you fine. She's mad at me. And I don't want anything to do with her right now."

"Why?" Pilar asks.

"Why what?"

"Why she mad?"

"Never mind."

"I not never mind. Why?" Recklessly, she leans at me.

"Forget it," I snap.

Pilar steps toward. She pushes her head out angrily. "I *not* forget."

"Hold it, folks," Clyde says, putting up a hand. "Let's start over."

"If you're going to calm somebody down, Clyde, why don't you calm Shelly down?" I charge. "Or are you afraid of her?"

"Damn right I'm scared of her," Clyde says. "It's pretty stupid not to be scared of a charging rhino." He doesn't seem the least bit insulted. He nods at Pilar. "Shelly thinks Arnie has taken advantage of you."

"Advantage?" Pilar murmurs. "Oh." She marches off toward the house.

"Pilar, we're going," I call.

"No," Clyde says, "let her go. Maybe she can do some good in there, change Shelly's mind."

"Shelly doesn't have a mind. With a mouth like that, there isn't enough room for a mind. You agree with Shelly or you would've said something in there."

"Settle down. Shelly has strong feelings about plenty of things. It's the way she is. I won't change her, and outside of a lobotomy, she won't change me."

Pilar calls from the backdoor. "Arnie, come," she hollers in Spanish. "I can't explain in English. Come tell Shelly what I'm saying."

"No," I shout. "I won't translate anything for her. I'm not going back in there."

Pilar steps out of the door. She shakes her head impatiently. "Come on, Arnie. She wants to know what I'm saying. You don't have to say anything. Just translate. I think you're afraid of Shelly."

"To hell with you, Pilar."

"I'm going to tell her that you're afraid of her if you don't come."

"What's going on?" I yell at Clyde. "Why is everybody after me?"

"Nobody squawks like you do. You make a good toy. Go on in with her," Clyde says. "You can always leave again."

My drink still sits absurdly on the sofa cushion. Pilar scoops it up, gulps half, and delivers the rest to me.

I drag my eyes over to Shelly. She sits where she was when I left. Her face is stony.

"Tell her these words," Pilar says with authority. She speaks rapidly in Spanish: "I came from a village where the people are killing each other. I had to leave my father and my brother, because Shining Path would have killed me. Without my village, my family, my life there can never be as much me as it should be. You tell her that now." She takes my drink.

Woodenly, I obey. Shelly's face is impassive.

"So I learn. This is what I do without my family, my past. I learn. I learn Spanish. I learn the life of a cholo and a mozo. You tell her what those are. And now I'm learning English, and I'm learning about the people in this country. It's what I can do if I can't go home. Tell her that."

Again, I do as told, but this time something in me resists. I manage to finish. Shelly seems to sense this. "Go on," she says to Pilar.

"In our bed I want Arnie as much as he wants me. I know what I want. Nobody fights for me. I fight for myself."

I realize what's bothering me. I look at the missing finger joint on Pilar's upraised hand. Here she is again, taking on the foe, while I watch from the sidelines.

"No, I'm not going to tell her anything," I say to Pilar in English. "Let her live with her own arrogance."

"Oh, come off it, Arnie," Shelly says casually. "I think I know what she said anyway, something about getting as much as you do or something like that. Maybe I did jump in too fast. I probably did." With a limp wrist, she twirls her hand. "So I apologize. You know how I feel about women getting taken for a ride. I get carried away."

"You forgive yourself. Just like that. I wish I could do that with my faults."

"If I hadn't touched a nerve you wouldn't be in orbit."

"You'd piss anybody off, pointing your finger, dropping condemnations like multiple warheads." I sip my drink and point my glass at her. "I accept your apology. But I don't want to hear another one. Your apologies are as cheap as your judgments."

"And your skin is thin as cellophane."

"Enough," Clyde says. "Halftime." He is standing behind me where he has been listening. "I'm going to call Jeff in for intermission, and we'll eat dinner. You all right, Pilar?"

Pilar has been watching our argument in the manner of watching a tennis match. She is swaying. "Whiskey . . . head?" Her eyes are large and looping.

Hastily, Shelly rises and leads Pilar to the table. Over her shoulder, Shelly frowns some remonstrance at Clyde. Clyde shrugs and goes out to fetch Jeff. In the kitchen, Shelly trucks out plates and bowls of food. Dazedly, Pilar watches. We sit down to platters heaped with pieces of fried chicken, scalloped potatoes, and garlic bread. The smell of blue cheese and garlic drifts from a green salad.

Pilar knocks her chair over getting to the bathroom. We hear her retching.

"You shouldn't have given her so much whiskey," Shelly jumps at Clyde.

"That's what she wanted, Shelly," he says placidly as he picks up the chair. "She said she wanted to learn about whiskey. She's doing that. And I think she'd rather do it her way than your way, so you can just butt out. Again."

When Pilar reappears at the door, she peeks her pale face around. "Not eat . . . sorry . . . must go to house under . . . thank you. Tomorrow to see you, Jeff. And Shelly, Clyde. Sorry."

I walk her downstairs, help her undress and get into bed. She asks for a bowl, and I bring her one. I kiss her on the forehead. Her eyes seem swollen with regret. Going back upstairs, I realize it was probably only nausea. Pilar is not one for regret.

6

*U*NDER THE SUN of an early October afternoon, the wildlife biology picnic takes place in Dr. Ikeda's backyard. The keg sits in a tub of ice overlooking Rattlesnake Creek, a clear, near river-sized stream running over colored stones at the edge of Ikeda's yard.

Pilar and I are filling our plastic cups at the keg. Mazie Kline, a new student who works on grizzlies in Yellowstone, fills hers, too.

"For Pachamama," Pilar says, and she sloshes a little beer onto the ground.

"Who?" Mazie pounces.

"For Mother Earth. In Peru, we share our drink with the mama. The mama who make . . . makes everything."

"Pach?"

"Pachamama."

"For Pachamama," Mazie says and pours a little beer onto the lawn.

"Waste not, want not." Eldon Sundling approaches with an empty cup. The way he holds his cup shielded behind one hand reminds me of a child who has stolen a sweet and suspects surveillance.

"We're not wasting it," Mazie tells him. "It's an offering to the earth mother. It's what Peruvians do to show respect."

Eldon draws the cup out from behind the shield of his hand. "I show my respect for the beer by drinking every last drop." He doesn't look at Pilar. Except for Mazie and Ikeda, the other graduate students and professors have made little attempt to talk with Pilar, to welcome her. She doesn't seem slighted.

"So this is the bear-people corner?" Eldon says. He moves to stand near Mazie, his back facing us. Eldon's intentions are showing. Mazie sidesteps enough so that Eldon has to acknowledge us. "Arnie's back with his bags of shit, and you have yet to gather yours?" he asks her.

"I got a bagful this summer," she says. "It's a start."

"Mazie is studying grizzlies in Yellowstone," I tell Pilar, "and she's doing pretty much what I did in Peru with the spectacled bear."

"I want to see the grizzly," Pilar says to Mazie.

"When the bureaucrats and the biologists quit fighting over the Yellowstone grizzly, there aren't going to be any grizzlies left," Eldon says with authority and stares at me.

"Maybe so, maybe no," I reply. I'm tired of this fight.

"I have hope for the grizzly in Yellowstone," Mazie tells Eldon. "Because I think the people will choose to keep them there."

"You mean people like the ranchers and the trophy hunters and the tourists who don't want to get eaten? People like that?" Eldon bends at the waist. I don't think he's going to get far with her, not with this approach.

"Yes," Mazie says, "I believe that. I believe there are tourists who want to visit the haunt of an animal that scares the hell out of them. There aren't many places like that anymore. I think people, most of them anyway, want to believe there are places where one enters as other people enter churches. People need to be respectful like that. It has its own meaning."

Dr. Ikeda, who has been filling a cup at the keg, turns to listen. Mazie pauses. "Go on," he says, "don't stop."

Mazie goes back to Eldon. "I don't think hunters should be allowed to shoot grizzlies," she says, "or outfitters allowed to guide hunters for that purpose, but I believe there'll always be those who want to go with outfitters into the places where grizzlies live. Every day Los Angeles gets more and more like itself, and every day another thousand malls make every different place into the same place without any breeze or birds or smell of its own. People want more than that. They'll want a place for grizzlies. A place that is like a grizzly." Mazie stops, glances about uneasily at the lull.

"Mazie, you're just another lobbyist," Eldon teases, trying to shade the tone of differences.

"Maybe you're just another graduate student," I say, mocking his offhandedness.

"And you're not?"

I follow Dr. Ikeda to the keg. There are questions I won't answer anymore. Dr. Ikeda fills his cup, then mine.

When I return, Pilar is waiting. "This talking," she says so quietly that I have to press near her, "this talking about the bear is like for me thinking about the Runa, my people. They are caught between different people who want all the things to change. But the Runa want nothing to change."

I glance at Eldon and Mazie to see if they've heard Pilar.

"So you think I'm cynical about your bears?" Eldon says to Mazie.

"What do you mean, Pilar?" I jump in. "Do you mean the Runa are like the bear? They won't adjust to outsiders?"

Eldon stops to listen. "No," Pilar says, "that must be different, I guess. The Runa have ways of living with most invaders. The Incas, the others, all those come take what they want from the Runa. They stay, live with the Runa. Like the priest and the other foreigners on plaza. But not really do they live there, not like we do. The village . . . how would you say? In our home, in our fields, in our magic, in all the fiestas that they only watch."

"Magic?" Eldon rouses. "What kind of magic?"

Pilar touches Mazie's shoulder. "That grizzly bear is your magic."

"My magic, the bear? How?" Mazie cries.

"Magic?" Eldon sneers.

"The item you don't have," I say to Eldon.

"You're into magic now, Arnie?" he says, escaping toward the barbecue grill.

"Tell me what you mean," Mazie says, tipping her face into Pilar's.

"I don't know how to say it. Not in English."

"Please try. Your English is very good." Mazie stirs one hand in agitation.

"No," Pilar says in her serene way.

Mazie looks to me for help.

"While you're evading questions, do you want to avoid the ones about the Incas?" I ask Pilar.

She laughs and puts a finger across my lips.

~

For a few weeks, I'd tried to help Pilar with the alphabet and the first stages of reading, but I had to quit. The swarm of utterly simple details frustrated me to a point where I could not move past incredulity. Without protest, Pilar found another teacher.

Barbara is Clyde's secretary at the clinic. She has two daughters, one in fourth grade, the other in first, and she brings some of their used school materials to the office. She even gives Pilar homework. When Pilar is washing windows, mopping, stuffing bills in envelopes, or doing any other work in the front office, Barbara quizzes her. Sometimes she asks Pilar to spell words or to pronounce the words that she spells. Clyde told me once that Pilar stuffed and stamped envelopes while reading from a workbook page taped to a cabinet.

Clyde hired Pilar the week after we came. He had intended something little, several hours a day on the cleaning and feeding detail for the dogs and cats that were patients or boarders. In less than a week,

Clyde said the clinic depended on her. She went full time and got a raise. Pilar serviced the kennels faster and better than others had. She dug a pit for composting out by the garbage rack and reorganized the bags and cans of feed to occupy half the space.

At the same time, Clyde discovered another, more significant talent of his new employee. The noise level diminished. Even though Pilar could not fully alleviate the terror of imprisonment and absent masters, the barking and mewing dropped both in volume and tone. Pilar made frequent visits to the kennels. From that, it followed that Pilar was the one assigned to take the cat or dog or bird from the client and deliver the animal to its kennel or cage. When the owner returned, Pilar delivered the pet.

"She's smooth as a wet rock," Clyde tells me. "These pets sense something about her." Noisily, he scratches the back of his neck with two thick fingers. "And she's just as good with the people. Most of them come in there pretty upset, and she does a lot for them. Even the people who bring in a dog or cat for the last time. It's something to see. They're saying goodbye to their friend in a sterile place that smells like Lysol. Pilar does something tilting her head and pushing out her lips. I don't know what the hell it is. She's sad for them. But firm. She won't let them make a scene. How does she do that? I'll tell you one thing, it's no good with words. You can't be telling people things then. Their ears don't work. It's like she shows them that they have to be dignified for their old dog. Brave for the one they're leaving, so that the animal won't feel worse. She doesn't let them linger too long, but there's nothing business-efficient about it either. Skinny little line there."

"Saint Francine of Assisi, eh? What's she doing with the animals out back?"

"One thing is that she talks to them in her own language, sumarini or whatever she speaks. Some things she chants and other times kind of sings to them. And I notice she's careful with her eyes, doesn't stare.

I think she's reading them to see if they want to be stroked or sung to or scratched or whatever." He grins his crooked teeth at me. "Watch yourself. You're just another old dog."

"Yeah, well at least I came with skin instead of alligator hide."

"There's something else," Clyde says slowly. "I didn't ask Pilar about it, because I don't think it was for anybody else except her, but there've been times out there when she's had these conversations with herself. I've heard her a couple of times, and it was strange, not like talking to herself, but like a play she was reciting."

"Do you remember what she was saying, any words?"

"The other day I heard her say her name was Mayo and that she lived on the bottom of the river where snakes swam in and out of her mouth. And something about somebody who sees all. It was pretty broken, as if she were translating it as she went." The heavy skin on Clyde's forehead squeezes into folds. "What do you make of it? Is that what Peruvians do?"

"Peruvians are different, different from each other. I mean the cultures. I don't know what it is. I know there's a lot more to Pilar than meets the eye, and she's happy to leave it that way."

"I can understand that. Minding my own business is something I can never do enough of."

"Yeah, well, I think you could say that Pilar is my business. I'm married to her."

"So you are, but you don't call her your wife."

"We're trying it out for a year. That's how we arranged it."

⌇

We still live in the Goligoski apartment and will remain for the year. Pilar has persuaded me not to look for another place. She has become obsessed with Shelly's pregnancy. Every day she feels Shelly's belly with both hands. She never asks permission. She just does it, closes her eyes and feels about and waits for movement and then feels for more, as if she's divining the baby's personality or conversing with it. Early on, I saw Shelly jerk at the invasion. But gradually, she's given over to it and, lately, seems more than willing to let Pilar handle her. For her part, Pilar acts as if the belly and the baby are her own.

At first, Pilar and Shelly got along peculiarly. Shelly treated Pilar as if she were mentally retarded. She spoke with maddening slowness and overdone emphasis. "Pilar, this . . . is . . . a . . . mixer. Mixer." Pilar was unfazed. Sometimes I had the feeling that she sensed the underestimation, the condescension, but enjoyed it. She seemed to view Shelly as someone who would come to understand. In time. And Pilar went into each day as if she had all the time in the world.

But that was an illusion.

⌒

The day Mazie phones is the day the arrow is notched. The call itself isn't a first cause; it just happens to be where it all starts. And some things begin to end.

Mazie's voice is solemn. "I hate to be the bearer of bad news, Arnie, but Celeste was at Lake again. She tore up a trailer behind the hotel. They caught her yesterday, and it's the last time. Bond called. They're not going to release her."

Dr. Lawrence Bond is the head of the Interagency Grizzly Bear Study Team, the one who makes all such final decisions. In this case, he's like the governor who considers commuting a sentence.

I swallow. "What are they going to do with her?"

"She's coming up here. To Fort Missoula. One of the graduate students will do some work on repellents and aversive conditioning this fall and spring." Aversive conditioning is academese for making a renegade bear sick by feeding it something awful to train it to quit killing sheep or cattle or eating garbage. *Clockwork Orange* for bears. Trials with repellents involve spraying a bear with something like Mace to turn away an attack. I could imagine the spray would be marketed under a name like Git-Grizzly or Bomb-the-Bear. I had to admit such work might help grizzlies ultimately, if it ever worked; fewer injured people means fewer bears killed. But, as a means to that end, Celeste would be tortured.

"Then what?"

"They're sending her to Churchill next summer. Somebody up there is doing something with physiology. Treadmill stuff." Churchill is a bear lab in Canada.

"Then what?"

"They'll kill her. It's part of the treadmill study."

"Fuck."

A pause. "I'm sorry, Arnie."

"I know you are. I'm sorry. It's all I can think to say. They can't find any zoos that will take her?"

"No."

Alarmed, Pilar watches me. She sits on the bed reading a primary-school book. When I hang up, she asks, "What's wrong?"

"They're going to kill Celeste."

"Who's Celeste?"

"She's a bear I know."

Pilar closes her book. "Why haven't you told me about her?"

"Why haven't you told me about the Incas?"

"It's different."

"Why is it different?"

"The Incas are dead. Tell me about Celeste. I'm listening." Pilar leans toward me, pats the bed, and beckons me to sit beside her.

"I was eighteen when I met Celeste." I sit. "And she was only two. That was in 1967. I'm thirty-four, so that makes her . . . eighteen. In those eighteen years, Celeste has raised thirteen cubs in four litters. She's one of about fifteen females that the Yellowstone population of grizzly bears depends upon. Other females are too young or too old or too carefree or careless or something." I pinch my forehead. "It ends up that a population of one to two hundred bears owes its existence to a handful of good mothers."

"So why are they taking her?" Pilar asks crossly.

"Celeste doesn't avoid people like she used to, so she's dangerous. She's been trapped and hauled miles away twice before, but she's come back again. Her number is up. She's never attacked or charged anybody, but she's a grizzly bear, and a good one, so that all it would take is someone strolling behind Lake Hotel to find out too late that they've blundered into a no-man's land between Celeste and her cub."

"Where did you get that name?"

"We named her after a pretty waitress in Firehole."

"How pretty?" Pilar leans at me. Her eyes turn smoky.

"Real pretty."

Pilar grabs a chunk of my side and squeezes. "Ouch!" I yell. Her strength always surprises me. "Not as pretty as you. Let go." She releases me, after a parting twist.

"You want to tell some of the other names?"

"Are you kidding?" I rub my side.

"Tell me about Celeste, the bear."

I tell her about the can on Celeste's foot and about finding her den. I tell her about my summers in the park's Pelican Valley and the parallel events of Celeste's life and mine as a student then. When I mention that I was studying English then, she is puzzled that I would study my own language.

"Studying English means reading all the important literature and learning how to write professionally, or well enough to teach literature or writing. I thought I wanted to be a sifter of the culture . . . a keeper of the songs. But that bit of innocent romance didn't last long."

"Keeper of songs? What is that?"

"Oh, I don't know much about it, something from the American Indians I think. It refers to the one in the tribe who keeps track of all the songs and stories for the rest. A native clerk and recorder. That's all."

"I like that name, keeper of songs."

"Are you a keeper of songs, Pilar? Clyde says he has heard you reciting long poems or something to yourself at the animal clinic."

"In a way." She waves her hand dismissively. "Tell me the songs of Celeste."

"Songs of Celeste. That's nice. But tell me, Pilar, do you keep these secrets about yourself just to be provocative? Just to drive me nuts?" I lie on my side and run the back of my hand along the curve of her hip and waist.

"Everybody has secrets. It's like their magic. They need them to live good."

"You mean it's good for me to know you have secrets, but only if I don't know what they are?"

"The corn sends down roots to grow tall. First, the broom comes, then the threads. Every day the corn shows another part of itself, another secret. I don't tell you the words I say, not the ones that Clyde heard. They are my magic, but every day you see them in other ways and in other words. I can't hide myself, not my heart." She pulls my hand through her robe and puts it on her breast. "Those words are what I grow in."

"But I'm telling you my stories. I'm telling you about Celeste. Should I keep that story secret?"

"No." She puts her face so close to mine that I can't focus. "If something terrible happened to her . . . or you . . . then maybe you wouldn't be able to tell me that part. And I would understand, I think."

"Are your accounts, poems, whatever these secrets are, a collection of tragedies?"

"No, they're just important in some way that can't be said out loud. I loved a man, Alejandro. I saw a woman put a knife into his chest, and I watched the life fall out of his eyes. I've told you about that, but the words that go into your ears are not same as those burning out my mouth. I see Lazario and Oqoruro and the other camayocs and all the people of the village throw their hats in the air over the new bridge and the flowers fall out of hats, and what you see, when I say it, is not what I say. But they aren't secrets I mean to keep from you. Put your hand here." She pulls my other hand down between her thighs and presses. "My secret, all the secrets de mío, are in me. I'm here, all of me. I am Pilar. A name in front of the sun. I love you more and better, because I have my secrets. Magic falls out like rain."

"Jesus Christ, Pilar." I draw back so I can focus. And I pull my hands from her body. "You are so persuasive. You won't even let me *want* to talk you out of your secrets. You're a lap ahead of me, in *my* language."

"Not the language. It's the story. Like Celeste's. Now tell me more about her. And when they bring . . . send her to Missoula, take me to meet her."

"I tell you about Celeste, and if I ask you about what you haven't told me, you'll simply put my hand between your legs?"

Pilar wrinkles her nose at me. "Do you think she will remember you?"

"Celeste?"

"Yes."

"Oh, I don't know. At one time I thought she might recognize me. She even had a greeting of sorts. I'm sure she did it in other contexts, but when she'd see me, she would stand and stir the air with her right foot, the one with half a pad, and then at the end of that stirring, she would raise that paw. It was as if she were waving. It probably had to do with that old wound, but it was fun pretending that she knew who I was and that she was greeting me."

"Why wouldn't you believe it? I believe it."

"It's the way of science. You can't go around believing everything you want to believe."

"But it could be true with you deciding already that it isn't."

"It's a little more complicated than that. Do you want to argue epistemology?"

"I don't understand those big words. But you're a sad believer, I'll say that. Tell me about Celeste making love."

"Yeah, well, when people believe everything, they end up with nothing but popcorn, puffy white shit."

Pilar rolls her eyes. "I don't believe in puffy shit." She smacks my arm with an open hand. "Do they make love like dogs and llamas and horses? Does he get on her back?"

"Yes. But they do other things like people. Standing, for instance. And the females nurse like people. They lie down on their back or sit and let the cubs nurse from the front. Face to face."

Pilar smiles broadly.

"Let me tell you about one of Celeste's cubs, from her first litter. She had three cubs then. One of them a male with a white collar, we called Hipshot after a cartoon cowboy. Even as a cub, he had more than an average amount of personality. He seemed to enjoy clearing the dump of bears, for instance. He'd sit on the highest mound of dirt in the dump, near where Celeste positioned him and his two siblings, and there he would find a big enough can, at least gallon-sized, and he'd beat on it like a drum. No preliminaries, just all at once, he'd start banging. Bears scattered everywhere. Even thousand-pound boars. Then he'd wait until—"

"What were they afraid of? People?"

"Yes. Grizzlies run from humans, almost always. Run from the sight, the smell, the sound of man. Except when they've been startled at too close a range, or if a female has cubs, that's when they charge. Or if they've gotten used to being around people—in campgrounds, for instance—then they're dangerous, because they don't run away anymore.

"Anyway, Celeste had her paws full defending Hipshot. He was always wandering off. A half dozen times, I saw Celeste attack big boars to keep them away from Hipshot, who'd gone a-visiting."

"Did Hipshot get to be a big boar?"

"Pretty big. But he never stopped being himself. Once I watched him chase a black bear off an elk carcass. The black bear went up a tree, and Hipshot, who was three or four then, went halfway up after him." I grin proudly, as if I were telling a story about my son.

Pilar is puzzled.

"Grizzlies don't climb trees. Grizzlies, except for Hipshot. Their claw are too long. They have digging claws. But the tree that black bear went up had low limbs, and Hipshot used his jaws to pull himself up. The black bear climbed to the top of the tree, high enough to tip the crown of the tree. Leaning out sideways, there was that black bear gazing down at crazy Hipshot.

"One year the Park Service trapped Hipshot at Fishing Bridge. They released him one hundred miles away. He was back in three days. We trapped him once as a seven-year-old. He was long but getting heavy, on the verge of becoming a dominant boar. When we went up to the trap, he went into a rage and attacked the steel grid of the door. He bit and held the bars and then twisted his head. All four of his big canine teeth popped off." I wince and swallow. "It made me sick to see what we were doing. That was the day I saw that we would probably have to say goodbye to the grizzly, because neither one of us was ever going to change. And that kind of mutilation could not go on long before the bear lost."

"What happened to him?"

"He beat the odds again, one last time. Without those teeth, he still gained enough weight to winter through in good shape. But that was his last trick. A hunter shot him in Wyoming the next year. He was eight, and he weighed six hundred pounds. But he never made it to the heavyweights, even though he was already a kind of heavyweight to begin with. The killing was illegal, but the taxidermist found a tattoo on the hide and reported it. After the guy got caught, he told us where he left the carcass. Ikeda sent me to Wyoming to bring back what was left. Which I did, for the most part. I told Ikeda that I hadn't found the skull. But that was a lie.

"I remembered that the Indians, some of the tribes somewhere, painted the skull of the bear they had killed, and then they tied the skull to a tree and left it. I also remembered that when the Indians killed the bear, they apologized to its spirit, and they never bragged or in any way ever described the killing. They believed the bear gave himself to them. I didn't have any paint, so I smeared stripes of huckleberry juice on Hipshot's skull and I tied it to a big Douglas fir snag on a ridge above Pelican Valley. I haven't told anybody but you."

"That's your magic, Arnie."

"Magic, pooh. I only did it because I couldn't think of anything else. It didn't matter much, and I didn't think it would change my luck or anything."

"You think Hipshot's skull is still there in the Valley of Pelican?"

"I do. You like that?"

"Yes. That's a place of power."

"*I* made it a place of power?"

"In a way. But it's more like you found it. That's the bear's home. And you brought him back to it. Some people will go there and see the power. They will be quiet when they feel it. The ones who are loud and laughing, those who have no secrets, find nothing there."

"So how do you know all this?"

"I just do. And so do you. Everybody with secrets knows it."

7

W E H A V E Thanksgiving dinner upstairs with the Goligoskis. Barbara and her two daughters, Kim and Jill, are there. Also, Mazie Kline. The preliminary conversations and the mealtime palaver among the eight of us have been polite and circumspect, exemplary in their inclusion of everybody, and empty as eight balloons. We have retired to the living room, and Clyde is serving brandy. Mazie and Pilar seem unaware of the starchy ambience. Mazie is grateful to be in a family setting, and Pilar has been fascinated with new foods and another new drink—brandy.

Our conversation languishes aimlessly until we wander into the topic of sexual differences. Pilar wades in with an observation about courage. "Men aren't strong like woman are. Men have more muscles in the legs and arms, but women have other muscles."

I can see the mischief on Mazie's face. "Arnie?" she probes.

As I hesitate, Pilar sails in for her usual rescue. "For a woman to be as strong as she can on the inside, there has to be a man showing his strength on the outside, one who works hard, saying yes he will do this, he will do that and that. There are two kinds of strong . . . strength for the family. One kind makes another."

"Yes, but you meant more than that," Mazie accuses her.

"That's all right, Pilar," Clyde laughs, coughs, and clears his throat with a whacking, rubbery noise. "Everybody knows Shelly wears the pants here. I don't care. Helps a lot when salesmen call on the phone or when Mormons or Jehovah's Witnesses show up on the front steps."

Shelly hasn't said anything. She's been listening for once. Squeezing one eye at her husband's comment, she studies Pilar. "I think women put up with pain better than men," Shelly says finally. "I had a saddle block when Jeff was born—that's a drug that makes you numb from the waist down, Pilar. With this baby, I'm thinking about dropping the drugs and trying it with breathing exercises. I haven't said anything yet to you, Clyde, but I'm considering a home birth. Women do it all the time, right?" she asks Pilar.

"Oh yes. And I will help," Pilar says. "I've helped with many babies. I know when the baby comes, I know how to . . ." she moves her hand in a washing motion, "so you will not tear."

"No deals, yet. I'm not committing to anything." Shelly shifts her weight in her chair, draws her legs up on one side. "What about you, Pilar? What about children?"

Pilar looks at me and smiles enigmatically.

I have no idea what she is thinking. I say, "We haven't even talked about it, Shelly. Don't be nosy."

Shelly holds up her hands. "Down, boy. I'm just curious about what Pilar thinks about home birth. I would imagine she's never considered any other alternative."

"I would have my baby at home, on the same bed where we made the baby."

There is a silence, a lapse that does not intend awkwardness but gains it in increments. Simultaneously, Clyde and Barbara move to fill the emptiness. They blurt something, laugh at their collision of words, and then they both refuse to proceed.

With inimitable ostentation, Shelly moves to draw out Mazie, "Why would you ever want to study bears?"

"I've always liked animals. And nature." Mazie rolls her eyes. "Terrible clichés," she apologizes, but then starts, "Oh, I just remembered I brought a little item for Arnie." She darts to the closet, retrieves a clipping from her daypack, and returns. "Have you, Arnie, or any of you ever heard of Ishi?"

None has.

"Can I tell you a little about him?"

"Shoot," Clyde says.

"It's the story of a small California tribe all but wiped out by the white man in the 1870s. For nearly forty years, one family escaped detection and lived in hiding not far from Chico. Eventually all died but one man, Ishi. He lived alone for three years. Desperately lonely, he gave up and walked out into the white man's valley where he expected to be killed. But instead, when he was found—this was in 1911, I think—they put him in the jail in this small town. When word of the wild man got to San Francisco, an anthropologist from the museum there was sent out to examine him. Ishi ended up living at the museum, and that's much of what's so interesting, the kind of man he was. Polite, gentle, meticulously neat and clean. One of the professors' wives complained that her husband wasn't as civilized as Ishi."

"How could he live with his people gone? All of them?" Pilar's face is heavy. "How could anyone live with that sadness? Could you?"

"I don't know. Yes, he was sad. He believed talking about them would disturb their spirits. When the museum people asked about his family, Ishi wouldn't say anything. Their questions alone would depress him for days."

"How long did he live without his people?" Pilar asks.

"He was alone for three years in the wilderness. He died five years after coming out. From tuberculosis."

"I don't think so," Pilar says, shaking her head. "I think he died from being sad."

"Ishi means man in his language."

"His name was man?" Pilar asks.

"No. That's the name his anthropologist friends gave him. He wouldn't tell them his name. So they called him Ishi, which was fine with him."

"His name was a secret," I say. "Pilar, you and Ishi might have understood each other very well."

Pilar cants her head and her eyes soften, but she does not smile.

"Anyway," Mazie proceeds, "when the whites were killing all the Indians, one of the posses even went so far as to visit a few of the white ranches where some of the Yahi worked as servants. Yahi is . . . was the name of their tribe. They dragged the Indian servants outside and shot them. They shot them even while their white masters fought to save them."

"Why?" Shelly nearly yells.

"You know, Shelly," I say. "In those days, the only good Indian . . ."

"And it all began with the whites killing the Yahi and taking their land," Mazie says. "The Yahi responded by burning down some of the settlers' places and killing a few people. So the whites proceeded to wipe them out, servants, children, all of them except Ishi's family, who hid out in these canyons near Mount Lassen. They didn't use the trails. And they hid their camp beneath remote cliffs in a dense woods loaded with poison oak. They lived on salmon they speared and deer they shot with bows and arrows — sometimes a bear — and in the winter they ate acorn meal. They swam almost every day in Deer Creek."

"They didn't grow anything?" Pilar asks.

"No. They were hunters and gatherers. Which ended up helping Ishi's family, because without gardens, they could hide better. Nobody found them until a team of surveyors went through the Deer Creek canyon. It really was a fluke, because if the surveyors had gone only fifty feet or more to either side, they wouldn't have found a thing."

Arnie groans.

"Think of it," Mazie goes on. "They'd been extinct for forty years.

That's what everybody thought. Then, at the same moment, the family is both rediscovered and destroyed. Three of them ran off in different directions, and two of them apparently drowned trying to cross Deer Creek below the camp. An old woman with a badly infected leg got left behind in a little cave. The surveyors tried to speak to her, but they couldn't understand what she was saying. The crew helped themselves to the Yahis' belongings. A bobcat robe, some baskets, bows and arrows, other stuff. They took everything the family needed to survive. When they went back to their own camp and told one of the cowboy packers what had happened, the packer was appalled. He went back the next day to help the old woman, maybe leave some sort of gift for them. But she was gone. Apparently, Ishi had come back for her. She was his mother."

"You're embellishing this," Shelly says. "Nobody would just up and take all their belongings, especially in front of the old woman. I know the moral to this story is that white people are horrid, but I don't believe this all happened."

"It did." Mazie says simply. "In fact, Ishi was surprised to see all of his things years later in a museum. Anyway, the old woman died soon after, and Ishi was alone, really alone. Surrounded by white killers—as far as he knew." Mazie glances warily at Shelly.

Clyde offers everyone brandy. Only Barbara accepts. He fills her snifter a third full. "Let's you and me get smashed," he says to her. Then he falls back into his chair and, lifting his glass, signals Mazie on.

Mazie unfolds the scrap of paper. She glances at me shyly. "When the whites were hunting down the last of the Yahi Indians, they often came across grizzly bears." She smooths the paper and reads:

Breckenridge threw a shot into a huge grizzly and it ripped at its side with its teeth and sent up a terrific bellow. Hi and I let go at the wounded beast and we soon had it down and out. Then on to the next. For a time we kept mighty busy loading and firing, but the bears never seemed to know where the shots were coming from, and so our trees were not put to use. We killed four and sent the fifth one off badly crippled.

They were huge creatures, weighing, I should judge, a thousand pounds each. We carefully removed their galls, which we knew we could sell to Chinamen. The Chinese use them in preparing some kind of medicine and in those days often paid as high as fifteen dollars apiece for them. The feet we also lopped off. They were to serve as food. After being roasted in hot ashes, they make a most toothsome dish. The sixteen feet made a considerable pack in themselves. The carcasses and skins we left.

Mazie looks up.

I whistle. "There's a lot of work with all this killing. All these bears and Indians that need to be destroyed. It's the white way, having dominion and all. I think they killed the last California grizzly in 1924." I say this to Shelly.

"That's pretty simplistic, Arnie," she says. "You filter the world for your prejudice just as any racist would. One could probably make lists of Yahi sins. And of course, you must disregard any kindnesses ever done by the white race."

I ignore Shelly and say to Mazie, "I don't think it's very likely that each of those bears weighed a thousand pounds, but the rest is all believable enough. It's interesting about the gall bladders and the Oriental market way back then in the 1870s. It's a big problem today." I'm looking at Clyde, who seems a little sleepy.

"Are you trying to ignore me?" Shelly asks me.

Clyde jumps to his feet. He stands between us and blocks our view of each other. "Don't start," he says. "Who needs another jigger of this stuff?" Holding the bottle by the neck, he gestures at us around the room.

Barbara holds out her snifter, and Clyde chugs in a generous measure. Barbara lights up another cigarette; she pops her lighter with a flare and sucks in the first drag as if to take it all in one draw.

"So your friend Bridget's gone to bed for the winter?" Clyde asks me.

"Celeste," I tell him. "Yes, she's asleep. She gets to wake up in the spring, be tortured for a month or so, and then she's off to Churchill, where they'll perform another battery of experiments on her. Then they'll kill her."

"Why do they torture her?" Barbara asks, her expression pained.

"They're testing bear repellents on her." I defer to Mazie for details.

"Celeste is in a cell at Fort Missoula," she says. "A graduate student is working with her. He stands on the other side of a barred door and provokes her to charge. When she does, he sprays her through the bars with different chemicals to see which ones are best for turning her away."

"It's so terrible." Pilar scowls. "They should spray that man there instead of Celeste."

"What kind of spray?" Barbara asks.

"Different things. A Mace-type stuff called Halt, an artificial skunk spray, and the crystalline extract from red peppers—an alkaloid called capsaicin. The pepper one burns them good," Mazie tells her.

"Doesn't that injure them? What about their eyes?"

"That's where they aim." Mazie is talking about something she has not seen. But Pilar has.

When Celeste arrived in Fort Missoula, Pilar, Mazie, and I went down to see her. It was still October, and Celeste was winding down for the big sleep. To reset Celeste's clock back and keep her awake a few weeks longer, they left the lights on for a while when it was dark outside.

Nonetheless, when we went into the fort, Celeste was curled up in the back of the cell, half buried in a pile of a hay. We couldn't see much more than part of her back and rear. Pilar was excited to see the gold and silver tips on her hair, the basis for one of the grizzly's nicknames, silvertip. We didn't want to disturb her, so after about fifteen minutes, we left. We were crossing the cell compound yard when Bob Miner drove in. He was the first-year graduate student assigned to the bear-repellent project. He invited us to watch a trial.

"I don't want to watch this," Mazie said. "I'll wait in the car."

"Me neither," I told Pilar. "Celeste's a friend of mine."

Pilar didn't say anything, but I could see she wasn't leaving with Mazie and me. "We'll wait," I said.

"Okay," she said, "I want to see Celeste. I want to see if he hurts her."

Pilar, Pilar, I thought, you're the one who'll find out everything, see everything. Mazie and I are in graduate school to find out things, but we don't want to look.

"All right," I said, "I'll go with you." Mazie went to the car alone.

Bob set up his camera and tripod in front of a barred window by the door. I agreed to snap pictures for him. He filled his spray bottle with the chile-pepper alkaloid. Pilar stood beside me at the window when Bob began the trial. To wake her up and provoke her, Bob began stomping his feet in a slow, loud, unwavering cadence.

Celeste awoke in an instant. She stood and stirred the air with her right foot, the one with the half pad. I could see that she was going to wave, that if Bob would quit pounding the floor, captive Celeste might let us pretend that we were both back in Pelican Valley. But she did not wave. Roaring, she dropped to all fours and charged the door. Bob shot her in the face with the alkaloid. Celeste raced to the back of the cell and rubbed her eyes with her paws. Bob did not quit stomping. Celeste charged again. Bob sprayed her in the face. But this time she stood, towering over him on the other side of the steel bars. He shot her again with the spray. Still standing, she swung from side to side and made great moaning sounds.

Bob moved to shoot her again, but Pilar snatched the bottle from his hand and flung it against the wall where it shattered. Pilar's face twisted with fury. Bob backed away from her and out the door into the compound. With the stomping gone, Celeste dropped to her fours and moved back to the rear of the cell where she rubbed her eyes again.

Pilar said nothing to Bob. In long strides, she arrowed her way across the compound, back to the car where Mazie waited. When I looked back in the cell, Celeste was lying on her side moaning and biting and chewing at her back paws. Bob said such behavior was normal for captive bears when they were stressed.

"I'm sorry, Celeste," I said to the moaning bear. Bob looked at me warily.

Pilar had told Mazie what had happened. On our drive back to the university, they were both quiet.

In the Goligoskis' living room, Pilar still doesn't care to talk about it. Her eyes are dark.

"Can't they try other things first?" Clyde asks. "Flares or Roman candles or something."

"They have," Mazie says. "Air horns, flares, even opening umbrellas."

"Doesn't work?"

"Some bears, female black bears, for example, are submissive to start with, and those treatments just make them more submissive. But with the few aggressive boars, black-bear boars, it just seems to make them more aggressive. I'm sure it will be the same with any grizzly."

"Uff da. Pissing off an already pissed grizzly." Clyde scratches his head. "I wonder how much you can learn from stomping at a caged bear," he says.

"Not enough," Pilar says vehemently.

8

I T I S J A N U A R Y. Inside the University Center, Mazie and I sit at a small table under a three-story forest of tropical trees and vines and ferns, a breathing green scaffold that makes the air moist and fecund. Behind a screen of date palms and cycads and umbrella plants, I can see winter through the big windows—horizontal lines of blown snow and bits of ice. We are waiting for Pilar. She drives a car now, her own, a Pinto beater. She has a driver's license and a new kind of independence, a zeal that shows in the way she stands or walks, how she plows ahead like a hood ornament, even the way she slants into her food when she eats.

Shelly taught Pilar how to drive. Their friendship has matured. Pilar is to assist the midwife with Shelly's home delivery. I imagine she will be doing what Clyde will not, that is, serving as a coach, somebody to coax the lioness from one piece into two. Shelly and Pilar attended birthing classes for a few weeks, but Pilar convinced Shelly that the midwife and Pilar will help Shelly find her own best way.

These days, Shelly asks Pilar as many things as she tells her. Pilar has become her confidante.

I can see Pilar coming through the storm, all the colors of her winter garb. Through the door and into the woods she finds us. "Would you like some hot chocolate?" I ask as she sits.

"Yes." Her eyes probe my face, then Mazie's, then mine again. I can feel them like fingers.

"What is it?" Mazie asks.

I am standing, searching my pocket for enough change to get the chocolate. Pilar winks. I am wary of her exuberance.

When I return, Mazie is laughing. She tells Pilar to ask me. "I'm at the Cenex for gas," Pilar explains. "Two men are standing at the coffee pot. One says 'Fuck me frankly, if the cables hold.'"

"Huh?"

"What's that mean? 'Fuck me frankly, if the cables hold.'"

"He's talking to you. Fuck *you* frankly?"

"No. Not me. Fuck *me* frankly."

"No, I mean you, Pilar. Fuck Pilar frankly? He said that to you?"

"No. He's not talking to me. Fuck me . . . he says the word 'me' . . . frankly. Not Pilar."

"I don't know what it means, Pilar. He must have said something else. Nobody fucks themselves frankly."

Mazie sniggers.

"He didn't say something else. This isn't my language. This is your language. Next time, I'll ask them. I'll say my husband doesn't understand his own language."

"I don't know the context, Pilar. I don't know what they were talking about. And neither does Mazie. Is this what you wanted to tell us?"

"No." Pilar rustles through her coat pocket and extracts an envelope. From it she draws out what looks like a small brochure and a map. Patiently, she unfolds and flattens them on the table. Mazie and I lean over to see.

"Ishi Wilderness?" Mazie reads and looks wonderingly at Pilar. The enclosures have been sent from the Forest Service in California.

"Yes, the place where Ishi lived is a wilderness place."

"How did you get this?" I can see the envelope is addressed to Pilar. "I mean how did you know to write for it? And why?" Pilar's secretive ways continue to exasperate me. I feel like an irrelevant accessory in her life.

Pilar has spent every Saturday for the last two months at the university library, presumably to practice her reading and writing skills. Several times, however, I found her in the map room where she was pouring over maps of South America. Several of these she xeroxed. One day in the apartment, I happened onto the copies and found they were maps of Ecuador, not Peru.

"I found this other book about Ishi," Pilar tells us. "In the library. Then I looked at the map, an old map in the book. And then at a new map. There's a line around the Ishi canyons, and it says 'wilderness.' I wrote to the map place. They told me to write the forest people in California. This came today."

"Why, Pilar?" Mazie asks. "Do you want to go there?"

"Is this another secret?" I ask bitterly.

Pilar snatches my face in both hands. "Yes," she says passionately. "It's a secret. Our secret. Arnie, Mazie, Pilar."

"You want us to go there?" I shake my face out of her hands. I'm not going to fake excitement for a trip to California. There are wildernesses in Montana I would rather see first.

"Yes. Four of us will go there."

"Who else?" I ask.

Pilar will not say. She looks at Mazie, as if Mazie is the one who can guess. I look at Mazie, too.

Mazie *is* the one to guess. The surprise goes off like a flare in her face. She shakes her head weakly. "No," she murmurs.

"Yes," Pilar says. Her eyes are grave and penetrating.

"But how?"

"All right, goddamnit—" I'm sick of the game.

"Celeste." Mazie floats the bear's name to me. "She wants us to take Celeste."

"Celeste?"

Pilar's study, her level scrutiny of my reaction, has a distance to it that is almost medical, as if she has cut me open and is sorting through my guts to see the color of my soul.

"How do we steal a grizzly? How do we get a live bear from Montana to California? How do we keep from getting caught?" I fire the questions at her. I'd like to have a thousand questions and shoot them at her one at a time, riddle every answer she's got. She has her hands on the table, and I see the missing joint of her little finger.

"What about Sernylan?" Mazie asks. Sernylan is one of the drugs used in the darts to anesthetize bears.

"We can't get our hands on Sernylan," I snap.

"*I'll* get the Sernylan." Pilar replies with perfect evenness.

"How? From Clyde? You want his hide on a barn? Not just yours or mine? Or Mazie's?"

"I want to do it," Mazie says.

Pilar doesn't seem to notice she has a recruit. She watches me. "You want that man to put more pepper in her eyes? Do you want them to kill her? Ishi is gone. The grizzly is gone in Ishi's home. Celeste can live there with the spirit of Ishi, with the spirit of dead grizzlies."

"We don't have any way of moving her. I don't have access to a culvert trap."

"We don't need a trap. Celeste is already caught."

"We can send her down UPS?"

"In a trailer, a Haul-U."

"In a U-Haul?" Mazie sits back.

"Yes, we pull it with my car."

"An adult female grizzly in a U-Haul?" I smile the most disdainful smile I can manage.

"Celeste can sleep in the U-Haul. The Sernylan will make her sleep."

"And how do we steal her? It's pure idiocy."

"It's not impossible," Mazie says. "We can get the keys, or get duplicates made. With a dart gun—"

"At night," Pilar tells her.

"We can get to California, to the area even . . . in twenty-four hours . . . maybe."

"Who will know where Celeste has gone?" Pilar shrugs. "Nobody knows. The U-Haul trailer looks like everybody else's U-Haul." She grins.

"No." I say. "I'll never do it."

Pilar takes my face in her hands again. "And if cables don't hold . . ." She is laughing.

I pull her hands down.

"If they don't hold, you can fuck me frankly," she says.

9

i DON'T WANT TO get caught burgling a bear. Pilar and Mazie don't want to get caught either, but neither of them stew about it like I do. Pilar cares only that we get Celeste out of her cell before Bob Miner shoots red pepper in her eyes again. And Mazie wants a bear back in Ishi's California homeland. She wants the substance of a grizzly bear to weigh in against the misconception of better living through chemistry. She talks about it as if an original denizen, in the form of Celeste, will inoculate that California nest of altered states and other superficiality with a germ of something real, something potent. Just the concept is enough for Mazie.

I'm going along with the idea of a U-Haul. It would be a two-day rental, three at the most. After running the trailer through a carwash a time or two, we return it to the dealer in the same condition we get it. I went down to the lots to satisfy myself that Celeste would ride in one. There are two kinds of construction: one with a fiberglass box and an older all-aluminum model. We'll rent the metal one. The dealer will supply a hitch with a bumper attachment.

I'm satisfied that Celeste won't break out of a trailer, even one with light-weight walls by bear standards. I know that Celeste is capable of piercing the metal of a trailer with her teeth, but in the windowless trailer there's nothing to get her mouth around, no place for any purchase.

Anybody working with bears or involved with the wildlife biology program will, I know, be the first suspects in the theft. Second on that list will be the ecotage people, the bullhorn environmentalists who chop down billboards and spike trees. We intend to imitate the way in which this second group might go about kidnapping a grizzly bear. We won't use any departmental gear. I'll order a dart gun out of the Palmer catalog for tranquilizer guns, have it sent under a pseudonym to my father in Tucson, and then supply him with a wrapper to forward the unopened package to me. He'll live with his curiosity on my account.

We won't use keys to enter. We can cut the chain on the compound gate with a hacksaw. We can break out the door on Celeste's cell with a sledge hammer and a crowbar, unless I can round up a cutting torch and learn how to use it. We'll take her during spring break when it's easy to account for our absence. The break-in and the untouched gun and darts and drugs in the departmental storeroom ought to divert suspicion from anybody in wildlife.

Pilar and Mazie are content to let me work it all out. I'm in charge of planning, logistics, and the generation of stomach acid in quarts. Late at night, sleepless, I review the scenarios again and again and wonder if I can survive the zealotry of my partners.

It's a cloudy, surly afternoon on Groundhog Day when I meet Clyde coming home from work. I catch him on the sidewalk before he gets to the door. I don't want Shelly in on any of our plans. Clyde stops when he sees me. "I don't like it," he says, "not one little bit." His eyes clamp down on me.

"So Pilar has talked to you?"

"You know what kind of consequences we're looking at. She doesn't. You've got to have better sense than that." He looks like he's talking to my nose.

"Do you think knowing the consequences would make a difference with her? Or Mazie?"

"No. Where do you come up with these women?"

"You don't have much to say on that account, Clyde."

"Jesus Christ, they want to break enough goddamn laws."

"No more than they need to get the job done. Can we steal the Sernylan from you? I mean do you have it in stock? Pilar could steal five bottles, transfer the drug, replace it with water and then have an accident the next day bumping those five bottles off the shelf and breaking them. We don't want to implicate you."

"Got it all mapped out, don't you?"

"I'm working on it."

"You got any idea what kind of shit will fly if you steal that bear and the press gets wind of it."

I hadn't thought of the press. "Yes," I lie without hesitation. "I don't think anybody involved is going to want the press to know. There ought to be enough red faces to keep it under wraps."

"How much money you got for a lawyer?"

"You know how much money I have."

"As much money as you have sense. Pilar's got your balls in both hands, and she can squeeze them any time she wants."

"You like Pilar. She works hard for you."

"What's that got to do with the price of sharkmeat? Today, she wants to tear up a clinic bill for surgery on a dog that got hit by a car, because the dog's from a single-parent family. She's got her nose in everything. Look at this home-birth thing. She's got Shelly talking about squatting on the floor when the time comes—like a whelping bitch. I feel like there's a big leak around here, one I can't find." Clyde turns to go in the house.

"What about the Sernylan?"

"Yeah, what about it?" Clyde yells over his shoulder and slams the door.

The next day I find five vials of Sernylan in our mailbox.

⌒

It's February. I'm sitting at my desk and thinking about how tired I am of short days, of living in cooked air among gloomy walls, when Pilar tells me Shelly wants to talk to us. "She knows about the plan," Pilar says.

"How? Who told her?" I squeal.

Pilar doesn't know. I gallop up the stairs. Oddly, I find some relief in this mini-emergency.

Clyde and Shelly sit at the kitchen table. Jeff has gone to school. A pot of coffee perks on the counter.

"Did you tell her, Clyde?" I point at him.

"She knew something was up."

"Don't keep secrets from me," Shelly says. "And don't implicate my husband in your stupid escapades, and don't tell him he can't tell his wife about it."

Pilar comes into the kitchen. In one lithe motion, she draws herself up to sit on the counter. "Don't be mad, Shelly," she says, "we didn't want you to know and get mad at everybody."

"You're playing in a fantasy world. What a terrific adventure! How romantic! What about going to jail?" she asks me. "Can you pay a big fine? What about having a record as a felon?"

"Felon?" Pilar asks.

"Shelly, this doesn't involve you," I say, measuring out my words. "That's why we didn't tell you. You would never do something like this. You need to be safe."

"And you can't resist the grand gesture. It's such a nice way to imagine yourselves. A hero and two heroines out to save the life of the condemned."

"Stop," Pilar says quietly. "Don't fight. This isn't for fighting about. Shelly doesn't want to save Celeste. She doesn't know Celeste. That's all right. We think we're doing the right thing. Maybe not, but that's all right, too. Even if we get in trouble."

"That's one way of looking at it, I guess," Clyde says. He pours himself a cup of coffee. "Sounds like Pilar's ready to take her lumps. You best butt out, Shelly. And Arnie, he has his own good reasons for doing what Pilar tells him to do."

"Piss on you, Clyde." I rise up. "You've got—"

"What about the birth?" Shelly sniffs. "The baby is due the same week you want to steal that bear. You stay behind, Pilar."

"No, Shelly, I have to go with Celeste. It's like another birth. But I'll only be gone two days. You make that baby wait. You tell it to wait for Pilar."

"You won't be gone only two days if you get caught. Damnit Pilar."

"I'll tell them you helped to steal Celeste. Then we can have the baby in jail." Pilar giggles.

"No jail would put up with her noise," I say.

"You're gutless, Arnie," she says calmly. "You wouldn't last two minutes of labor. Godamighty, think of it." She shakes her head. "Wouldn't you squawk?"

⌒

A week has passed. I'm in the lab helping Mazie analyze shit. She has a batch of turds that look like tar caulk, the dried remnants of the runny stuff bears purge just before they hole up for the winter. Sitting side by side, we each work under a dissecting scope. When I find some remnant embedded within—roots, seeds, insect parts—I show it to her. When she finds something she doesn't recognize, I try to identify it for her.

We are on the last bag of bear shit when Ikeda comes into the lab. "There's news from the fort," he tells us. He pulls up a stool and sits comfortably, as if what he has to tell us will take some time.

"Celeste?" Mazie clicks her tongue.

"Yes," he says. "Celeste. She has three cubs. They saw them this morning when they were cleaning out her cell."

"They can't kill her now, can they?" I slam down a pencil.

"Sure they can." Ikeda sighs. "They can still kill her."

"But what about the press and the public? 'Grizzly Bear team kills bear family, mama and three babies.'"

"No, they wouldn't kill the cubs. They'll just keep them until late summer and then release them. The press can't make much of it, because they know there are no zoos left that will take bears. They can't release Celeste because she's dangerous. Besides, the cubs would pick up her bad habits."

"Goddamnit." I stand up and go look out a window. Mazie doesn't say anything.

"You know," Ikeda says, "I don't know what to do about Celeste. I know you two have been thinking about it, too. She's the one who has been through everything with us. But I can't see any way out of it. I called all the zoos again myself. Then I thought we could get a petition or something going, but that would only send the Bear Team out for our heads. She can't live at the fort anyway."

I glance at Mazie and see the warning there.

If Ikeda has any questions, he'll have to ask them. As he watches us, I am wondering what three more bears will do to our plans. I dare Ikeda to read my mind. Mazie's mind speaks loudly, insists I keep my mouth shut. Ikeda follows my gaze to her. She looks right back at him with perfect flatness.

Ikeda rises dejectedly. He looks at us for a moment, and then he leaves.

When he is safely out of earshot, Mazie thrusts her face at me and whispers, "It doesn't change a thing. Not one thing. In fact, it's better, especially if there's a little male in that trio."

I am thinking about another male, the one in our trio.

10

*i*t's Saturday, the day before we will steal Celeste and her triplets. Pilar is working at Clyde's clinic. Mazie and I are hiding in the Goligoski apartment. We've scheduled our break-in for the third night of spring break so that we have two days for preparations and unforeseen complications. But we have nearly everything ready the first day, and no complications have arisen. We'll wait anyway to avoid weekend revelers out late at night.

At the university, everybody in our department thinks Mazie is visiting her folks in Minnesota, while Pilar and I are pretending to head to Tucson to see mine. We've all told colleagues that we'll linger on our way. Shelly's imminent birthing gives us an excuse for coming back earlier than planned.

A glitch arose when Eldon Sundling pursued Mazie enough to become a pest. More than a pest. Eldon's friend, a graduate student in anthropology, lives in the same apartment complex as Mazie. Because our vacation plans are common knowledge in the department, Mazie cannot be seen. So for two days she has to stay with Pilar and me.

Last night, I slept on the floor and left the bed to Mazie and Pilar. When Pilar got up this morning, she told us she was going to work.

Mazie and I protested. "You worry too much," Pilar chided us. "Nobody from the university will see me."

Mazie suggests that we go for a walk. "Let's drive out of town," she says. "Go up to the reservation. I know where there are some Indian pictographs and a nice path along the river."

"How do you know about Indian pictographs?"

"I've been there. Eldon and Lawrence took me." Lawrence is the anthropology student who is Mazie's neighbor.

Her Volkswagen is parked in the alley. She drives. After an hour on the highway, we turn off and follow a dirt road—twin paths through the grass—for a mile along the north bank of the river. She stops where a stone ridge runs into the river and squeezes out a donkey-tail of current, below which corklike chunks of driftwood litter a swoop of backwater. We follow a path away from the river up to one of the bluffs. Protected by an overhang, the pictographs array themselves on a stone face just above our heads. In rust-orange paint, four stick-figures resembling deer walk above several handprints.

"So Lawrence and Eldon brought you here?"

"Yes," she says. "Lawrence said that the Indians used to leave money here, folded up bills and coins stuffed into the cracks between the rocks, but the whites took it all. They used thin sticks and fish hooks to pull it back out. The Indians still visit here because it's a sacred place, but they don't leave money anymore."

"Money seems an odd offering for an Indian to leave."

"It's an offering. Like a tithe."

"Yeah, but you can give a tithe to somebody who needs it."

"Then it would be like money. Stuffed in the rocks, it's gone, something they've denied themselves. It's a value of another sort."

"Is that your circular interpretation, or theirs?"

"I don't know. You're crabby because you're nervous about tomorrow."

We climb over the ridge and walk on along the river. "Was Lawrence the one who first told you about Ishi?"

"Yes, he lent me the book."

At length, Mazie asks, "Are you and Pilar all right? You don't have to answer that."

I pause. "Pilar seems distant to me. I'm jealous of her secrets, even though there's something about them that doesn't intrude that much. I think the fresh way she sees things makes her seem closer than she really is. Everything we do together—eat, go to a movie or a concert, walk around the block and look at crocuses—all that is fun because of what she does with it. When she saw a crocus in the snow she said it was like a happy little boy with his pants off."

"Sometimes I think Pilar is more like me than I am," Mazie says. "We like the same things, but she has more guts. Nothing stops her."

Going on, we find a few buttercups. On one, within the circle of waxy petals, a honeybee roots around in the nest of stamens. When the bee flies off, its drowsy hum stabs me with a nostalgia for summer.

⁓

The next day I take Pilar's car, pick up the trailer, and drive to Barbara and Will Stedman's place. I don't want to risk killing Celeste with multiple doses, so the plan is to immobilize her only twice, once to get her in the trailer and once again to let her out. Because she'll be conscious during the trip, I'll need a peephole that can be closed. In this way, I can keep an eye on her and the cubs, and in California I can dart her through the hole.

A week before I had asked Will about cutting through the roof of a U-Haul trailer. He said to use a drill and a saber saw.

"And to repair it again?"

"You can rivet on a plate of aluminum, seal the crack with aluminum roof repair, sand and paint it. If you were looking for it, you'd see it easy, but I imagine anybody would think it had been repaired by some other dealer."

"If I could borrow your tools to cut it out and then repair it later, I wouldn't need your help."

"All right," he said simply. Barbara had told me that Will would help me, no questions asked.

"I get there through the alley, and the key is hanging on the back of the birdhouse?"

"Yeah." He dug at his ear with his little finger. "I'll leave out a chunk of aluminum, too. And some roof patch."

The saber saw makes a terrific racket hammering against the trailer roof. I muffle the sound a little by leaning hard into the saw. Sweating, I cut out the little window in a one long, noisy pass. I drill two holes, one through each end of the aluminum flap and on into the roof with the flap fit in place over the hole. I run back into Will's garage and rummage around until I find a nut and bolt to secure one end of the sliding flap and a bolt with a wing nut, which I thread to the head, to insert in the opposite hole as a latch.

I drive back to the apartment and park in the alley behind Mazie's Volkswagen. I leave the cutting torch in the trailer. Pilar and Mazie are making tunafish sandwiches and filling two thermoses with coffee.

It's three o'clock in the afternoon.

Sunday.

Eleven hours to go.

⌒

Mazie and I are playing a game of cribbage and Pilar is knitting a baby sweater when Shelly comes down the stairs slowly.

"I don't think it's fair for you to say you'll be my midwife and then leave the same week I'm due," she tells Pilar for the hundredth time. Shelly looks impossibly bulbous. Her hands are always propped somewhere around her midsection.

"The baby will wait. She will be okay," Pilar says.

"It's too late. The kid's too big to fit out the hole," I say. "Fifteen two, fifteen four," I count my cards.

"Arnie," Pilar's voice rises; she points a needle at me. "You quit that."

"You're a talker, Arnie," Shelly says. "You need women who will pretend you're in charge."

Mazie intercedes. "Come on, Shelly, this is as much his doing as ours. He's the one who got the trailer today and cut the hole, and—"

"Yeah, well, he just goes where you point him."

"Go away," I tell her.

Pilar puts her knitting down and rises. "Shelly, we'll be back in three days. You won't have the baby for another four or five days. At least. I will be here. And I'll finish this sweater I'm making for her. Let's go back upstairs. It's good for you to go up and down the stairs. You do that every day. It will help when she comes." Pilar is certain the baby is a girl. She leads Shelly toward the stairs.

"I'll bet you've got another month or two to go," I say.

The lights are out upstairs when we leave. We take sleeping blankets and pillows, the sandwiches, coffee, and a hacksaw I borrow from Clyde's work closet. I have a tent, too. The gun, darts, drugs, and flashlights are already in the trunk of the car. We're all carrying extra cash.

Neither Mazie nor Pilar wants to drive with a trailer, although I know that either one would do it if I weren't here. The streets are empty. On the way to the Food Mart's parking lot, a sign blinks twenty-nine degrees, 1:40 A.M.

"Let's go," Pilar says. We were going to wait in the lot until two o'clock, but nobody argues.

We drive down the lane to the fort and up to the steel gates in front of the compound. I turn off the lights, and it's dark. The first-quarter moon has set.

"Let's go," Pilar says again.

II

*P*ILAR HOLDS the light while I am sawing the chain. Mazie stays in the car and loads the dart gun. I try to steady the chain link I'm cutting against the gate frame. But it wants to wobble; there isn't enough to hold with my fingers. Sweat seeps out of the folds of my body. My glasses fog up. Pilar says nothing, but I can smell the contagion of her uneasiness. Mazie comes to watch. She, too, says nothing. Frantically, I work. The chain link gets hot, and I burn my fingers through the glove. "Goddamnit." I shake my hand.

Mazie murmurs sympathetically. Pilar remains silent. Then the saw binds in the cut. "Move the chain," Pilar says. "So I can help." I sit back on one leg to rest. Pilar hands the light to Mazie and twists the chain around a bar so that by twisting and pulling she gains enough leverage on the neighboring links to widen the gap of the first cut. I lean back and start sawing again. The saw no longer binds. When I cut through one side of the link, Pilar twists the chain enough to open the link a little. She smiles at me. "Enough," she says and slips the adjoining link through the gap.

Mazie pushes the gate open. I drive into the compound, back the trailer up to the cell block where Celeste and her cubs live. Mazie guides me with the flashlight. I rush to fetch the cutting torch from the back of the trailer.

"Wait," Pilar says to me. I'm dragging the tank and the torch to the cell. Mazie has the loaded gun. Pilar puts her hand on my arm. "What about the key?"

"We decided not to do that, Pilar. We've got to stick to our plans." I know that she's alarmed with how long it took to cut the chain. I pull away from her hand. Mazie has the flashlight on us. I don't like my anxiety in the spotlight.

"Wait," Pilar says again. "Mazie knows where the key is. But I don't. Do you?"

"No."

"There's too much work to cut the door before looking for the key. Anybody would look for the key first."

"She's right," Mazie says.

"Wait, Mazie," I put down the torch. "Why didn't we decide this before, Pilar? Why are we changing what we decided to do? This isn't the time to change plans."

"Things change when you're there," Pilar says. "We can't stop thinking. You and I look for the key. We can cut the door if we don't find it. Mazie won't tell us where it is; that way, we will be like anybody else who would look first."

"She's right, Arnie. Nobody would cut that door without poking around first. And besides, it would be better not to have to damage the place and give them another reason for needing to catch us."

I throw up my hands. Going through the motions, I scuttle about for a quick search. I'm feeling along the top of the wall between the rafters when Pilar calls, "Got it." She finds it hanging on the casement of the door in the portico leading to Celeste's cell.

"All right," Mazie cheers. Pilar taps me on the nose with the key and grins. I haul the torch back out and throw it in the trunk of the

Pinto. Inside the colonnade, Pilar and Mazie wait for me before shining the light into the cell.

"Do you want to shoot her?" I ask, looking at each of them. Neither does.

Mazie gives me the rifle. Pilar waits until I check the gun's setting for the short distance. When I slide the barrel through the cell window, she shines the light in. At first we see nothing but yellow blots of straw in the far corner. Then, gradually, we make out an undefined bulk of animal. Celeste's body seems to suck away all the light within the boundary of her outline. I can't tell one part of her from another.

We hear the sound of a car. Pilar flicks off the light, and we freeze. The car sounds near. "Son of a bitch," I mutter.

"It just sounds close," Pilar says. "Because it's so quiet here." She moves down the colonnade and out into the compound. We follow her. In the open, the motor sound swiftly recedes. Pilar leads us out to the gate. We can't see the lights of the car or tell which road it is on. The sound is gone.

"It sounded like it was coming in here," I say.

Pilar turns back. "Scared ears hear too many things," she says. We return to the cell, and once more I search Celeste's bulk over the gun's sights. She seems dead. I stomp my foot. Her head rises. Like cleary marbles in moonlight, two spirit eyes reflect back at us. She woofs once lightly and rises up a little. I aim at her neck and shoot. She leaps up, and we see other eyes beneath, tinier and intermittent. Celeste bites toward her shoulder. I can see the red tail of the dart in her neck. We make no sound, and she does not attack. I can hear a cub crying. Celeste sits. She looks down at her cubs and then at us. We wait. At length, her head sags. Her feet slide out away from her, and she slumps to the floor. Her eyes are fixed, lost, yet wilder somehow, as if realization of what has happened to her body has nowhere to escape but through her glaring. Head up, she struggles weakly. Gradually, her head wilts to the floor. She lies there a while, her jaws working, and then she is still.

Pilar unlocks the cell door. "Let the cubs be," I tell them. "Let's get her first. Then we'll look at the cubs."

Celeste is completely immobilized. Her eyes are open but she can't move. From a vial of mineral oil, Mazie eyedroppers a little of the oil onto each of Celeste's unblinking eyes so they won't dry. I pull out the dart and lay it on the floor to the side. The cubs race back and forth in the gloom on the other side of the cell. Pilar unfolds a square of canvas and slides it up against the bear's back. I take a front leg. Briefly, Pilar and Mazie blunder about trying to manage the other front leg without hindering one another. We roll her onto the canvas. I take one end, Pilar and Mazie each of the opposite corners.

We carry the sow grizzly in ten- to fifteen-foot lunges. The smell of bear stirs old memories in me. At the door, Mazie waves a broom at the cubs to keep them back and then latches the door on them. We go on moving Celeste. I marvel for a moment to see that this is really happening.

When we get to the trailer outside, I unhitch it. We struggle to get the bear up onto the inclined floor. I back into the trailer, while Mazie and Pilar, on either side behind, drop the canvas and push Celeste. Once in, I keep the bear from sliding out while the women tip the trailer forward and hitch it again. Celeste slides easily on the level aluminum floor. We take her to a far corner and roll her off the canvas onto her side.

When we return to the cell, the cubs are puling and snuffling through the straw. "Each of us take one," I tell them. "Grab them by the scruff of the neck, so you don't get bit, and get them up away from the floor and yourself, so they can't get a foot on anything. They're a lot stronger than you'd think."

We chase them toward each other. Pilar snatches one up. It bawls and flails about. Pilar laughs. Mazie and I corner another one in the straw. The cubs thrash and bite at us. An infant grizzly bear is an oxymoron of sorts. Pilar gets clawed on the wrist. She changes her grip without letting go. I shine a light onto Mazie's ward. She turns its wriggling belly toward the light and pokes her face down the twisting groin. "Male," she says finally. His ears and eyes and muzzle are tiny, his white teeth catlike, but he's as fat as a watermelon. Mine is a female. Pilar's is another male. They weigh ten to fifteen pounds and are about the size of terriers.

We fetch them out to the trailer, push them toward their unconscious mother, and hastily shut the door. Ten minutes later we're on Interstate 90.

By the time we reach St. Regis, we have been driving an hour and Celeste should be reviving. In this March frost she could stand in an hour; for some reason, the effect of the drug lasts longer in warmer temperatures. I slow the car, and we roll down the windows. We hear only the rush of cold air. I am waiting for a tremor or some clue that she is moving about in the trailer.

We cross Lookout Pass into Idaho and descend toward Wallace. Pilar is leaning over the back of the front seat chatting at high speed with Mazie. You could never tell they've missed a night's sleep. I'm still fretting, waiting for the brakes to burn up or for Celeste to burst through the side of the trailer.

"You two should be sleeping. We've got plenty ahead."

"Yeah, but we've the crossed the Rubicon," Mazie says. "I'm too excited to sleep."

"You drive, and we'll talk to you," Pilar says.

They talk about Australia, something Lawrence told Mazie about the Aborigines. I can hear the tone of fascination in Pilar's questioning. "What are those songs about?" she is asking.

"I don't know. I don't think anybody knows but the Aborigines. Maybe they're secrets of that clan, I'm not sure."

"But no girls?" Pilar asks crossly. "There are no girls walking on those lines, remembering the songs?"

"I don't know, Pilar. I probably shouldn't be talking about this stuff secondhand," Mazie back-pedals. "Maybe the young women could, too. I don't know. But these young men, when they go, follow these invisible lines for miles all across the country, sacred lines, and they sing these songs as they walk. They're gone for a long time, days." She glances at Pilar and apparently anticipates her question. "I don't know how long. I don't know much about it except what Lawrence told me. I do know that this concept of sacred lines makes it hard for all the developers and miners and engineers. The whites ask the natives the location of sacred places so that they might find a way around them to punch through the power lines or roads or railroads or whatever. But with songlines, it ends up that the entire continent of Australia is sacred. The lines go everywhere. So the whites pose the question by saying they can put this power line or railroad here or over there. Which is least sacred?" Mazie puts her hands on the back of the seat and scoots forward. "But there is no least sacred."

"Tell him about the Japanese," Pilar says.

"Oh yeah. There is, or was, a race of people in Japan called the Ainu." Mazie speaks to the back of my head. I watch her in the mirror. "They're supposed to be Caucasian. They've lived in remote valleys of Japan for hundreds of years. I think, for the most part, they're gone now. But the curious part of their tradition involves these long poems, lots of them, many thousands of words long that they have passed down generation to generation, word for word. The Ainu had no written language, but did have this oral tradition where each generation memorized these incredibly long epic poems."

"But those people are gone?" Pilar asks.

"I think so, absorbed into the other Japanese culture."

"That's a bad word, 'absorbed.' They're gone because their secrets are gone," Pilar says vehemently. She looks away, out the window.

"So you think their culture would have survived if they'd kept everything secret?" I ask.

Pilar does not answer.

"Is that what you mean?"

Pilar looks at me, again with that disturbing gaze of nonrecognition. Then, on legs folded beneath her, she pivots to face Mazie. "When I read about Ishi, I found out that most of the Indian tribes in this country called themselves by one name, The People. All in their own words, they are The People. The People carry their secrets like a woman carries a baby. Without their secrets, there are no people, just a lot of persons who live in the same place."

"Goddamnit, Pilar," I sit forward, tap the steering wheel with a fist, "secrets are for excluding. I feel excluded. People who think they must have secrets need people like me just to have somebody they can keep something from. I get to be necessary because I'm a priceless unit of ignorance. I'll bet secrets wouldn't be worth a wooden nickel if nobody else cared about them. Secrets just make for another kind of class system, like Runa and mozos and cholos, only it's not economic. It's more exclusive."

Pilar frowns.

"I think this is about religion in many ways," Mazie says. She's looking at the back of my head again.

Pilar puts her hand on Mazie's shoulder. "That is so different here. In Peru, we call white people peeled ones because they don't have their own skin, their own secrets. Their church wants everybody. The white church wants to tell everybody the same thing, wants everybody everywhere to believe the same things."

Mazie laughs. "That's true. Evangelizing is just the opposite of a secret."

"So what makes a secret?" I ask Pilar.

"All kinds of things. Runasimi is like a secret to me. In dreams I hear the words of my people. They are all around me like a blanket, the only words I knew as a child." Pilar sways, rocks her head, and then leaning toward me, whispers, "You and I have our secrets."

I look at the amusement flickering in her eyes.

It's nine in the morning when we get to Spokane. We need gas. At the exit, I see a truckstop on our side of the interstate. Slowing to a stop at the bottom of the off ramp, we turn to watch the trailer and listen through our open windows. Nothing. Gently, I turn into the truck-stop. I find a pump for regular gas farthest from the building and pull in alongside. No one else is in the adjoining lane. A man in a blue pickup is pumping gas two islands over. He doesn't look at us.

The three of us get out and listen. Attending to nothing but our ears, we look at each other blankly. "Christ, we look like bank rob-bers," I say. I take off the gas cap. "You two need to do something."

Pilar is looking above where I cut the hole into the trailer. "Okay," she says. "I have to go pee."

Mazie tugs the wrinkles out of her jeans. "Me, too." They walk off across the lot. I lift the handle on the nozzle and wait for the rush of gas. I wish I knew what Celeste was doing.

A little red foreign car approaches. The car zips up into the adjoin-ing lane and stops at our pump. A middle-aged woman wearing dark glasses and a salon tan—orangish, rubbery, and impossibly uniform—glides to the pump, takes the nozzle, and moves to the rear of her car.

Inside the trailer, Celeste moans and stirs. I can hear the sound of her claws clicking against the metal. I leave the nozzle in the tank and walk back to the trailer. "That's okay, Fido," I call. "Be there pretty soon."

The woman, nozzle in hand, is watching the trailer with obvious consternation. "Just the dog," I tell her. "Getting tired of this trip."

She looks at me for the first time. One eye is narrowed. "A Saint Bernard," I say, "too big to ride in the car."

"Why don't you let him out for some air?" she asks snippily. She moves to replace the nozzle she holds.

"Oh, I will," I say, "at the next rest area where there's a little grass."

"He'll suffocate in there." She flings this out as a parting shot.

"Oh no," I call, sniveling still. "It's got a special vent on the roof."

But she doesn't look back to see where I am pointing. Not until she gets to the building where she meets Pilar at the door. She pauses a moment to watch Pilar coming toward me across the lot. I clamp down on the handle and shoot the gas into the tank at high speed.

"She heard Celeste," I hiss at Pilar when she reaches me.

Pilar doesn't seem to hear. She finds the squeegee and washes the windshield.

The tank fills to the top, and I replace the nozzle. "Stay," Pilar says quietly without looking at me. "Mazie will pay. We saw her watching the trailer. Mazie is staying in there to see what she does. What did you tell her?"

I open the hood and check the oil. "I told her it was a dog."

"Yes. Good."

"Shit, Pilar, it wasn't a dog sound."

"She doesn't know, not a woman like that. Celeste is awake. She's going to California. Everything's good." Pilar peeks under the hood and smiles pertly at me.

"We need to go," she says. "Before Celeste wants out."

"Nice to hear a little concern from you. I get tired of doing all the worrying for us."

Pilar wrinkles her nose, leans over, and kisses my ear. "I like your worries."

The woman, followed by Mazie, leaves the truckstop building. Neither seems aware of the other's presence. In the car, I turn the mirror to watch Ms. Sunglasses when she gets in her car. She glances at the trailer but doesn't slow. Mazie gets in. I start the car and pull away. I follow the sports car out to the street; she turns right, we go left.

The next time we stop is in Kennewick, again at the most distant island of pumps. It's two in the afternoon. The sky is overcast, and a stiff wind blows from the west. No one intrudes this time, and we hear nothing from the bears. Pilar drives from there. I crawl in the back seat and eat a sandwich. Three states back, a crew of some sort is looking for four stolen bears. In a few minutes I close my eyes and sleep fitfully.

"Arnie, wake up." It's Mazie. "We have a flat tire."

I bolt upright. Wham, wham, wham. We are on the shoulder. Pilar is slowing the car. The Columbia River is alongside, a huge river, rasp-like with whitecaps. Cars rush by on the other side. My heart beats like a fist against a door.

"Arnie, we have a flat tire," Mazie says sympathetically. She tries to penetrate my vertigo. Pilar gets out of the car. Momentarily, the wind lashes at Mazie's hair. It's quiet again when the door closes. I get out. The wind nearly knocks me down. I go around to the trunk where Pilar is waiting. "Can you work the . . . the lifter?" She pumps her hand up and down.

"Yeah," I yell at her. My head is clearing. "I'll do it."

The trailer is quiet, as much as I can tell. I get the jack out and hook it up under the front fender. I loosen the nuts and jack up the car. The tire is warm, but not broken. Pilar unthreads the nuts. I pull off the tire and put on the spare. Mazie throws the flat tire in the trunk while Pilar and I finish the job in front. Before getting back in, the three of us put our ears against the trailer. We can't hear anything but the roar of wind.

In Biggs we find a service station attendant who will repair the tire, but being the only man on duty, he is continually interrupted with customers wanting gas. We've parked the car and trailer behind the station at the farthest end of the lot alongside a wreck on blocks. When the attendant gets it repaired, we insist on replacing it ourselves. The spare is nearly bald.

We leave Biggs and the Columbia River and drive south on Highway 97. Hours later, we have to get gas again. Eventually, lights appear. From a distance, Klamath Falls seems quiet. Twelve-thirty A.M. on a Tuesday morning. Gas? Can we buy gas at this hour? Why didn't I bring two cans of gas? "Shit," I whisper, "shit, shit, shit."

"What?" Pilar asks thickly. She lifts her head and pinches her face, then rubs her eyes with her knuckles.

"Nothing. I thought I was talking to myself. We're in Klamath Falls, and I don't know where to get gas at this hour."

She doesn't say anything.

"So what do we do if there's no gas?" I ask her.

"We look for gas first." Pilar searches ahead. She rubs away the condensation on her side window with the back of her hand.

At the junction with the strip, a Town Pump and Market is open. "Hey, okay." Pilar slaps the dash, then reaches over the seat and jostles Mazie. I pull up alongside the outer island.

While I fill the tank, the women go in to buy coffee. The bears are quiet. I finish with the gas and check the oil. Then I go into the store. Mazie pays while I use the men's room. When I come out, I hear the attendant ask Mazie where we're headed. He's college-aged, lean, with a keen raptorial face and impish, darting eyes.

"California," Mazie says awkwardly, self-consciously.

"Big state," the kid says. "Just moving to California?"

"Oh no," Mazie mumbles, "we're not moving . . ." She follows his gaze out to the trailer. "Oh, that," she gropes.

"We're going down to pick up some stuff we bought," I intercede.

"Going to California for stuff," the boy summarizes. "Keeping all your options open."

"You always issue questionnaires with your coffee?"

"Only with people on their way to California for stuff." He grins at Mazie.

"We have to go," Pilar says. "Now." She's looking at the trailer, which is shaking. We dash out of the store.

Celeste is roaring. The trailer rocks.

"Get in," I yell. "We can't do anything here." The sound of ripping metal cuts through the bellowing. Our three doors slam, and we lurch out of the lot to cross the main avenue of the strip. Mazie and Pilar look stricken. Around the corner, I can see the partial darkness of a residential area. "Gun, light," I holler.

Pilar already has the light. Ahead, a large tree on the boulevard blocks much of the streetlight. I pull up underneath it and vault out. Celeste is still rampaging. Her roaring makes a terrible racket. Across the street a dog starts barking.

I duck back into the car. Pilar shines the flashlight into the backseat where Mazie fumbles at loading one of the emergency darts. I try to stop shaking, but I can't. Mazie gives me the gun, and I load a cartridge and the dart. I snatch the light from Pilar and jump back out into the street. Clambering up from the hitch, I climb onto the trailer roof. Celeste is still bawling.

"Don't hurt her," Pilar yells up at me.

"Shut up." The dog across the street is raising a fuss. Nausea wells up, gathers at the top of my chest. I pull the bolt on the peephole cover, slide it open, and stab in the flashlight. The beam of light is deformed, a fragile cone eclipsed by lunging blots of animal darkness. Against the formlessness of bear, the gleam of teeth, spittle, eyes, and claws flares up, dies, and flares again. A torn strip of metal behind the bear shines silver behind the massive roving darkness of the bear. I slide the gun barrel in the hole. At the first movement I point the gun and, without aiming, fire.

I pull out the gun and press my face to the hole alongside the flashlight. I can see Celeste half standing. The dart is in one of her hindquarters. There is blood on the floor of the trailer. A lance of aluminum has impaled one of the cubs. The little bear lies by the door. Celeste moves over the cub and obscures it from the light. The sow has ripped a rail loose from one side of the trailer. I put the light on the wall. The rails, something like furring strips, are riveted to the walls for tying restraining ropes. Somehow she has bitten or clawed one loose, and it has stabbed one of her cubs. Celeste's roaring ceases.

Pilar and Mazie are shouting at me in hoarse, sibilant whispers. "I shot her," I tell them. "One of the cubs is hurt. He's by the door. She tore off one of the tie-down rails. Is there anybody around?"

"What happened to the cub?" Pilar demands.

"I saw blood."

"I'm going to get the cub," Pilar says.

"Wait." I hear her rattling at the door. Then she rushes to the front of the car where she rustles through the jockey box for the key. "Stop her, Mazie. Celeste isn't down yet. You've got to wait, Pilar."

I slide around again to the hole and peer inside. Celeste has quit moving. She is sitting. I look at the cub. It is partially covered with straw, but blood runs in the channels of flooring. I hear Pilar and Mazie arguing.

"She's sitting," I whisper down. "It won't be long."

"What about the cub?" Pilar snarls.

"I think it's hurt bad, maybe dead."

"I'm opening the door."

"Wait, Pilar," Mazie tells her. "Wait till Celeste is down."

"At the fort she was down by now."

"We've got to wait a few minutes," Mazie says.

"There's no time if the cub's dying."

I can hear Mazie whispering, but I can't make out the words. I look over the edge. Pilar's head is bowed, her chin propped against one fist tucked in her neck. She fidgets with her feet.

Mazie looks up with pleading eyes. "What happened?"

I shake my head.

"I'm getting the cub," Pilar says. She looks at me defiantly.

"Wait," I say. "Let me check." Celeste is still sitting near the rear of the trailer. Vainly, I look for the other cubs. They must be in the straw. "Wait," I call down.

"No," Pilar says. "She's drugged enough not to get me. I can just pull the cub out quick."

"Not yet," I hiss.

"I'm not waiting for the cub to die," Pilar says.

"You'll wait, Pilar, because there's nothing else to do."

I hear the rattle of the lock. "Pilar!" Mazie chokes, "not yet. You . . ."

"Pilar, goddamnit," I yell, "stop it, goddamnit, let me look." I can still hear her rattling the lock. I scramble back to the hole and poke the light in. Celeste is not down. The rattling at the door has aroused her. She's moved nearer the door where she sits watching it. I hear Mazie's voice imploring. The bear struggles to stand.

"No," I holler into the trailer, "she's by the door!"

Celeste is upright. The door swings open. Staggering a little, she leaps from the trailer, sheds the puny clutching beam of my light, and vanishes.

12

i PUT THE LIGHT ON MAZIE. "I couldn't stop her," she says. "She wouldn't listen." The dog across the street is in a frenzy, its barking staccato and incessant.

Pilar has the cub on the ground. "Cub's dead," she whispers, her head bent. She cradles the little bear. "A metal part of the trailer went through the baby bear like a spear." Pilar's white blouse is smeared with blood.

Pilar looks up at me, her face twisted. "Arnie, I'm sorry. I didn't think she could get up and run. And I almost lost the other cubs when they tried to follow her. I don't understand. At the clinic when Clyde gives a drug, the animals go down. And when you shot her at the fort she was down in that much time." She holds out an open hand, as if pleading. "Where will she go?" The question bursts out of her. "You shot her. How can she run away? I thought you were being too careful about making me wait."

"I shot her in the rear, not the neck. The dart must have gone into a fat deposit, where the drug didn't do anything. I don't know for sure. We have to call the police, though. I know that. She's loose. She might kill someone."

"No!" Pilar jumps up, then stoops to lay the cub on the ground.

"Listen, Pilar, you've done enough deciding for us." My voice cracks in and out of an upper register. "Celeste is loose. She won't leave her cubs. She might kill somebody. That's manslaughter. And the three of us would go to prison. Is that what you want?"

Pilar snatches my arm. She has touched her cheek with a bloody finger. "I did it. I lost her. And I'll find her and shoot her with the dart. No police. They'll kill her."

"We can't wait till morn—"

A door slams across the street. We move from behind the trailer to see someone coming off the lighted porch behind the barking dog. The silhouette stops at the bottom of the stairs. "What's going on over there?" It's the voice of an elderly man.

"No." Pilar squeezes my arm.

"What about him?" I whisper. "What if Celeste is over there? What if she attacks him? Or somebody like him?"

"Not yet," Pilar croaks.

"What's going on over there?" the man cries out.

"We've had a little trouble with our dogs," Mazie returns.

"Mazie, goddamnit—" I move to step in front of her, but Pilar jerks me back. My arm is numb with her clutching.

"We had to stop to let them out of the car," Mazie goes on. "And then they got in a fight. And one of them ran off. As soon as we get her, we'll leave. We're sorry for the disturbance."

"Can we—" I call.

"No!" Pilar blasts in my ear. "Maybe she won't hurt anybody. But the police will kill *her* for sure."

"There won't be any more noise," Mazie resumes evenly, "and we'll be gone as soon as we get her. She always comes back."

Looking at Pilar's bloody, haunted face, I hold my tongue.

Apparently uncertain, the man doesn't move. Behind him, his dog goes on with its hammering racket. "Hush, Ambrose," the man says finally. The dog stops. Silence reverberates. After another prolonged vigil, the man turns without saying anything, and accompanied by the dog, he mounts his porch steps and goes into his house. But he doesn't turn off the porch light.

A block away, another dog starts up. "The police will be here anyway," I tell Pilar. "You know that, don't you?"

"I didn't see where she went," Mazie says, as if to herself.

"What will Celeste do now? Where is she?" Pilar asks.

"She's nearby. Lurking. She won't leave without her cubs."

Pilar and I look at the dead cub. "It was the little girl," she says quietly, then looks up. "Will Celeste come back here?"

"Probably, if there's nobody around."

"Can we hide?" Mazie asks. "Hide and wait and shoot her again when she comes in?"

"I'll wait." Pilar stands with the cub. "I'll hide. I'll shoot her. I lost her. I'm doing this. You go."

"Go?" I mock. "Where do we go, Pilar?"

"There's only one gun. I'll hide. You go. Stop the police from coming. Tell them we're looking for our dog. Show me how to use the gun. Mazie, put the dart in now." In the trailer, a cub cries.

"Forget it, Pilar." I turn and survey the area, search the hedges and shadows for the shape of bear.

Pilar opens the back of the trailer again and slips in. She returns with the rail that Celeste ripped from the trailer wall. "Open the trunk," she tells me. She points at the cub's body. "I'll bury her in Ishi's home. Open the trunk, then fix the gun for me."

"I'm going to call the police before somebody gets killed."

Pilar closes the trailer doors, turns, and kicks me hard on the side of the knee. I yelp and fold. "Arnie, you can call the police when morning comes. I'll get Celeste before the morning. I *lost* her," she cries through her teeth. "I'll get her. *You won't stop me.*"

Mazie steps between us. "Let her try, Arnie. Give her two or three hours. That leaves another couple hours of darkness before people are up."

"Shit, Mazie, you too? You think that's enough time to find a flipped-out grizzly in a town neighborhood? You really think that?"

"I don't know," Mazie answers. "Everything looks bad right now. But give her a chance. Do you think Celeste would come back to the trailer right away if it was quiet around here?"

"I'll wait in this tree." Pilar points up into the heavy overspreading limbs of the tree we are parked beneath. "I'll wait over the trailer. She'll hear the cubs but won't see anybody. I'll shoot her in the neck. Then we'll go California, and everything will be the same."

Across the street, a door slams. In guilty reaction, I flick off the light. We do not move but watch the old man's profile descend the stairs again. Watching across at us, he pauses at the sidewalk. Nobody says anything. The man turns and walks toward the strip.

"Shit, shit . . ." I shake my head. "There's a candidate for you, Pilar. You want to go to jail? This is big time now."

"Where's he going?"

"Who knows?"

"Maybe he's going to that gas station," Mazie says. We watch him go on toward the lights of the strip. "I wonder if anyone has called the police yet."

"There's no time," Pilar commands. She picks up the cub. "Arnie, open the trunk. Mazie, fix the gun. You push me up the tree. Then you go with the old man and talk to him. Talk to the police. Talk to everybody. Tell them I'm finding the dog. Everything's fine. We don't need help."

I don't answer or move. Pilar puts the cub in the trunk. Mazie brings the gun and another light. Pilar takes the gun, and Mazie goes back to load another dart. Equivocally, reluctantly, I show Pilar how to put the safety on and take it off, how to view over the sights and aim.

She aims across the street at a mailbox on the man's porch, and I caution her about flinching. "Use part of the tree to steady the gun and gently squeeze the trigger. If you jerk or flinch, you'll miss." All the time, she is nodding.

Mazie brings a dart she has just loaded along with the other emergency dart. I load the gun. We push Pilar up into the crotch of the tree where the first limbs radiate outward. The limb is wide enough so that she can lie there mostly concealed. I crawl up onto the trailer and hand the gun, extra dart and cartridge, and light up to her. Mazie throws a coat up to her. "Go," Pilar says, "hurry. Find that man. Stop the police."

I don't say anything to her. I jump down from the trailer, and Mazie and I start down the street. I walk backward for a ways to watch. Pilar is not visible. Near the strip, Mazie and I embellish our story with what we hope are persuasive details. I turn my fleece jacket inside out to hide the stained sleeve where Pilar's bloody hand gripped me. As we cross the strip, we can see through the store window that the old man is there with the attendant. Unabashedly rapt, the two of them study our approach.

When we enter the store, the old man steps back against the counter as if we're holding a gun on him. The attendant's smile is enigmatic. "You folks raising a little hell tonight?"

Mazie and I collide, both talking at once. I barge on. "Had a dogfight in the trailer. And now one of them has run off, a big brown Newfoundland. She's done it before, but she always comes back. We're really sorry for disturbing everybody."

The old man's expression does not alter. "You flew out of here, all right," the boy says. "I guess you didn't want them fighting here where they might knock over a gas pump or something." His eyes are mocking.

"We don't mean any harm," Mazie entreats, "and the last thing we wanted to do tonight was disturb anyone."

"Miller and I were just discussing that very point. We were noticing that you were having a lot of trouble being as invisible as it looked like you wanted to be." The boy grins at Miller.

Miller is a tall, spare man whose thick-lensed glasses make his eyes blurry and enormous. He looks like a locust. "We called the police," Miller announces.

"The police?" I say this with all the innocent surprise I can muster.

"Maybe they can help you find the dog," the young one offers disingenuously.

"No," Mazie shakes her head. "No, they can't. She's half wild. We have to catch her. She was feral once and she's afraid of lights. That's why we moved to the side street before we let her out."

"So here you are." The boy throws up his hands. "But she's not here. She's afraid of lights."

"We . . . we were afraid that we'd caused such a ruckus, that we needed to explain," I tell them. "The other woman is looking for the dog. Her name is Celeste . . . the dog, that is. I'm Arnie, and this is Mazie, and the other one looking for Celeste is Pilar." I move over to shake their hands.

Reluctantly, limply, Miller shakes it once. "Saul," the boy says, his manner skeptical.

A police car appears at the mouth of the street where the trailer is parked and approaches the gas station. Mazie and I glance at each other.

"Lively evening," Saul says happily.

"You don't know how much I wish you were bored," I say.

"This is my night." Saul grins.

"I'd like to be asleep," Miller grumps.

"Go home and go to bed," I tell the old man. "We won't disturb you anymore."

"I'll go when I'm good and ready, thank you very much. It's your cousin, Herman," he says, watching the policeman get out of the car.

There's no partner. "I'm going to stay to see what you tell him." Miller looks back at me, fixes me testily with his colorless eyes.

Herman, a stout man with a large belly, walks through the door. "Whatssup, Saul?"

"These two have troubles." He points at us. "They woke up Miller's neighborhood. They say they're on their way to California to get some stuff."

"Stuff?"

"We're helping a friend move," I say with an exasperation half genuine.

"Our dogs got in a fight," Mazie tells him.

"I didn't see anybody around your outfit," Herman tells us. "You say your . . . uh . . . partner—"

"Wife."

"Your wife's wandering around looking for the dog? Why aren't you helping her?"

"The dog's hers. She goes to Pilar," Mazie says. "Maybe we'd see the dog, but she won't come to us. We just have to wait. It's happened before. It'll take an hour or two, but we won't be making any fuss, and then we'll be gone again. She'll get the dog sooner if there's no commotion. We came down here to explain what all the racket's been about."

Herman contemplates Mazie for a while. Then, his head tipped back skeptically, he looks at me. Scratching the back of his neck, he walks back to the beer cooler. "Saul," he jerks his head. Saul joins Herman for a short conference. Miller wanders back to the two cousins, as if to demonstrate which team he's on.

In a few minutes, Herman moseys on back past us to the front door where he turns and stops. "If I hear or see anything about that dog, I'll let you know." He looks at Saul. "And I'll be in touch with you." Herman goes out to his patrol car. We watch him drive across the strip and back up the street where Pilar waits to ambush Celeste. We make no attempt to conceal our interest in Herman's destination.

"Maybe I can help," Saul says. "Miller here will tend store, and I'll help look for your dog."

"No, please, you'll only screw it up," I beg. "We told you that the dog's wild. It's best if we leave Pilar alone. That's why we're here." He's got to believe me. For once, most of what I am saying is true.

Saul goes into a side room and comes out with a jacket. "Well, I'll just range out a little farther. It can't hurt. I know you'll understand that I have to get out of here for a little fresh air." Smiling inscrutably, he bows slightly, makes a salaam, and goes out the door.

"Goddamnit." I glower at Miller.

"Whenever I can't sleep," Miller says, "I come here to chat with Saul, and sometimes I tend store while he goes for a stroll."

We watch Saul cross the strip two blocks down from Miller's street. He disappears around the corner. "I'm going to look around the area here," I tell Mazie.

"I want to come."

"I don't see how we can do this, even if Pilar gets her," I tell Mazie outside. "Not with everybody watching us. They all know we're liars. They're just waiting to see what happens."

"We've got to wait it out, that's all."

We don't go far. We return to the gas station to wait for Pilar.

"You ever read *The Hound of the Baskervilles?*" Miller asks.

"A long time ago," Mazie says.

"Is Miller your first name?" I ask him.

"Yep."

"What are you going to do if she can't find the dog?"

"She'll find her," I tell him firmly. "It's just a matter of when."

"Then you won't be leaving without the dog?"

"No."

Miller thumbs through a magazine. He looks up. "How wild is half wild?"

"Half is half, you know, like a half hour is thirty minutes. And a half peanut, two of them make a whole peanut. Are you asking if she's dangerous?"

"I am."

"No." I pace to the door and back and then to the door again. "I'm going to walk laps around the gas pumps," I tell Mazie. "So my legs will be what are getting exercised."

On my second pass around the islands, Pilar appears, running across the strip.

"I shot," she gasps, out of breath. "Celeste came twice. Both times, she watched from the bushes across the street. The first time a policeman car came, and she ran away. The second time she was in the street. I heard a dog coming. Celeste was going to run. She was far, but I shot. She ran. I didn't see the dart. I jumped down and hunted in the street for the dart, but I couldn't find it. I looked in the bushes, but Celeste wasn't there." She puts a hand on my chest. "How far can she run? Did the dart work if I shot from a long ways? Is she down somewhere?" Pilar's voice quakes. "What do I do? What do we do? Arnie . . . Arnie . . ." I put my arms around her.

She pushes me away. Mazie runs up behind us. "We have to go," Pilar says. "We have to go fast and find her. We need another dart ready. Maybe she's asleep. If she isn't, maybe we can shoot her."

The three of us run across the strip and down the street toward the trailer. Pilar recounts for Mazie what has happened. I learn from this second telling that Pilar doesn't think the policeman saw the bear and that Celeste ran through Miller's yard.

Pilar and I search the alley behind Miller's, while Mazie reloads the gun. All of us have flashlights; I worry that Herman will be getting another call about prowlers. Mazie finds us. I change my mind about the gun. "Let's leave the gun," I tell them. "Either Pilar hit her or she didn't. If she didn't, there's no way we're going to get another shot. She won't let us get near her. The only shot we'll ever get will be near the trailer."

"What if she's only halfway down?" Mazie asks me.

"Another dose might kill her."

"But that's a risk. Not getting her means somebody else will shoot her dead."

"We don't have time to talk." Pilar snatches the gun from Mazie. "It won't hurt to have the gun. There's no time. Maybe she's sleeping."

"What about Herman? How do you explain a gun to him?" I look at Mazie.

"Herman?" Pilar says. She shakes her head. "There's no time. I'll take the gun. And I'll take trouble from the policemen. But I'm not talking anymore." Pilar rushes off. I see her poking her light into the hedges and under garbage can racks.

Mazie and I follow Pilar. The three of us fan out, each in a separate yard, three lots at a time, back to front, then return through another three yards, front to back. We move quietly and keep our lights down. No bear. We go to the next block along the same bearing Celeste had taken when she fled Pilar. No Celeste.

Pilar, her eyes half crazy, resembles some overwrought drama character, Antigone or Lady Macbeth, toting a gun. I sit down on the curb.

"Get up," Pilar snarls. She jabs me with the muzzle of the gun.

I get up. "Tell me where to look, Pilar, and I'll go look." I can hear how beaten I sound.

"You quit giving up," she shrieks in a whisper. "You look by those houses. And look hard." She points the gun across the street. "Mazie . . ." Pilar swings the gun to the block catty-corner from the streetlight. Mazie and I obey. Backing away, I watch Mazie move out of the light. She, too, seems hunched over, hopeless.

"Arnie?" Pilar calls. "How many minutes?"

"I'd guess fifteen minutes, a half hour, but she'd have to be in the trailer by then."

"No," Pilar whispers.

Mazie calls, "Watch out, it's Herman!"

Two or three blocks down the patrol car turns onto our street but away from us. The three of us fade into the darkness of the trees on the boulevard. We watch the car proceed to the strip, turn, and vanish.

"Hello, folks. Don't shoot. It's just me, your local service station attendant." Saul walks out under the streetlight. He has his hands up.

Nobody moves or speaks. Approaching, Pilar moves into the light. "Have you seen a dog?" Dangling the gun at arm's length, she lets the muzzle wander carelessly.

"Maybe." Saul nods at the gun. "You want to point that somewhere else."

"Oh," Pilar grunts. She turns the gun away. Mazie and I stride quickly toward them. "What did you see?" Pilar demands.

"I saw a huge dog crossing the street." He tips his head, pointing. "I couldn't see much in the dark, except it looked like the . . . dog was trying to keep from falling down."

"Where?" Pilar has her face in Saul's face. She clutches the collar of his jacket in one hand. "Where?"

I pull Pilar away. Saul backs up a step and straightens his collar. He frowns at Pilar.

"Tell us where," I beg.

Saul points down the street behind him. "Two and a half blocks down, crossing from this side," Saul gestures, "to the other. Almost in the middle of the block. I was—"

Pilar and Mazie race down the street.

"I was going to look to see if it was all right. But there was something I didn't like. Big dog, and you said something about it being wild. I didn't have a light, so I decided to look for your—"

I'm backing down the street. "Saul, don't tell anybody anything.

Keep them away from us if you can. I promise to tell you everything tonight, and if you still want to tell anybody else, you can."

"Herman, you mean?"

"Yes. All right?"

"You need help?"

"No . . . yes. Just keep Herman off our tracks for fifteen . . . thirty minutes."

No answer.

I stop. "All right?"

No answer. I turn and run.

Mazie meets me on street. "Celeste is down," she says, "but she's coming out. Her jaws are moving. She's on a front yard lawn." Mazie points.

I'm running again. When I round the corner by Miller's house, I pivot and dodge back from the light and the surprise waiting there. Herman's patrol car is parked alongside the Pinto. Herman stands behind the trailer and is shining his light on the pavement, apparently at the blood spilled there.

He flicks his flashlight off. I can't see very well, except to know that he isn't moving. I imagine he's just gazing around, listening. Then, he walks out from behind the trailer. Slowly, he circles back around the patrol car and gets in. Nothing happens. Finally, he starts the engine and inches away. Creeping down the street, the car turns at the first corner.

I leap into the Pinto and start it. No lights. Herman turned the right direction. Away from where I'm going. I pull ahead slowly. At the intersection, I see Herman turning two blocks away. In the next block, I turn on the lights and stomp on the gas pedal. Three straight stretches, two corners.

At the last corner I can see Pilar and Mazie in the middle of the street with Celeste. The bear's head is roving, searching drunkenly. The two women are dragging the bear's hind legs. I pull up alongside, slam on the emergency brake, and then stupidly, I pop the clutch and kill the motor.

The faces of both women ripple with turmoil. Head reaching, jaws snapping, Celeste is dangerous. "Herman was back there," I blurt, attempting the briefest possible explanation. I run back to the car for the broom. "Here, Mazie, keep the cubs back when you open the door." I trade places with her at the back leg of the waking grizzly. Pilar and I pull the bear's hindquarters up to the trailer doors. Mazie opens the door on one side. With a light in one hand and the broom in the other, she watches for the cubs and swats at them. Momentarily, they retreat. I get one foot up onto the trailer. I have to shove the other door partway open. Pilar gets a foot up. We yank and hoist at Celeste's back legs. The cubs can't get around us. Simultaneously, furiously, Pilar and I yank up and backward, jerking the forward-leaning bear upward over the end of the trailer.

We are in, but the front of the enraged bear keeps us from the door. Although Celeste still has no control of her hindquarters, there's no place for avoiding her wide-awake front half. Freshly baffled, Pilar looks at me. But then a cub bawls behind us. The bewildered sow turns her head at the sound, catches a front foot on the trailer side and half turns herself. I spin Pilar toward the bear's rear end and shove with all force I can summon, at the same time vaulting us up, over, and out. Our legs strike the end of the trailer, but we land all the way out with me on top of Pilar. I hear the wind blast out of her. Then the slamming of the trailer doors. Rolling to the side, holding my aching shins, I see Mazie snap the lock.

Across the street, a porchlight flicks on.

I push Pilar toward the car. "Hurry, Mazie. Pilar. We've got to keep hurrying. Herman will be here in a minute. We've got to get to Saul before Herman finds us, or all of this will go to hell."

"Saul? Saul?" Pilar, gasping, cries from the back seat. "What're we doing? Who's this Herman?" Her voice is hoarse, strangely bitter.

"Listen, you have to listen fast. The policeman will want to see what we have in the trailer. He's seen the blood. The only way we can save Celeste now is with this other guy. You have to believe that, Pilar. Herman will be here in a few minutes. It's all got to be done by then. Let me talk." We're pulling into the Town Pump lot. I can see Saul at the counter, but I don't see Miller anywhere.

Pilar doesn't speak. I look back at Mazie. Her mouth is open, but nothing comes out. I stop the car in the lot and run for the door. Pilar and Mazie are on my heels.

Saul starts to say something, his head slanting. Looking down alongside his nose, he smiles and opens his mouth. Holding up a hand, I stop him. "Just listen, Saul. There's no time. Herman will be here in a minute."

Saul closes his mouth.

"Inside our trailer are three grizzly bears. Stolen bears."

"Arnie!" Pilar screeches.

"Shut up, Pilar. It's our only chance. If you don't shut up, she's dead."

Saul's eyes bug a little.

"Celeste is an old sow with three cubs. One of the cubs was killed tonight. Here, when we were getting gas. Celeste escaped when we tried to help the cub."

"Arnie." Mazie points out the window. Herman is coming down the strip.

"Saul, nobody wanted Celeste anymore. No zoos. Nobody. She was going to be killed. They were testing repellents on her, too, shooting her in the face with red pepper and Mace. We want to let her go, with her cubs. In California in a wilderness where grizzlies used to live."

Herman drives right up to the door. For a man built like an egg, he's in the door quickly.

"You've managed to bother a lot of folks tonight," he says, slowing abruptly.

"We apologize for that," I say, "and we won't disturb anyone here again."

"I want to know what's in that trailer and about the blood out there and . . ." He points at the blood on Pilar's face.

"It's from the dogs fighting. One ear got sliced and—"

"Don't lie anymore," Saul stops me. He turns to the policeman. "Listen, Herman, you don't want to see what's in the trailer."

"I don't?" Herman looks like Saul just slapped his face.

"No."

"Are you telling me that you know what's in there and that I shouldn't even ask you?"

"That's right. I'm telling you that."

Herman's eyes narrow. "You're making that decision for me?"

"Yes."

"What you're saying is that if I knew what was in there, I'd have to do something I wouldn't want to do?"

"Yes. That's right again."

"But I want to know what's in there, goddamnit. They're lying. There's blood."

"They *were* lying. There *is* blood. But they didn't lie to me, and this is one time you're just not going to want to know what it's all about. You'll have to trust me, cousin."

"Look at the blood on her face."

"Quit talking about it. It's not human blood, I can tell you that. Just let this one go."

"Sonofabitch, Saul . . ."

"You don't want to know about this."

Herman takes off his hat and squeezes one eye shut as if he has a headache. "So you're telling me the best I'm going to make out of this fiasco is to tell them to get out of Klamath Falls before the sun goes . . ."

"Comes up."

"I'll never know what's in that trailer?" Herman puts his hat back on. "You'll never tell me?"

"That's right. Just quit thinking about it."

Herman approaches me. "I'd like you folks to be on your way before the sun comes up."

"Yes, sir," I say.

Herman squints at Saul. Then he pivots, strides weightlessly, and at the door, whirls. "Someday, you're going to tell me?" he asks Saul.

"I don't think so, Herman."

"What about the statute of limitations? Five years or something?"

"I'll tell you in five years."

"Goddamn right you will." Herman thrusts himself out the door. In the car, he turns off the blinking, spinning lights and departs slowly.

"Thank you, Saul," I say.

Saul points at Pilar. "You better wash your face before you talk to anyone else. Go use the rest room."

Perplexed, Pilar touches her face.

"Blood from the cub," I tell her. "Hurry, we need to get out of here before somebody changes their mind."

Pilar runs to the back of the store.

"What happened to the cub?" Saul asks.

"Celeste went beserk and tore off a rail inside. In the melee, the cub got stabbed with it."

"So it could happen again?"

"Yes. It's another reason why we're in a hurry. U-Haul trailers are not good grizzly habitat."

"Where you coming from?"

"Missoula, Montana. We started last night. We had the bears in the trailer around 4 A.M., I think." I look to Mazie, and she nods.

"Herman called in the number of your plates and got nothing. Apparently, nobody is looking for you," Saul says.

"No. They don't know who they are looking for, or where we are going."

"Where are you going? Where in California?"

"We aren't going to tell you that."

Saul's head recoils a little. "You're only going trust me as much as you have to."

"That's right. I just figure you won't want to know where they are."

"Maybe in five years."

"In five years I'll send you a postcard. Where shall I send it?"

"Not here. Send it in care of Herman Bishop, Klamath Falls Police Department. I won't be here, I hope, but he'll be there. We'll swap stories. In the meantime, I'll be watching the newspapers."

"Let's go." Pilar curves back through the store.

"She wears the gun in your family?" Saul asks.

Pilar swoops up to Saul, hugs him, and then kisses him on the end of the nose.

Saul follows us out to the lot. He waves as we drive off, which brings Mazie to observe that sometimes life imitates the movies.

13

WHEN I WAKE, Pilar is driving, and we are between Red Bluff and Chico. The Ishi Wilderness lies just east of us. "We just crossed Mill Creek," Pilar says. She grins. "The whites used to call Ishi's people the Mill Creeks. The water's pretty. Clear. Good water for grizzly bears to drink."

I rub my eyes and look in the back seat where Mazie is stretched. She has one arm beneath her head, the other hand is tucked between her thighs. Outside, rows of almond trees are downy pink with blossoms. We pass an orchard of walnut trees, magnificent reaching giants, their long limbs smoothly muscled and flung up at the sky like the arms of dancers. A few miles beyond, a yellow spray plane banks low over the highway. Poison for Eden.

I lean forward and try to make out the foothills above in the wilderness area. "We're almost there?"

"We're close now. I've been looking at the map. In a few minutes we cross Deer Creek," Pilar says. "Then we come to Chico. After we get gas, we drive up to the mountains, back to Deer Creek." She looks at my watch. "We'll be in Chico by nine. It will still be morning when we let Celeste and her cubs go." She squeezes my wrist. "Today is here. It all happens today."

"I wonder what kind of road goes up there." I'm still cranked forward, looking out the window past Pilar trying to divine something, anything about what it's like upstream from where we are. "I hope it isn't too bumpy," I tell her. "A bad road might set Celeste off again. We've been lucky since last night." Time to fret. "Then again, we don't want a real good road, or it will mean traffic of some sort."

"We want a good road nobody uses. Look."

The sign on a small concrete bridge says Deer Creek. A small river, the blue-green water is clear and deep with twisting warp lines.

Mazie wakes when we slow down entering Chico. When we find a gas station with distant pumps, Pilar pulls in. Mazie and Pilar cross the street to get groceries, while I pump the gas. There's no sound from the trailer. I go in to pay for the gas and get directions for Cohasset, a satellite community near the edge of Deer Creek Canyon and the Ishi Wilderness.

Twenty minutes later, we're out of Chico. The two-lane pavement ascends through oak savannas shelved on beds of lava. Swards of green are lined with gold poppies and the lavender-scarlet of cranesbill. We're drinking bottles of orange juice and eating peanut butter and raisin sandwiches that Mazie has made for us. I'm driving again. Above the oak and grass openings, we enter thickets of pine. "Letting them go will be complicated," I say. I glance at Pilar.

"Why?" Her face clouds.

"We'll have to drug her again. And we have to drug the cubs, too."

"Why? We open the door, and out they go." The muscles around Pilar's eyes pinch.

"No. If we don't drug Celeste, she might attack. There's a good chance of it, in fact. In the park, when we released grizzlies out of traps, they sometimes attacked the trap or the truck towing the trap. Or the guy on top of the trap. We've tried to outrun them. Then you get the guy on the trap trying to keep from getting bounced off into the bear's lap. We can't do that with cubs anyway. She might charge the trailer or the car and kill herself.

"We have to drug her and get her off the road, out of sight. That means somewhere downhill from the road, a place where we can watch from a distance. And we have to drug the cubs. Otherwise they might freak out and wander away before she comes to. That's happened. They all have to revive about the same time, the cubs a little sooner, if possible. So we give them a light dose." I look at Mazie. "Tell her, Mazie. It's the safest way."

Mazie nods glumly. "He's right, Pilar," Mazie says. "Sows with cubs are tough. She's dangerous. To us and to herself. And we have to be careful about getting them split up."

"I don't like that gun," Pilar says. She quits eating and puts her sandwich back in the bread bag. Mazie gives her what's left of her sandwich, and Pilar bags it up, too. I've already eaten mine. "It's just the last big step, that's all," I tell Pilar. "I'll shoot her in the neck this time."

Intent upon the road and the unforeseen complications of the impending release, nobody says much. Except for one grocery store, the village of Cohasset is no more than a small community of new residences tucked into a pine forest. Outside of Cohasset, the paved road turns to dirt. A quarter of an hour beyond, the dirt road levels and crests the ridge. The forest here has been logged recently. Slash piles, skid trails, rutted spur roads, dented fuel cans, and broken chunks of cable array a wasteland of stumps and pools of mud. This is not grizzly habitat, and yet the boundary of the wilderness can't be far.

After meandering through a quilt of clear-cuts, a sign at a fork in the road directs us to the left for Deer Creek Canyon. Abruptly, we descend into a dense, uncut forest of pine. The road switchbacks downward, then deteriorates. I have to crawl over ruts and moguls and dodge the holes. We haven't seen another car or person since we left

Cohasset a half hour earlier. Mazie hears a noise from the trailer. We stop and get out. Celeste is moaning and roaming about inside the trailer.

"Why don't you load up the gun, Mazie?" I ask. "We're going to need it soon."

Pilar has put her hands on the trailer as if to comfort those inside. She turns and asks me, "Shoot her now?"

"I don't want to if we can help it. We might need the whole hour to get her situated. And we'll have to knock out the cubs when we do her."

"You want syringes loaded for the cubs?" Mazie asks from the car.

"Yes." We are all acting as coolly as possible, trying perhaps to telegraph some calm to the bears inside. In the trailer, Celeste has slowed, but she's still pacing. We drive on. We can hear her moaning again.

"We'll have to do it pretty quick," I say. We are about two-thirds of the way down into the canyon. Ochre cliffs and escarpments lift up to meet us at the end of each switchback. At the bottom, the river cuts deeply through rock. The water cascades white around blue pools. Between the cliffs and river, the pines thin out and eventually give way to crooked oaks and buckeye wearing new, lettuce-green leaves. A few steep, golden savannas fit into the paisley of forest thickets.

At the bridge we can no longer ignore Celeste's mounting racket. We stop to wait her out, but she doesn't quiet.

"It's Deer Creek. Can we do it now?" Pilar asks. She has the side of her head pressed against the rocking trailer. "Now, before something happens to another cub?"

"We can't release them here. They might get in the river, half-drugged, and drown. We've got to go up this other side a half mile or so." Celeste thrashes and bellows. "Goddamnit! Shall I shoot her now?" I look at the women. "When she sits, we'll just race up the road?"

"I'll get the light," Pilar says.

Once again, I'm on top of the trailer, a light in one hand and the rifle in the other. The light of day makes it more difficult to make out anything but the most obscure movement. Light coming through my peephole seems to aggravate her more. I tell Pilar to throw up our coats, climb up, and drape them over me. Covered, I can see a little better but Celeste won't quiet down. I call out. "Celeste!" She stops. I get the light on her head. Quartering toward me, she watches the light. I find the rear part of her neck over the sights, and I fire.

Celeste roars and rears up. I slide the peephole door shut and latch it. It sounds like she's about to come through the side of the trailer.

"Get in the car," I yell. "She might break out."

Mazie has the car started. "Drive," Pilar says. Mazie slides over in front, I jump in, and we barrel up the road. Pilar and Mazie hang out the windows to watch the trailer and listen. After the second switchback, Mazie ducks back in. "It sounds like she's slowed down."

On the slope above I can see a big clearing. I decide to stop on the next switchback if it cuts above the clearing. When I see that it does, I make the corner and slow. A wall of live oaks shields the view below, so I have to guess when to stop. When we get out this time, the trailer is quiet.

"I want to look through the peephole to see if the cubs are all right," Pilar says. We wait while she looks in. "Celeste is down. The dart's in her neck, and the cubs are okay."

Mazie whoops. "Go catch the cubs, and I'll give them their dose."

We open the trailer. Celeste seems completely incapacitated, inert but breathing. I pull the dart out of her neck and pass it out the door to Mazie. Pilar and I each catch a cub. Standing in the open doors of the trailer, we hold them by the scruff of the neck and dangle them one at time while Mazie, holding one hind foot, injects each youngster in the buttocks. While Pilar and I wait for the writhing, bawling cubs to wilt, Mazie brings a dropper of mineral oil for Celeste's eyes.

Shortly, the cubs become quiet and limp. We put them back in the trailer at the rear where Mazie administers mineral oil again; then we roll Celeste onto the canvas tarp and lower her to the ground. I'm amazed that Pilar and I could muscle her weight up into the trailer the night before. Half lifting, half dragging, we step on each other's feet, slide, fall, scoot our way through the live oaks into the meadow beneath. We place her on her side in a swale behind a rock outcropping. Pilar stays with her while Mazie and I fetch the cubs. We each carry one cradled in our arms. In the meadow, we lay them near Celeste. Pilar whispers something in the ear of each bear.

Because it is a sunny, warm morning, the effects of the drug are prolonged, and we must wait several hours before the bears begin stirring. When Mazie says that the cubs are up, the three of us bang heads pushing to see down through the window in the trees where the cubs stagger around in front of Celeste. She is lifting her head, then lowering it. After a few minutes she waves her front legs and then, after several attempts, uses them to prop up her front. The bears don't seem alarmed.

Their departure is anticlimactic. After another quarter hour, Celeste struggles to her feet and wanders off out of view. Her cubs follow, and that's it. They're gone.

~

Pilar wants to go back to the bridge where she saw a place along the river to bury the dead cub. At the river, Pilar wraps the cub in the canvas with a yellow poppy and a spray of forget-me-nots. With sticks, we dig a shallow grave. We each put a rock on the grave. Then we clean out the trailer. Mazie gives the floor a rinse with water ferried up from the river in juice bottles.

Mazie tells us that the location of the hidden camp of the last Yahi family is across Deer Creek on a high ledge about nine miles downstream from where we sit. I try to imagine living here and always hiding. The place is so beautiful, but it seems to me that hiding would have obscured that beauty. I'm exhausted by the events of the last day and a half, the secrecy required, the fear of getting caught.

"I'm going to take a sponge bath," Mazie says, animated suddenly.

"Me too." Pilar stands.

They go down around a bend. I take off my shirt and halfheartedly splash some of the cold water onto my chest and face. Through the brush downstream, I can see the naked backs of the two women, one back dark and solid as mahogany, the other pale and tapered.

I follow two happy people back to the car. Before getting in the car, we look at the canyon. "I can't believe we did it," Mazie says dreamily.

⟿

We stop at a Mexican restaurant in an old building with high ceilings and oak wainscoting. Our booth and table, both of darkly stained wood, are decorated with bright silk flowers and burning candles. We order enchiladas and stuffed peppers. Pilar asks me to telephone the Goligoskis' to find out about Shelly.

Barbara Stedman answers. "Oh, Arnie, we've been waiting for you to call. Shelly's in labor. She started at noon. You're supposed to go to the nearest airport and fly Pilar out on the first plane. Clyde will pay for it. He's a mess. And Shelly hasn't stopped cursing about Pilar being gone since it started."

"Jesus, there's no let-up on the emergencies. Aren't you going to ask how we are?"

"How are you? Hurry."

"Fine. Bye."

"Hurry. Bye. Oh, Arnie, Arnie . . . wait. You still there?"

"Yes," I grunt.

"A man came by today. He wouldn't leave his name. But he said it was important that you call him. Here's the number. Got a pencil?"

"What did he look like? Never mind. Yes, I've got a pencil."

I tear off a corner from the phone book, scratch down the number.

The number is familiar, but I can't place it. Barbara tells me to call her back with Pilar's arrival time once we know it. I hang up and call the airport in Chico. The connection we want is in Red Bluff. I call there and make a reservation for a plane that leaves in an hour. If we can get to the airport in time, Pilar will fly to San Francisco, then Salt Lake City, and be in Missoula in three and a half hours.

There's no time to call the mystery man. I go back to our table with my message. We scramble, pay the waiter for a meal we'll never see, and once more, the old Pinto and the U-Haul fly out of a parking lot.

When I was on the phone with the airlines, I had the presence of mind to get directions to the airport in Red Bluff. It happens to be just the edge we need. They're closing the door on the departure gate when we gallop up. Mazie and I pay for the ticket. Pilar jumps over a velvet cord fence and runs past the attendant and through the gate. She carries nothing. Then she reappears, waves, and yells goodbye.

~

This is the last time I see Pilar. "Goodbye, Arnie, goodbye, Mazie. Goodbye, Celeste," she shouts joyfully.

Goodbye, Pilar.

~

Mazie goes back to the car which is still idling at the curb in front of the doors. I find a pay phone and call Barbara to confirm the arrival time. When she hangs up, I dial the number she had given me earlier.

Dr. Ikeda answers.

"This is Arnie," I tell him.

"Arnie!" he seizes my name. "You know about Celeste?"

"Yes," I say guardedly, letting the ambiguity drift.

"You know that she's gone, that she and the cubs have been stolen?" He seems perplexed by my reticence.

"Yes."

"Well, what have you done with her?"

"What have I done with her?" The back of my neck is hot. I stretch it out a little.

"I know it was you. I knew at once."

"Why do you say that?" Even in the face of his certainty, I can't admit it yet.

"Listen, Arnie, don't worry about me. I want to help. I want to be an accessory. I already am. I've lied about who I thought did it. And I'll keep lying. I'll do everything I can to make this work. And if you get caught, I want to be implicated. I didn't have the guts to do what you've done, but it's all I've wanted. Have you released them? Are they free?"

"Yes."

There is a long silence. "Thank you, Arnie." Again a long pause. "Listen, Arnie, it's been bothering the hell out of me about the work we did and the bears that died, some as a direct result. The price is too high, and we rationalize it as a means to an end. I've been changing my thinking."

I can't think of anything to say. I'm still afraid to confirm a secret of which I am only a third. "Why did you think that I was involved?"

"It was just like you to do something like that. There was never any question. Can I ask you . . . can I ask where you are?"

"Not yet. But I'll talk to you soon."

"Yes. Of course. Listen, call if there's anything I can do. Anything. I have my own ledgers to balance. You understand?"

I say yes and hang up.

But he's wrong. I wouldn't have done this. Disoriented, I find myself standing alongside the Pinto. Mazie is in the driver's seat. She leans over and calls through the window, "Want to drive?"

"No." I get in. I tell Mazie about Ikeda. I tell her that he guessed that I had something to do with the theft but that he doesn't know yet who else was involved. She laughs giddily. Leaving out the parts about me, I go over the conversation piece by piece.

Finally I realize that Mazie and I are alone in Red Bluff, California. Neither of us suddenly has anything to say. "Shall we just hoof it for home?" I ask her. "We can pick up some groceries, take turns sleeping, get the hell out of California, and drive straight through."

"Let's do it."

We trade two-hour shifts of sleeping and driving and then double that to four-hour stints when it gets light. A few gas stops, one rest stop, punctuate an otherwise uneventful trip. We arrive in Missoula the next day just at dark and drive straight to the Goligoskis'.

They are in their living room, all four of them. Shelly is on the couch in her bathrobe with her infant daughter, Holly. Alongside, Jeff shakes a tiny plastic rattle for her little sister. The baby's eyes are soft, empty and receptive as the morning sky. Clyde sleeps in the recliner chair. The midwife, Barbara, and Pilar have left. The baby was born in the morning, and Pilar had arrived in time to help.

"No thanks to the two of you," Shelly grouses.

"Can I hold her?" Mazie asks.

Reluctantly, Shelly gives up her baby. Mazie holds the tiny, blanket-wrapped package as if she were a grenade.

"So, were you brave?" I ask Shelly. "Or did you cry, scream, cuss, and abuse everybody?"

"Yes, she made a lot of noise and said awful things," Jeff answers for her, "until Pilar came."

"Pilar slapped you up a little?" I can't help grinning.

"Quit gloating, Arnie. Do you have to do everything vicariously? Getting even, too?"

"She taught Mom Runa chants and made her say them during the contractions," Jeff says.

"What did you think of seeing your sister being born?" Mazie asks Jeff.

"I was scared. Especially before Pilar came. Because I could tell Mom was scared."

I open my mouth for another dig, but Shelly interrupts. "Shut up, Arnie. Just shut up."

"Is Pilar downstairs?" Mazie asks her.

"No, she left to do a bunch of chores. She borrowed your car, Mazie. She said to tell you that if she wasn't back when you got here, you were supposed to take her car. Arnie, she left you a note." Shelly points at an envelope on the mantle.

"How long has she been gone?" I ask Shelly. I unfold the little note.

"Three hours."

The message is brief: "Arnie, Will do a few jobs while you're gone. I have Mazie's car. But I won't be back tonight. Not if I get all my jobs done. See you tomorrow. Mazie can take my car. Holly is such a pretty baby. Shelly was good. She had to work many hours. I love you. I love Mazie. Goodbye. Tomorrow."

"Jobs? Did she say anything about anything?"

"No," Shelly says.

"She sure hugged me hard," Jeff says.

"What?"

"She hugged me hard. I couldn't breathe."

"What the hell?" I look at Mazie.

She seems depressed. "I better go."

I take Mazie home. When I get back to our apartment, it's dark outside. I'm feeling a little spooky.

The next morning, I wake alone. I decide to get the trailer fixed and returned, do something while I wait. Nobody is home at the Stedmans'. I use his tools to repair the damage and their hose to give the trailer a good washing. I take the trailer back to the dealer. He doesn't look at the outside of the trailer, just glances inside to see if it's clean. We do the paperwork, and I pay him.

With that hurdle out of the way, I go back to look for Pilar. But she's not there, and I know something's not right. My stomach knots up. Then, the mailman comes, and there's a letter for me from Pilar. It's postmarked Missoula.

In the instant that I see it, I know what's happened. My hands tremble. I take the letter downstairs and sit on the bed. I can't open it. I go back outside and walk down to the children's park. There's nobody on the swings. I sit on one and open the fat envelope. If I let myself, I could throw up. There are separate notes to me, Mazie, Shelly, Jeff, Barbara, Clyde, and a little one to Holly. I can't bring myself to open mine. I open the note to Holly.

> *Holly, I saw you coming out. I saw your head inside your mama and I thought you were coming to a good world. You have a strong mama and a strong sister. A good papa. Ask your mama to tell you the stories of her mama and grandmama. And keep those stories for the little girl who will come out of you. Pilar loves you.*

I fold the note and open mine.

> *I love you, Arnie. Goodbye. I am going now. I didn't know that when we were at the airport. I can't say goodbye to everybody. You would stop me. Mazie, Shelly, Jeff, now little Holly, you would all stop me. But I have to go back home. I live there. You live here. It's right. It's hard and it's sad. But when it's all over, it will be right. I love you and Mazie. I'm glad I married you. Thank you for being my husband. In little while I'll send you directions from Ecuador where I am going so we can do the papers for getting unmarried. Mazie's car is at the airport. You have my car. I left a little money in Mazie's jockey box to pay for the apartment. I took the rest of my money from working at the clinic. There were many dollars left over after I bought the ticket. I will thank your country when I'm flying over it. It's been very good to me, your country. But it's not my country. That is all I know to say now. My heart tells me to go home.*

Pilar

*t*HIS OLD MAN is a sorcerer. He doesn't smell very good. Maybe
he never takes a bath. His wool pants could walk by themselves,
I think. The teeth in his mouth are rotten. No gold there, yet he has
more gold than anybody in this part of the country, this old Indian
sorcerer.

"Can I see the gold?" I ask.

"Not even my sons have seen it," he says.

"I have five hundred American dollars, and I want a gold figure that
belonged to the Inca once."

"Why?" He sits on a wooden box and pokes at the ground with a
staff. His poncho is unraveling at the neck. He has oat porridge in the
corners of his eyes.

"It is the last money I have, and I don't want it anymore." Maybe
I can never return to Wasi, but the daughters I will have can — or
the granddaughters. The gold could pay their way better than paper
money.

"I don't want money either," he says.

"Your sons can make use of it. Let them buy a plot of land with it."

He smiles at me. "You've made use of my sons, I'm told."

"I have. Luis and Miguel are good workers. They helped me build my house."

"You paid them well. They have never worked for a woman before. And for money, dollars. You've done much in four months." He looks off in the distance. The sound of water and wind comes out of big canyon of the Juanuru. The sorcerer's hut is halfway up the canyon, on a lip of a cliff. The stream that goes by the old man's hut falls off over the rocks. It falls so far that I think only half the water comes to the ground. The rest floats away to make pieces of cloud. "And my son, Marco? You've made use of him?"

"No, but I look at him." Marco doesn't want to work for my money. But he would like to lie with me. He has a laughing face, eyes like a fighting cock, those eyes that watch the women. And children, too. They like him, and the games he plays with them. Maybe he doesn't work so much, but he makes people happy, I think. So I let him watch me. And I watch back.

"They say you are a sorceress."

"They say you are a sorcerer."

"I am a sorcerer. Are you a sorceress?"

"I know the stories of my old people."

"You are clearing ground where the crying spirit lives."

"I haven't heard the crying."

The old man smiles. He makes a line in the dirt with his staff. "They say the crying spirit was waiting for you. You knew the name of the spirit. And that the ground there was the ground of your old people."

"Yes, but I only know the stories. I knew the place was where the two rivers met. Back then, the big river was still called Juanuru. And the stone point called El Cuntur, that was the name then. Three of my old mothers lived where the shadow of the stone condor crossed when the sun was highest. I found that place. It was part of Ceferino's land, but nobody tilled it because of the ghost's voice at night. Ceferino kept his cows there. They said the ghost's name was Titu María, that she has been there as long as everybody's old people remember. One of my old mothers was Titu María, who lived when the world was crazy with killing. Maybe she came back, I don't know. Maybe only her spirit came back. But I know that I found the place where my people began. I bought that piece from Ceferino—"

"He said that you gave him more than he asked."

"I don't want the money. If he can use it in the village, that is good. I had enough money to buy the plot and to get lumber and rock and tiles for my house and to pay your sons to help me build my home. I picked the place to build, and when we started to dig, I found pieces of pottery. I think those pieces had been in the house of my old mothers. I'm living in their home. It's home, too, for Titu María, whose spirit can sleep now. Once it was a place called Pomba."

"You lived in America. You bring their money. And they say you can speak that language."

"Yes. And I speak Runasimi, the Indian language, which I will teach my daughters."

"And your sons?"

"If they wish to learn it."

"Is there any man here who will marry a sorceress?"

"I think there's one."

"Ha!" the old man cries. He farts, but takes no notice of it. "You lived in America. You brought money from there. Is there anybody in this valley who would come back as you've done? They dream to have the things you could have had."

"I've seen many kinds of people. In my old village there were the Runa, the priests, the merchants. In my stories, I know of soldiers, of tax collectors and corregidors, of Incas, of The One Who Sees All. In America I knew people there. What I can say about most people is that they believe their way is the only way. And I'm often the same. I don't believe that many of the ways in America are good. It's too clean, too busy with empty work. It's not a place for ghosts."

The old man does not understand.

"Life can't leak in around all the cleaning. There's no smell there, no smell of shit, of death or birth, of rotting and growing, no smell at all. They give each other money so that they don't have to help each other."

It had happened one day in a supermarket. I knew I couldn't live there anymore. The floors were polished tile, the shelves heavy with shining jars. The people hurried by with babies in polished plastic carriers. They didn't carry them against their bodies where the babies could hear the hearts of their mothers.

"But I left people I loved there, good people," I tell the old man.

"So are you sad?"

"Yes. But I know how to be sad, all the way to the bottom sad, so that I can be happy, too."

The old man stands. He's bent. He uses the staff as a third leg. He peers up at me under the bone of his brow. "I will show you the Inca gold, but I have no use for the money. What will you do with that money if I don't take it?"

"I'll buy more of Ceferino's land around my plot. I have five hundred dollars left, but I don't know if he will sell it."

"Maybe he won't." The sorcerer starts down from his hut. He crosses the stream and follows a trail that neither rises nor descends on the side of the canyon. We walk for an hour, but we don't get far because the old man shuffles slowly. We come to a corral with rock walls and a pig inside. We dump a pile of straw and the tops of manioc plants into the corral. The pig, a boar, grunts and goes to the food.

The old man circles the corral to a place where a large rock makes part of the wall. He sits and then taps two of the stones in the wall with his staff. I understand. I lift them away. Beneath I can see other stones that are carved to fit tightly together. They have handles for my fingers. I lift them out. There is one large flat stone left. I move to lift it, but the old man stops me with his staff.

"You haven't told me two things. You haven't told me why you want Inca gold. And you haven't told me what you'll give me for one of the figures. I don't want the money. See if Ceferino will take your money for the other plots. But tell me these things before you move that stone."

I sit on the stone beside him. "I left the village of my people in Peru. There's a war going on there, and they will kill me if I go back. Maybe I can never go back to find my brother and my father. But if I can't, maybe my daughters can, or my daughters' daughters. I will leave them Inca gold. I want the Inca to pay for them to see this other home."

"And for me?"

"I don't know. I can tell you the name of your old father, maybe, but that's all. There was a man named Yataban—"

He blows through his nose and shakes his head. "The families of Ceferino and the other villagers are from Yataban's line. My old father is from the north, from the village where your brother and father are. The Inca brought them here. That's all that I know."

"Then I have nothing to give you, nothing I can tell you."

"No, that's true. But I've already shown you where the gold is hidden. So it must be yours now. The fathers of my line have not passed on what the mothers of your line have given you. Maybe your daughters will carry me with them somehow. Maybe Marco will plant my seed in you." He brushes my breast with one finger. "Lift the last stone," he says.

The stone is heavy, and the old man has to help me get it off. There is a hole carved in the native stone beneath. Inside are three gold figures, each the size of my hand. A woman, a man, a condor. I look at the man first, because he is the simplest. He has little expression on his face, but he holds a clear, blue stone in each hand. The stones gleam in the light, but not the figures; they are dark and splotched with age. And heavy. I pick up the woman, the heaviest. She has good strong eyes and a large, happy mouth. She stands with arms outstretched. Her breasts are full, her belly large with child. The condor is a female; her gold wings are half spread, as if she is about to fly. She is perched on a gold stone, part of which is her tail.

The pig has discovered the hole we have made in his corral. As he comes to explore, I stand the three gold figures on the stone lid. I place the condor and the woman facing each other with the man watching them both. They are a pretty threesome. Sniffing, grunting, the pig noses them and knocks them over into the mud. The old man and I laugh to see those things together. The gold, the pig, the stinking mud.

‿

Acknowledgments

I got a lot of help with this book. My wife, Janet McGahan, helped the most. For her eye, her convictions, her example, I am grateful. Thank you, Jany. A number of other readers improved my original manuscript tremendously. First among those are my editors, Barbara Ras, Matthew Specktor, and Emily Wheeler. Maggie Brown, Patricia Goedicke, Leonard Robinson, and Greg Tollefson provided page-by-page guidance. Doug Baty, Elizabeth Crumley, David Rockwell, Nancy Rockwell, and Jay Sumner also read, commented on, and shaped this book. In addition, Jay Sumner gave me a word processor and supplied information on bear behavior and handling. I also got help on bear handling from Jim Claar, Bob Henderson, and Harry Reynolds V. I thank Craig MacFarland and Adriana von Hagen for historical information on Peru, and David Rockwell for information on the Ainu, and for his original inspiration to liberate a captive grizzly bear. And thanks to Bounthavy Kiatovkaysy for her story of courage.

Many of the characters, places, and situations in this work are fictional, while others are actual. In this novel, I have used for my own purposes various spectacles and encounters, dilemmas and disputes, and even some phrasings from other writers and investigators.

From Billie Jean Isbell's *To Defend Ourselves: Ecology and Ritual in an Andean Village* (1978; University of Texas Press, Austin), I have taken descriptions of the interrelations among the villagers, the complicated system of reciprocity, various rituals involved, and the account of the dispute with a neighboring landowner. I modeled Wasi on the small village of Chuschi where Isbell lived with and studied the Runa on and off from 1967 to 1975. It may be only coincidental that Chuschi became the first target Sendero Luminoso chose; on the night of the national presidential election in May 1980, a group of students burned ballots and ballot boxes in the Chuschi plaza, and Sendero was born.

Other material on life in a Runa village came from Thelma S. Baker's "Child Care, Child Training and Environment" and Gabriel M. Escobar's "Social and Political Structure of Nuñoa" from *Man in the Andes: A Multidisciplinary Study of High-Altitude Quechua*, edited by Paul T. Baker and Michael A. Little (1976; Douden, Hutchinson and Ross, Stroudberg, Pennsylvania) and Alfonsina Barrionuevo's *Cuzco, Magic City* (n.d.; Editorial Universo S.A., Lima, Peru). My source material for the Ollantaytambo region came from Oscar Nuñez del Prado C.'s *Kuyo Chico; Applied Anthropology in an Indian Community* (1973; University of Chicago Press, Chicago, Illinois) and Ethan Hubbard's *Journey to Ollantaytambo: In the Sacred Valley of the Incas* (1990; Chelsea Green Publishing, White River Junction, Vermont). Whereas Titu María and Melchor are characters I invented, nearly all of the events in the description of the Runa rebellion are taken from Lillian Estelle Fisher's *The Last Inca Revolt, 1780–1783* (1966; University of Oklahoma Press, Norman).

Most of my background material on Sendero Luminoso came from an issue of the *NACLA Report on the Americas* entitled *Fatal Attraction: Peru's Shining Path* (1990–91; volume 24, number 4). I used the following articles: Carol Andreas's "Women at War," Jo-Marie Burt's "Counterinsurgency = Impunity," Carlos Ivan Degregori's "A Dwarf Star," Anita Fokkema's "There Is No Other Way: An Interview with Arce Borja," Nelson Manrique's "Time of Fear," and Jose Luis Renique's "The Revolution behind Bars." See also Raymond Bonner's "A Reporter at Large: Peru's War" in the *New Yorker* (1988; volume 63).

On the subject of bears, I consulted the following sources: Frank C. Craighead, Jr.'s *Track of the Grizzly* (1979; Sierra Club Books, San Francisco), Carrie Hunt's "Behavioral Responses of Bears to Tests of Repellents, Deterrents, and Aversive Conditioning" (1984; Master's thesis, University of Montana, Missoula), Bernard Peyton's "Spectacled Bear Habitat Use in the Historical Sanctuary of Machu Picchu and Adjacent Areas" (1984; Master's thesis, University of Montana, Missoula), and David Rockwell's *Giving Voice to Bear* (1991; Roberts Rinehart Publishers, Niwot, Colorado). Other sources included Juan Antonio Manya's *Hablando Quechua con el Pueblo* (n.d.; La Pluma Fuente S.A., Lima, Peru), Robert F. Heizer and Theodora Kroeber's *Ishi, the Last Yahi: A Documentary History* (1979; University of California Press, Berkeley), Loren McIntyre's *The Incredible Incas and Their Timeless Land* (1975; National Geographic Society, Washington, D.C.), and Ronald Wright's *Quechua Phrasebook* (1989; Lonely Planet Publications, Victoria, Australia).